ALSO BY JUDITH A. BARRETT

GRID DOWN SURVIVAL SERIES

DONUT LADY MYSTERY SERIES

MAGGIE SLOAN MYSTERY SERIES

RILEY MALLOY MYSTERY SERIES

DANGER ON THE ROAD

GRID DOWN SURVIVAL SERIES

BOOK 3

Judith A. Barrett

DANGER ON THE ROAD

GRID DOWN SURVIVAL SERIES, BOOK 3

Published in the United States of America by Wobbly Creek, LLC

2020 Georgia

wobblycreek.com

DANGER ON THE ROAD is a work of fiction. Names, characters, businesses, places, events, locales, and incidents either are the products of the author's imagination or used in a fictitious manner. Any resemblance to actual persons, living or dead, or actual events is purely coincidental.

Edited by Judith Euen Davis

Cover by Wobbly Creek, LLC

ISBN 978-1-953870-03-2

DEDICATION

DANGER ON THE ROAD is dedicated to the color red and to the angels who protect children.

CHAPTER ONE

Major and Stuart strode along the farm's fence line while Major's German shepherd, Shadow, dashed ahead. Major pulled up his collar to ward off the chill of the early dawn air as the dew in the tall grass dampened their boots and jeans. When Shadow growled, Major lifted the hunting rifle sling off his shoulder and tucked the rifle under his arm, and the men quickened their pace.

"Here's the break." Stuart scanned the area then examined the downed barbed wire and pulled away a clump of hair. "Our visitor might be a bull."

Major rubbed the back of his neck. "That explains why Shadow raised a ruckus a few hours ago. We patrolled around the house; I decided there wasn't anything close because the chickens and goats were quiet. He alerted in this direction, but I didn't want to surprise a predator in the dark."

Stuart examined the ground then squinted at the house. "Aimee Louise and Rosalie are running this way. Something's up."

Stuart raced to meet them, and Shadow matched his pace. Major jogged along behind Stuart and Shadow. When Stuart reached

Major's nineteen-year-old granddaughter, Aimee Louise, he hugged her then they ran to the house together.

Major's eighteen-year-old adopted granddaughter, Rosalie, waited for him. "Pops, we just heard on the ham radio that a small FBI team was ambushed thirty miles north of the Georgia state line. It sounds like it might have been Peyton, her partner Nate, and Nate's wife, Charo."

"No more details?" Major trotted to the house with Rosalie at his side.

"Aimee Louise asked for more information. One of the hams knows somebody near the state line. I don't know when we'll hear anything."

Major and Rosalie reached the former living room that now served as the computer and radio room and a bedroom for Sheriff and Molly. The breaking dawn provided its first light to the east-facing room, and the candle on the top of Molly's dresser added to the room's glow. Aimee Louise wore her headset as she listened to the ham operators on the solar and battery powered radio. When Rosalie sat in her chair next to Aimee Louise, Major headed to the kitchen with Stuart following him.

"Guess it doesn't do any good to hover," Major said.

Mr. Young brought a carton of eggs out of the pantry. "Good morning. You two were up early."

"Checking the fence. We've got repairs ahead of us this morning," Major said.

"Coffee?" Molly asked as she poured two cups. "The girls raced out of here to find you. What's up?"

"According to this morning's ham report, a small FBI team was ambushed north of the Georgia state line. We don't have any details yet. The girls were afraid it was the Cabellos and Peyton," Major said.

Mr. Young shook his head in disbelief as he dropped onto his chair's seat; Molly stared then stomped out the back door and slammed it behind her.

Stuart widened his eyes. "Is she mad?"

"She's scared. She'll find the sheriff," Major said.

Mr. Young pulled out his handkerchief and wiped his face. "Do we have any details?"

Rosalie hurried into the kitchen. "Two women and a man. Survived the attack but badly injured." She ran back to the computer room.

"Doesn't sound good." Mr. Young drank the last of his coffee, and Stuart refilled his cup.

Sheriff threw open the back door. "What's going on?"

Stuart caught him up on what they knew as Molly, red-faced and out of breath, hurried into the kitchen.

Molly put her hands on her knees until her breathing slowed. "Sara asked me to run with her. Guess I should." At the thundering sound of footsteps on the stairway, Molly grabbed her cast iron skillet to cook breakfast.

The four younger children trooped down the stairs and into the kitchen. Eleven-year-old Josh and nine-year-old Brett jostled each other on the way to their seats while Brett's twin, Sara, sat at her place.

Sara had curly, blond hair and blue eyes and wore pink and silver sparkled glasses. Molly called Sara her mini-me. Brett was taller than Sara, and his sandy-brown hair had the same cowlick that the sheriff's had. Annie's skin was a shade paler than Josh's dark-brown skin, but Josh was taller than she was.

Sara glared at the boys. "You know Mommy's rule. No breakfast until you settle down."

Thirteen-year-old Annie poured water into four glasses, and Mr. Young set them on the table. When Mr. Young picked up the coffee pot and waved it as he headed out the back door, Major, Sheriff, and Stuart followed him with their cups.

Mr. Young filled the cups as each man stepped onto the porch then he and Major sat in their rockers while the sheriff paced, and Stuart leaned against the porch railing. Aimee Louise sat on the porch near Stuart, and Rosalie sat next to her. Major's wife, Vanessa, opened the door for Molly, who carried a fresh pot of coffee. Molly set it on the table between Major and the sheriff, and Vanessa filled the two cups she had brought out. Molly and Vanessa relaxed in their rockers.

"It's quiet inside." Sheriff refilled his cup. "Bacon, eggs, and biscuits quiet the savages, don't they?"

Mr. Young chuckled. "Who would have thought that our vet was a smokehouse expert? Jody's bacon is excellent. Your strawberry jam is worth its weight in gold on the bartering market, Molly."

"Thank you," Molly said. "Annie told me you two might build a smokehouse for us."

"We're talking about it," Mr. Young said. "Annie has a design in mind. We may take a trip to spend a little time with Jody. Aimee Louise has been giving Annie driving lessons and said Annie is ready for a solo any time."

"What's the news on the radio?" Vanessa asked.

"A ham operator called for help on behalf of the farmer who is caring for the injured team, and a doctor named Scooter showed up from Atlanta. The doctor gave the farmer and his wife instructions on their care before he left this morning. He was there for two days," Rosalie said. "Pops, don't we know of a doctor named Scooter?"

"That's Phil's son in Atlanta. Phil organized the road block south of the state line," Major said. "I'm surprised Scooter hasn't left Atlanta yet to take his family to his dad's farm."

"It's light enough to leave." Stuart strode to the back door. "Rosalie, would you give me a list of what I'll need for three days' travel?"

"I'll help gather supplies." Mr. Young rose from his chair.

"Nobody travels alone," Aimee Louise said. "I'll go too."

"Hold up," Major said. "We've got some logistics to work out. Aimee Louise is right. Nobody travels alone. We need to decide who is going, and who will pick up their chores. Second question is which vehicle? We've got cars that are all in pretty good shape and three trucks."

"As far as a vehicle is concerned, my truck is fine for around the farm, but I wouldn't trust driving it anywhere farther than my old farm." Mr. Young resumed his seat.

"Isn't a truck less conspicuous than a car on the road?" Molly asked.

"Yes, it is," Sheriff said. "What about Pete's truck? Last time I went by his store, it was still parked in the back shed. It looks junky, which is probably why it hasn't been stolen, but Pete always took care of it."

"Aimee Louise and I will go into town after breakfast and check it out," Major said.

"I could go," Vanessa said. "Never mind. Sara and I have plans for this morning."

Major nodded. *Dodged that one. Someone else can tell my wife she's a hazard behind the wheel.*

"We could still gather supplies while you two are gone," Vanessa said. "Can we continue the conversation over breakfast? Sounds like the kids have finished theirs."

Sheriff grabbed the coffee pot, and everyone else followed him inside.

As Major waited for the crush at the door to clear, Stuart asked, "Go for a short walk?"

"Good idea."

"I can't go today," Stuart said as they sauntered to the barn. "We need to fix the fence before I leave."

"You're right." Major stopped and faced Stuart. "I'm impressed. I was worried you were going to dash out of here on some foolhardy, half-baked quest."

Stuart furrowed his brow. "And Aimee Louise would go with me to protect me."

Major resumed his stroll to the barn. "She would go along to protect you, but there is a strong bond between you two. I don't like it any more than any other father would, but I accept it."

"Thanks, but I heard your tone. In your heart, you are rocking on the front porch while you clean your shotgun." Stuart glanced at Major.

Major snorted. "Right about that. Let's eat breakfast. We don't want to get left out of any decisions."

When they stepped into the kitchen, Molly said, "About time. I was about to offer your eggs and bacon to my two bottomless pit sons."

"I called dibs on your biscuits, but I would have shared," Sara said.

"Would not," Brett said.

"You all clear out." Molly waved her apron, and the boys and Sara raced out the back door. Annie shook her head as she heated water to wash the dishes.

Mr. Young drizzled honey on his biscuit. "You said you needed to fix the fence, Major. We think you should do that right after breakfast, and the sheriff, Aimee Louise, and Rosalie should go to Pete's diner as soon as they finish eating. If Pete's truck is there and runs then Sheriff can drive it back, and the girls can come back in his truck. Don't forget to take a can of fuel. If I remember correctly, Pete's truck is diesel."

Major smirked, and Stuart chuckled.

"Too bad you came back so quickly," Vanessa said. "Molly and I almost had everyone convinced that she and I should go to Georgia."

Molly giggled. "Wouldn't that have been something?"

Major refilled his cup then passed the pot to Stuart. "Stuart and I will fix the fences after breakfast. Stuart and Aimee Louise can take our most reliable truck to find the injured team."

Vanessa cleared Aimee Louise and Rosalie's dishes while they collected their backpacks. Rosalie slipped in her waistband holster and picked up her rifle, and the two young women hurried to the sheriff's truck.

Sheriff finished his breakfast and carried his dishes to the sink. "We're leaving for Pete's diner. Here's another decision for you. Does Rosalie go along with Stuart and Aimee Louise?"

After the sheriff left, Stuart said, "Rosalie goes. I need the backup, and Aimee Louise and Rosalie work in tandem."

Major nodded. "They do. Good description." He turned to Mr. Young. "How would you cover the radio?"

"Annie will help me. She'll be my second set of ears and take notes."

"I think the sheriff and I can absorb Stuart's tasks, at least for a while," Major said.

"If Mr. Young and Annie take care of the radio, Molly, the kids, and I can handle everything else except the level of security that Aimee Louise provides," Vanessa said.

"Shadow's a good close second. We'll have to pay closer attention to him," Annie said.

Vanessa raised her eyebrows. "Good insight, Annie. I'll get started on a packing list. I have one that Rosalie created earlier to use as a template."

Major scooted away from the table. "Let's go fix a fence, Stuart."

"Can I come?" Josh asked from the back door. "I want to learn how to fix a fence."

"Grab some gloves," Stuart said. "You can ride on the trailer."

* * *

Sheriff swung by the fuel shed and picked up a can of fuel. When he reached his truck, Aimee Louise was in the front, and Rosalie was in the back on the passenger's side. *Makes sense to me. Aimee Louise is the lookout, and Rosalie is my backup.*

As the sheriff turned onto the highway that led to Plainview, he said, "I'll drive past Pete's first. If we think it is clear, we'll go back."

"I've been working on my list in my head," Rosalie said. "Can you think of anything we didn't take to the Newton farm in Georgia that we should have taken?"

"Now, I have to think," Sheriff said. "What about you, Aimee Louise? What would have been handy if you'd had it?"

"We could have used Georgia maps with more detail to find detours, but if the ambushed team isn't Peyton, Charo, and Nate, we'll need South Carolina maps if we plan to catch up with them."

"Hadn't thought about the possibility of continuing on and the extra travel time. Our packing list needs to have more than three days' worth of supplies," Rosalie said. "I'll sort through the maps that Dr. Jody gave us for South Carolina maps and secondary roads for Georgia and South Carolina."

"We'll need more than the supplies for us if we find the camp," Aimee Louise said.

"Good point. I'll talk to Aunt Molly and add extra water to our list," Rosalie said. "Annie and I can check Grandma Trish's storage closet for disposable or party cups."

As Sheriff approached Pete's diner, Aimee Louise asked, "Did you see him?"

"Yes," Rosalie said.

"See who?" Sheriff maintained his constant rate of speed until the diner was no longer in sight. As he turned right at a dirt driveway, Rosalie said, "A man crouched behind the swap table before we reached the property."

"Worried cloud," Aimee Louise said, "and sick."

Sheriff frowned. "Would a worried cloud cover up a danger cloud?"

"No, because if he was worried and dangerous, his cloud would show it. Clouds show lots of things."

"I'm not sure I knew that," Rosalie said, "but I never asked, right?"

Sheriff pulled into the overgrown parking lot and parked then dropped the truck keys on the floor board. "Stay out of sight, but cover me."

When he opened his door and stepped out, Rosalie eased out of the truck then she and Aimee Louise moved to positions behind the truck.

The sheriff shouted, "Hey, Pete? You around? It's the sheriff." He strode to the door and knocked.

"Pete? You here?" He tried the door, and it was unlocked. He frowned and unholstered his pistol. As he stepped inside, he said, "Anybody here?"

He scanned the room then shifted for a closer look into the kitchen. *Looks like the scavengers haven't left anything except a mess.*

He turned to the doorway at the sound of a cardinal whistle and narrowed his eyes as a man pulled himself to his feet by using a thick walking stick and the swap table for leverage.

"Sheriff?" the man called out.

Sheriff maintained his cover in the diner. "That you, Pete?"

"No, sir. It's Troy." The man leaned against the table. "I'm looking for Peyton." He shifted his weight and winced. "I left home early Saturday morning. Thought you might have seen her."

The sheriff stepped outside with his pistol drawn, and Troy leaned on his elbows as he raised his hands. He wasn't as tall and lean as the sheriff, but he was tanned and muscular. His jeans and jacket were grimy, and his dirty hands and face and scruffy beard added to the overall appearance of a homeless wanderer. He wore a Florida State University ballcap over unruly, curly, black hair.

"Show me your hands," Sheriff said.

Troy turned his hands to show the sheriff both sides.

Good. No rash. Calloused hands. Not an office worker.

"What's your daughter's name?" Sheriff asked.

Troy tilted his head. "What? I don't have a daughter—only a son, Brandon."

Sheriff chuckled and slid his sidearm back into its holster. "Aimee Louise?"

"Brandon's dad," she said.

"You can put your arms down, we believe you. You need any water?"

"I filled my canteen from the well out back and drank it. The well's okay, right?" Troy furrowed his brow as he gazed at the sheriff.

"It's fine. I didn't realize the well had water again. It ran dry, but that might have been from the entire community drawing its water over the first few months after the grid collapsed. I forgot it's an artesian well. Doesn't need a pump." Sheriff waved to Aimee Louise and Rosalie. "Come meet Brandon's dad while I look for Pete's truck."

"There's a truck out back," Troy said. "It started, but it's about out of fuel."

"Good news! I'll check it out."

Rosalie lowered the tailgate, and Aimee Louise lifted out the can of fuel then the two young women walked to the front of the truck.

"I'm Rosalie, and this is Aimee Louise. We know Brandon and Ms. Peyton. Our best stories are about Brandon."

Troy's smile was weak. "I can imagine. You know Brandon? Is he with you?"

'No, he's safe at a farm in Georgia."

Sheriff took the fuel can and hurried to the back. When Aimee Louise joined him, she reached into her jeans pocket. "I have the truck keys."

Sheriff's eyes widened. *Why did she bring my truck keys? Did Troy's cloud change after I left?* "I thought Troy was Brandon's dad."

"He is. I have the keys."

"Better safe than sorry." Sheriff nodded. "Let's check out Pete's truck; if it starts, I'll put in more fuel."

Sheriff jumped into the driver's seat. "No key in the ignition." He reached under the seat then stepped out to lift the floor mat.

"I have the truck keys."

You have my keys. What am I missing? Sheriff furrowed his brow then smacked his forehead. "Pete's keys! I completely misunderstood."

He accepted the keys then climbed into the truck, and it started. "Fuel is less than a quarter tank. I'll put in enough to get us to the farm. I'll keep the can in case I misjudged, and Troy can ride with me."

After he poured fuel into the tank, Aimee Louise jumped in and rode with him to the front.

When he stopped, Aimee Louise said, "Engine sounds rough. I'll check the oil."

Rosalie joined her when she lifted the hood.

"It's low," Rosalie said.

"Let's look in the diner. Pete might have had a stash of oil or other things we can use at the farm that have been overlooked," Sheriff said.

"I saw automotive oil under the sink in the kitchen," Troy said. "It struck me as odd. I worked construction in college and doubled as the onsite mechanic. I haven't slept more than twenty minutes in two days. Still no excuse to be so slow-witted. Can I ask what the plan is?"

"You'll ride to the farm with me in Pete's truck. Aimee Louise and Rosalie will bring my truck."

Troy frowned. "Is that safe? Two young women alone?"

Sheriff chuckled. "Yes. They'll be safer than you and I will."

"More stories?" Troy asked.

Sheriff chuckled. "Some of our farm family are master storytellers. Yes, more stories."

Sheriff carried out the case of oil while Aimee Louise scoured the diner. When he returned, she pointed to a door marked *Broom Closet*. "It's locked."

"Guess none of the scavengers needed a broom." Sheriff jimmied the door and peered inside. "Pete had such an offbeat sense of humor. Look at all the canned goods."

While Aimee Louise stacked cases on the counter, Sheriff carried them outside. When Sheriff and Aimee Louise lifted the last of the canned goods into the back of the pickup, Troy asked, "Rosalie's our lookout, isn't she?"

"More like a guard," Sheriff mumbled. "Here's a case of olive oil and another one of canned chicken. Molly will love this."

Sheriff and Aimee Louise returned to the diner to search the kitchen.

"Place has been stripped except for these pots and pans. These are good quality. If Molly doesn't need them, someone else might," Sheriff said.

Aimee Louise opened the oven. "One more thing." She pulled out bags of chocolate and hard candies and dropped them into a large canning pot.

"What a bonus!" Sheriff said. "Is that it?"

Aimee Louise scanned the kitchen. "We can go now." She carried out the canning pot, and Sheriff brought the rest of the cookware.

Aimee Louise set the pot with the candy on the backseat of the sheriff's truck then climbed into the driver's seat. After Rosalie jumped into the passenger's seat, she leaned out the window. "Do we lead or follow you?"

Troy leaned on his walking stick as he limped to Pete's truck. He climbed into the passenger's seat with the sheriff's help.

"Follow us," Sheriff said. "We'll let the old truck set the pace."

On the way back, Sheriff told Troy about Brandon and the farm in Georgia, the ambushed team, and the plan to check on the team.

"You think the ambushed team was Peyton, her partner, Nate, and his wife, don't you? I'm going too. I need to be sure Brandon is okay," Troy said.

"It's not yours to decide. The farm family discusses options and makes the decisions, but you need food and rest, or you'd be a liability," Sheriff said. "You can't go if you'll be a burden. While we don't make the decisions, Major and I have the right to veto."

"Have you ever used it?" Troy asked.

"Would you use your right to veto against Peyton and Brandon?"

Troy glanced out his side window. "Maybe."

"I hear ya." Sheriff chuckled. "You won't go if you can't contribute to the team. I know the family."

Troy leaned back. "Tell me more about the family."

As the sheriff talked about the farm family and how they came together, Troy nodded off.

Guess he finally feels safe. That's a good sign.

When Sheriff stopped at the gate to the farm driveway, Troy jerked awake.

"Farm already?" Troy yawned.

"Sure is. Almost forgot to warn you. You're going to be mobbed by a family of thugs. You ready?"

Troy smiled. "Looking forward to it."

"Watch what happens when we reach the house," Sheriff said.

Molly, Mr. Young, and the three younger children waited on the porch while the trucks parked. Molly rested her hand on her holstered pistol, and Mr. Young cradled his shotgun. Molly spoke to the children, and everyone remained on the porch.

"He's okay," Rosalie said as she stepped out of the truck.

"Thanks, Rosalie." Molly nodded, and the children raced to Pete's truck.

Troy's eyes widened. "Impressive."

"Yep. That's Molly, my wife. All the younger kids are ours."

Brett crowded Troy's door, and Sara jumped up and down to see inside. Molly and Mr. Young headed to the driver's side.

Sheriff stepped out of Pete's truck. "Give the man some space. Molly, we have a hungry guest. Do you mind taking care of that?"

"Breakfast will be ready in five minutes. Kids, back to your chores." Molly whirled back to the house, and the children scattered.

"Aimee Louise will drive your truck around back, so we can unload it," Rosalie said.

Sheriff nodded, and Rosalie joined Aimee Louise in the sheriff's truck.

"Mr. Young, this is Troy, Peyton's husband." Sheriff helped Troy out of the truck.

"And the famous Brandon's father." Mr. Young smiled, and his eyes twinkled.

Troy returned Mr. Young's smile. "Nice to meet you. Do you know Brandon?"

"I've never had the pleasure of meeting the young man. Stuart is the one with all the first-hand Brandon stories." Mr. Young raised his eyebrows as he examined Troy. "No offense, Troy, but you look awful. If Molly offers you a shower, take it. I have room in the camper for you to stay. I'll ask Vanessa to help me set up a bed."

"A meal, a shower, and a bed. You folks run a nice place." Troy's eyes twinkled.

"Best accommodations around," Sheriff said. "Ready to go inside?"

Sheriff helped Troy to the porch and up the steps. "I'd like to take off these boots. My feet might be swollen, and the boots are too muddy to wear into the house." After the sheriff helped him sit in one of the rockers, Troy struggled with his boots.

"Let me help." Mr. Young pulled off Troy's right boot then struggled to remove the left one. "Probably about time to get these off. We'll leave them out here."

On the way to the kitchen, Sheriff pointed down the hallway to the main bathroom. "Annie must have started the generators. You can wash in there. I'll be in the kitchen." Sheriff helped him to the bathroom then frowned. "Will you be okay?"

"I'll be fine; I've got my stick and the wall to lean on. This pain in my leg is slowing me down."

Molly handed the sheriff a cup of hot coffee when he stepped into the kitchen. As Aimee Louise and Rosalie unloaded the supplies from Pete's diner, Vanessa held open the back door and pointed to the kitchen or the wagon for each item. Rosalie loaded items into the wagon, and Aimee Louise carried the kitchen items inside and placed them in the pantry where Molly indicated. When the wagon was full, Vanessa said, "Take the wagon to the barn and stack the items out of the way." Rosalie pulled, and Brett pushed the wagon then they returned for the next load.

"Troy is Peyton's husband," Sheriff said. "He's been walking since Saturday to get here. We found him at Pete's. Glad we went to get Pete's pickup when we did. He's exhausted."

"After he eats, do you think he'd like a shower?" Molly asked. "We can find something clean for him to wear while we wash his clothes. He didn't have a backpack?"

"I'm sure he'd appreciate the shower. We'll ask him about the backpack."

When Troy hobbled into the kitchen, Molly said, "I'm Molly. Pick a seat, and I'll pour you a cup of coffee and serve up your breakfast."

Troy sipped his coffee then gazed at his plate and inhaled. "Eggs, biscuits and gravy, and bacon. I haven't eaten since Sunday morning, and that was a quick bite while I kept moving." He dug in.

"Did you have a backpack?" Molly asked.

Troy finished chewing and swallowed. "It's in the back of Pete's truck. I tossed it in when I thought the truck would run."

"Be right back," Annie said.

Annie returned empty-handed. "I left your backpack on the back porch, Mr. Troy. It was soaked. I'm Annie."

"Thanks, Annie. I dropped it more than once in the swamp and again when I crossed a stream early yesterday morning. I'll dump it out to see what I can salvage after breakfast."

"Annie, you're in charge of the kitchen. I'll find a change of clothes for Troy that he can wear until his are clean." Molly hurried to her bedroom.

"You care for another egg, Mr. Troy?"

"I couldn't eat another bite, thank you."

Annie cleared his dishes and slipped them into the warm, soapy dishwater. As Annie washed and rinsed the dishes, Molly returned to the kitchen with an extra-large T-shirt and an old pair of the sheriff's sweatpants.

"I'll put these in the bathroom for you. Check the clothes you packed, but if it's wet inside your backpack, your clothes may have mildewed. Our weather is famous for that."

Sheriff helped Troy to a chair on the back porch. Sheriff sat in his rocker as Troy dumped his backpack contents onto the porch.

Troy wrinkled his nose. "Whew. Your wife was right about these clothes. I'll bet I smell as ripe as they do."

"I don't have the best sense of smell, but I won't take that bet." Sheriff chuckled.

When the back of the sheriff's pickup was empty, Aimee Louise moved it to its usual parking spot while Rosalie waited on the porch.

"Unless there's something else, Sheriff, we'd like to go through the maps we have," she said. "If we can't find what we want, we'll take Number 48 to see if Dr. Jody has more maps."

"Go ahead. That's one of our top priorities."

"I'll tell Mr. Young that we'll need to plan for more than three days in case he and Aunt Vanessa are working on a list," Rosalie said before she and Aimee Louise hurried into the house.

When Troy's jackknife clunked on the porch, Sheriff said, "I'll get a towel from the kitchen that you can use to dry things off."

Sheriff returned with a small towel and wrinkled his nose at the pile of damp clothing. "I shouldn't have gone inside; now I can smell the mildew from here."

Troy caught the towel that the sheriff tossed to him. "Everything was wet."

"Do you wear a pistol? Did it get wet?" Sheriff asked.

Troy removed his inside waistband, brown leather holster and shook his head. "Not wet. My ammunition that was in my backpack was in a plastic storage baggie. A last-minute decision that was dumb luck."

"If you want to take your shower now, we can finish drying your knives. Anything else that needs special attention? I'll hang onto your pistol while you shower and change."

"Thanks. Shower sounds good."

Sheriff helped Troy out of his chair and to the bathroom. When he returned to the porch, Brett peeked around the corner. "Can I come on the back porch?"

"Sure can. I need your help."

Brett hopped up the steps and onto the porch. "Sara went to the camper to help Aunt Vanessa and Mr. Young. I waited to see if I could help you."

"Would you dry these knives?" Sheriff handed him the dry cloth then turned the backpack inside out. "I'll hang this to dry and air out."

As the sheriff headed back to the porch after putting the backpack in the sun, Major, Stuart, and Josh returned. Major drove the tractor to the barn with Josh and Stuart riding on the trailer.

Sheriff strode to meet them at the barn, and Josh grinned. "We fixed all the fences, Dad. Pops said I did good. Right, Pops?"

Major nodded. "You caught on right away. You were a big help."

Major parked the tractor and trailer in the barn then climbed down. "We found another section of fence down. By the time we got to the third section, Josh did most of the work on his own."

"It's not hard to fix fences, but it has to be done right." Josh puffed up his chest.

Sheriff smiled. *He's going to strut when he climbs off the trailer.*

Stuart hopped off the trailer, and Josh jumped off next to him.

As Stuart reached for tools, Major asked, "Anything new with you?"

Sheriff snorted. "Put your tools away then meet me in the kitchen."

Major narrowed his eyes, and the sheriff turned away.

"Is Aimee Louise okay?" Stuart asked.

"Yes," Sheriff answered as he went into the house.

* * *

The three of them hurried to the shed. Stuart and Josh passed tools to Major who hung them in their designated spots as quickly as his helpers handed the equipment to him.

"Let's go," Major said.

Stuart and Josh raced ahead as Major strode to the house. *Next time I'll ask for a head start.*

Before Major reached the house, Josh and Brett passed him as they headed the other way.

"Dad told us to check the chickens and the goats. We'll hurry," Josh said.

Sheriff rocked while Stuart paced as Major scooted his rocker out of the sun.

"What happened? Is everyone okay?" Major asked.

"Everyone's fine. Aimee Louise, Rosalie, and I went to Pete's diner to see if his truck was there. That's the red truck behind the barn; it needed fuel and oil. We also found Peyton's husband, Troy. He was trying to find Peyton. Long story, but the short version is that he walked here in only two days from their home on the Atlantic coast south of Jacksonville. He's exhausted."

Molly helped Troy out to the back porch. "Major, Stuart, this is Troy. Troy, sit in the rocker. I'll check the camper to see if your bed's ready."

After Troy sat in Molly's rocker, he said, "Nice to finally meet you, Major. I've heard a lot about you. Peyton told a friend she needed to find her lucky star and the hunter's big dog. Her friend didn't understand what she meant, but I did."

Major smiled. "Sounds like you and Peyton had your family codes just like Aimee Louise, Rosalie, and I did. After the rest of the crowd joined us, we added a few more. Lucky star—was that her reference to Sheriff Starr?"

"Sure was. As far as the hunter's big dog, Peyton and I loved to stargaze in our early college days before she was pregnant with Brandon, so I knew she meant Orion's Canis Major. Took me a while to get here."

Major snorted. "I don't mind at all being the big dog. Not sure if I'm going to tell my wife, though."

Troy chuckled. "Smart man."

Aimee Louise stood behind Rosalie while Rosalie opened the back door. "Excuse the interruption. Aimee Louise and I are taking Number 48 to Pastor John's farm to see Dr. Jody. We have only Florida and a few Georgia maps."

"I'll go too," Stuart said.

"No, we'll be fine," Rosalie said.

Stuart scowled then sighed. "Okay."

Major asked, "Troy, when did you leave the coast?"

"I was actually closer to Orlando. I left Saturday after breakfast. I somehow thought I could get here in twenty-four hours and planned to walk straight here. Seemed like a good idea at the time. It took longer than I expected because I realized after I started walking that I needed to stay away from the major highways, but I didn't think about all the rivers and streams."

Major examined Troy's hands. "No rash. Did you see anyone who was sick?"

"No. Is that why the sheriff asked to see my hands?"

Sheriff nodded. "There's a deadly virus going around. The most common symptoms are a cough and a rash on the hands. It has a high mortality rate. It's swept through the urban areas and seems to be following the interstates to rural areas as people evacuate to the country. Instead of running away from the disease, they're taking it with them to the older generation who are more vulnerable."

Troy frowned. "Sometime Saturday night I approached a rest area and considered going in to get out of the wind. I heard several people coughing. It was a wet cough, almost like they were drowning. It reminded me of a TB cough, so I kept going. After that, I steered clear of the highways."

Molly returned to the porch. "Bed's ready. I'll walk you to the camper."

"I'll help Troy, Molly." Stuart rose and offered Troy a hand.

Troy shook his head as he rose to his feet. "That shower and some food gave me new energy."

After he limped to the steps he said, "Guess I'll take you up on that offer for help, after all. My mind obviously is more energetic than my body right now."

"It's an honor to meet Brandon's dad. After you're rested, I'll tell you about what a hero Brandon is." Stuart took Troy's arm and helped him to the camper.

CHAPTER TWO

Mr. Young opened the camper door with a full garbage sack in his hand. "Right on time. Your bed is made. We'll wake you for supper."

Vanessa and Sara stepped out of the camper. "Hello, Mr. Troy. We made you a nice bed, and Aunt Vanessa cleaned the entire camper. Mr. Young will take the trash to the burn pile. Mr. Young is messy, but I don't think I'm supposed to say that. If you're messy, Aunt Vanessa—"

"Nice to meet you, Troy." Vanessa smiled. "Sara and I have work to do in the garden. Let's go, Sara." She took Sara's hand, and Sara skipped along while she chattered.

Mr. Young said, "Come in. I'll show you where you'll sleep. If you wake up this afternoon, come to the house, and Molly will give you lunch or a snack. I have a pitcher of sweet tea in my refrigerator, and your cup is on the counter. Sleep well."

Stuart lingered at the doorway after Troy stepped into the camper. Troy eased off the slippers but left on his socks as he lay down on the sofa that was his bed. "This is heaven. I'm clean. I have a full stomach, and a safe place to sleep. I'm so glad Brandon is safe." He closed his eyes and dozed off.

Mr. Young closed the camper door. As the two men headed to the house, Stuart asked, "Can we talk a minute?"

"I wouldn't mind a short walk to the barn."

"After Major and I left the house to fix the fence, was there any discussion about the trip tomorrow?"

Mr. Young shrugged. "You may know all of this, but it makes sense for the three of you to go. Vanessa and I decided to change the list for supplies from three days to a month. Molly updated the food list after she and Rosalie talked about South Carolina; I suspect the supplies from Pete's will be a big help. Nobody's mentioned this, but I wouldn't be a bit surprised if Troy wants to go too. What would you think about that?"

Stuart scowled. "I don't know. We know Peyton and Brandon. We don't know Troy. I'm not sure I'm convinced he is Peyton's husband, but even if he is, we haven't had a chance to assess his strengths to determine where he'd fit into the team. On the other hand, if we don't let him go, wouldn't he just follow us? I need to ask Aimee Louise something first." Stuart headed toward the house then paused as he turned to wave. "Thanks."

Mr. Young stared while Stuart hurried to the house. He furrowed his brow. "You're welcome. What did I do?"

Stuart rushed into the kitchen then stopped. "Sorry, Annie. I had something to ask Aimee Louise, but forgot she and Rosalie left to see Dr. Jody."

"Can I help?" Annie asked.

Stuart frowned. "I don't know. Maybe. You and Peyton rode together. Can you think of anything that Peyton told you that wouldn't be part of some data on the internet?"

"Let me show you the greenhouse."

Why the greenhouse? More privacy? Stuart tilted his head. "I'd like that."

When they stepped inside the greenhouse, Annie asked, "What do you think?"

Stuart scanned the greenhouse; he checked the seedlings in the pots on the shelf along the west wall and the jalapeno and serrano plants in large pots on the ground along the east wall.

"You've got water here too. Is it on a timer?"

"Not yet," Annie said. "Shortage of timers. Aunt Vanessa and I decided the garden had priority because I can water in here by hand."

"This is really amazing. And you built it by yourself. Did you draw up your own plans?"

"I did design it, but I had help with the construction."

"Peyton. I remember Peyton helped you."

Annie smiled as she pointed up at the roofline in the corner. "Look at the construction. What do you see?"

Stuart narrowed his eyes as he stared. "How are they joined? I need a closer look."

Annie followed Stuart as he walked to the corner of the building and stared. "That didn't help. I still don't know how they are staying together." He pointed. "This board is butted up against the other board at a ninety-degree angle. I give up. Is it Annie magic?"

Annie giggled. "Have you ever heard of mortise and tenon?"

"Easy question. No, I haven't." Stuart smiled.

"Peyton taught me. One board is the tenon. It has a peg or pin cut so the peg fits perfectly like a puzzle piece into the slot cut into the other piece of wood called the mortise. When they're put together, the joint has unbelievable strength and durability. Peyton said she learned it from Brandon's father. He always put at least one mortise and tenon joint in every new construction he worked on when he was in college."

Stuart's eyes widened. "Brandon's father would recognize the mortise and tenon and would know Peyton helped you."

"That's right."

"You could have told me that Peyton helped you, and Troy would recognize his signature style, but instead, you taught me about mortise and tenon. You are a brilliant instructor, Annie."

Annie picked up the hose and sprayer to water her plants. "I know. Pops taught me."

Stuart smiled as he hurried to the house.

"Good. You're here," Vanessa said as he entered the kitchen. "I've marked the boxes with the contents, but I need you to go through the boxes to see if there is anything that isn't needed. I've got the master list here." She handed him a notebook. "Check off everything. Do we know which truck you're taking?"

"I haven't heard," Stuart said as he read the first page.

Vanessa frowned. "You check the items in the box, and I'll find Sheriff and Major. I know where to find them. We need these boxes cleared out of the kitchen."

* * *

Major and Sheriff examined the engine and battery in Pete's truck. "Need to clean these cables," Sheriff said before he glanced up. "Watch out. One of us is in trouble. Hope it's you."

Major chuckled as he straightened his back and watched Vanessa stomp to Pete's truck.

"Knew I'd find you two here," she said when she reached the red truck. "Which truck are Stuart, Aimee Louise, and Rosalie taking on their trip? We have boxes of supplies that need to be loaded."

"We had talked about mine. What do you think?" Major asked the sheriff.

"Let's check the oil and tire pressure then fill 'er up. Both trucks are reliable, but we thought your truck would be more inconspicuous."

"Right. They'll take my truck, Vanessa," Major said.

"That's what I thought too." Vanessa hurried back to the house.

"Woman on a mission." Major chuckled. "I'll check the tire pressure and the flashlights. I dare you to ask Vanessa if flashlight batteries are on the list."

Sheriff snorted. "After you."

Major glanced up at the roar of Number 48. Aimee Louise pulled the side-by-side next to Major's truck; after Rosalie hopped out with a medium-sized box, Aimee Louise headed to the equipment shed to park Number 48.

"Dr. Jody was a big help," Rosalie said. "She found South Carolina, Alabama, and Tennessee state maps, and county maps for Florida, Georgia, and South Carolina." She cocked her head. "We're taking your truck, Pops? That's perfect. I'll put the maps in the truck close to where I sit then we need to talk."

After Rosalie loaded her maps into the document holder in the back seat, Major said, "Sheriff, I won't be long."

Rosalie ran ahead of Major to the equipment shed. The two young women were waiting for him.

"What's going on?" Major asked.

"Troy is sick," Rosalie said. "I thought he seemed fine at Pete's, but Aimee Louise said he is sick. At first I thought it could be exhaustion or exposure, but Aimee Louise doesn't agree."

"Troy told the sheriff he wanted to go with you to find the ambushed team. What do you think?"

Aimee Louise stared at Number 48. "No."

"What if he wakes up after his nap and is fine?"

"No," Aimee Louise said, and Rosalie raised her eyebrows.

"He won't be fine, Pops," Rosalie said.

Major furrowed his brow. "Okay. We'll quarantine Troy until we know he's well. Mr. Young can stay in the house. Stuart's bed will be available while you all are gone. I'll explain the situation to the sheriff."

Major reached his truck as Stuart loaded the last box from the wagon into the back of the pickup. Brett climbed into the wagon, and Josh pulled the wagon toward the house.

"Need to talk to you, Stuart. You too, Sheriff." Major told them about Aimee Louise's assessment of Troy. "We'll quarantine him until we're sure he's well."

"Mr. Young can sleep in my bed," Stuart said. "After Troy is well, Annie has a foolproof way to make sure he is Brandon's father, not an imposter. She can show you."

"Were you worried he isn't Troy?" Major asked.

"Yes," Stuart said. "Still am."

Josh and Brett ran to join the men. "Mommy said don't start anything else. Lunch is ready."

"Good timing, boys. We can finish up after lunch," Sheriff said.

"Can we move Pops' truck closer?" Josh asked. "Brett's getting tired, and I am too, a little bit."

"Should have thought of it earlier," Major said. "I'll move it right after lunch."

"I'll tell Aimee Louise and Rosalie," Stuart said. "We'll be right there."

* * *

When Stuart reached the equipment shed, Aimee Louise and Rosalie were arguing. He raised his eyebrows. *I'll bet this is a doozy.*

Rosalie glared at him. "About time you showed up. Maybe you can talk some sense into her."

I doubt it. "What's going on?"

"Aimee Louise said we should load up and leave after lunch. That's not our plan. We get more daylight for travel if we leave in the morning."

"Why?" Stuart asked.

"Why should we leave right away? I don't know, but we already planned—"

Aimee Louise interrupted. "The family has almost everything ready. If we leave right after lunch, we can be at the state line long before dark. We need to talk to Pops' friend, Phil."

"Why Phil?" Stuart asked.

"His son is the doctor who traveled to the farm where the injured team was taken. Phil will know where they are."

"With all that has gone on today, I'd forgotten about Scooter." Stuart shook his head. "If we waited until tomorrow morning, we may not find Phil until later in the day."

"Yes, but what if the roadblock has been abandoned?" Rosalie asked. "Sheriff said they have become difficult to staff. Trying to find Phil makes us lose the time that we could have spent traveling."

"Then we go into the nearest town," Aimee Louise said. "It wouldn't take long for the news to get around that we are looking for him. If we can't find Phil, he'll find us."

Stuart said, "Let's eat lunch. We can continue our argument on the road."

Rosalie's eyes twinkled. "Nobody's going to believe you if you tell them the three of us argued."

Stuart chuckled. "They would think I'd lost my mind."

"Yes," Aimee Louise said.

As they walked to the house, Stuart said, "Was I set up?"

"No, you just stepped into the middle of one of our discussions," Rosalie said.

"And we set you up," Aimee Louise said.

"You did not," Stuart said as they entered the kitchen.

"Did not what?" Molly asked. "About time you got here. We've finished eating. Sit. Sheriff and Major will finish loading your supplies. Annie checked the list for you. Read over it while you eat, Rosalie. Did you all pack your clothes? We thought you might want to leave right after lunch."

Stuart's eyes widened.

Molly frowned. "Didn't the girls tell you? Aimee Louise asked Pops if it was a good idea. Rosalie was lukewarm. We agreed there was no reason to waste any more time."

After they finished lunch, Stuart loaded his bags into the truck. While Rosalie read the list, Aimee Louise hurried upstairs then carried down the travel bags she and Rosalie had packed.

Rosalie said, "List looks good. See what you think, Aimee Louise. I need to refill my go-bag with snacks."

"It's been a while since I've checked my go-bag for the essential items that I'd need to get back home," Stuart said. "Won't take me long to pack my clothes into my backpack."

Aimee Louise and Stuart read the checklist together.

"List of Georgia and South Carolina repeaters?" Stuart asked.

"I added that," Mr. Young said. "The list is in the glove compartment. I programmed Major's ham radio, but the list has alternates in case one of the repeaters isn't operational."

"Thank you," Aimee Louise said.

"I packed supper for you. Here's a list of menu items that are quick to fix for those times that you don't have the time to prepare a meal." Molly handed the list to Rosalie.

"I used to have to cook for myself all the time. I'll enjoy pulling together meals for the three of us."

"We'll be your sous chefs, Rosalie," Stuart said. "Everything ready?"

After good byes and hugs, Stuart, Rosalie, and Aimee Louise headed to the gate where Major, Sheriff, Shadow, and Penny waited.

When Stuart lowered his window, Sheriff approached the passenger's side. "Major and I knew both of us wanted to go with you, so we're here to say goodbye together."

Aimee Louise and Rosalie lowered their windows on the driver's side. "Shadow and I hate that we're not going too," Major said, "but at least the two of you will be together." Major smiled. "Look after Stuart, would you?"

"Dr. Jody needs to look at Troy," Aimee Louise said in a quiet voice.

Major watched the plume of dust that followed his truck as it sped away. *Look after them, Lord.*

When he turned to the house, Sheriff said, "That had to be the hardest thing you've ever done."

Major exhaled. "It was, but Aimee Louise gave us an assignment. She wants Dr. Jody to examine Troy. I have an idea, but let's check with the family."

On their way back to the house, Josh and Brett ran to meet them. "We need a farm family meeting. Can you let everyone know we'll meet on the back porch?"

"On it," Josh said as he raced to the house, and Brett ran to the garden. Shadow trotted after Josh, and Penny loped along with Brett.

By the time Major and Sheriff reached the porch, everyone was waiting for them.

"Are we going to follow Aimee Louise?" Sara asked. "I can be packed and ready in five minutes. Mommy takes longer. Maybe she should stay here with the chickens. Will you take care of my chickens, Mommy?"

Sheriff smirked at Molly who raised her nose in the air.

"We're not going to follow Aimee Louise, Sara, but I like the idea," Major said. "Aimee Louise said Dr. Jody needs to check Troy. How do we keep the farm safe and go to Mr. Young's farm?"

"That's a hard one," Vanessa said. "I could go by myself, but we have the rule that no one travels alone. Does that have to be both ways? Because I'd have Dr. Jody with me coming back."

"Counts both ways," Molly said. "You and I have a lot to catch up on. We spent all morning getting everything ready for our travelers."

"True," Vanessa said.

Sheriff said, "I could go alone except for our rule that we have a driver and a guard. I couldn't be both. Same with Major."

"Annie and I can go," Mr. Young said. "Aimee Louise taught Annie to drive Number 48, and I can ride shotgun."

Sheriff raised his eyebrows at Major. "Is that what you were thinking?"

"Sure was. Aimee Louise told me Annie could drive with a guard along."

Annie beamed.

"I'll check on Troy to see if he's any better, and if not, Annie and I can leave right away unless there's something one of us needs to do first."

"No," Molly said. "If Aimee Louise said to get Dr. Jody, it's important."

Mr. Young hurried back from his camper with his shotgun. "Troy said the pain in his leg is excruciating. I believe him; we'll leave now."

After they left, Molly said, "I'll check on Troy then we have laundry and garden and animal chores for starters."

Vanessa accompanied Brett and Josh to the coop for the day's chicken chores.

"Daddy, would you carry the laundry outside for me?" Sara asked. "I can hang it up for Mommy."

"Sure will. I can help you with it too, if you like."

"I can do it by myself, Daddy, except for the heavy things,"

"You can tell me which ones you want me to pin up." Sheriff took Sara's hand, and the two of them went inside to take the laundry out of the washer.

Major headed to the barn but stopped when Molly called him. She was out of breath by the time she reached him. "Mr. Young was right. Troy's leg is swollen, and he is in a great deal of pain. We have some strong pain killers, but I want to wait for Dr. Jody. I told him we were getting him help."

"Do you want me to sit with him?"

"I don't know. I got the feeling it took as much effort to hide his pain from me as it did for him to deal with it. I do think it would be wise to cut off his sock. It seems to be cutting off circulation. I have trauma shears."

"Let's get those shears."

Before Major reached the camper, he heard Troy's moans. When he stepped inside, Troy lay on his side in a fetal position, and his skin was ashen. Troy's dull eyes stared at Major until a flash of recognition softened them. He struggled to sit up then gave in. "Having a little problem with my leg, Major."

"That's what I understand. Molly wants me to cut off your sock. Can I look?"

"Yeah." Troy writhed in his effort to roll to his back.

"Easy, son," Major said. "You don't have to do anything. I'm here with you until Dr. Jody comes. Shouldn't be much longer."

Major cut the left leg of the sweatpants up to Troy's knee then cut off the sock.

"How is it, Major?" Troy tried to raise himself on an elbow to see.

"It's swollen. Molly was right about getting that sock off. It was constricting your leg and probably added to your pain."

Major examined the swelling and frowned at the deep purple wound in Troy's midcalf. "Did something bite you?" he asked.

"I don't think so. I thought I'd scratched my leg one time when I slipped and fell."

"In the water or in the woods?" Major asked.

"River bank. I think I slipped getting out of the water. Might ease the throbbing if we can raise it."

"Let's sit you up a bit, and I can help you sip some water. You're pretty dehydrated."

Major grabbed the pillow off Mr. Young's bed and the sofa pillows and pulled Troy into a sitting position. After he poured cool water from Mr. Young's camper refrigerator into Troy's cup that was next to the sink, he held the straw close to Troy's mouth. "See if you can sip some water."

Troy's lips were cracked, but he opened his mouth enough to take the straw into his mouth and sip. He leaned his head forward for another sip then fell back against the pillows.

"Doing good," Major said. "Rest a minute then you can have another sip. Sure am glad Molly got some food in you too."

Troy raised his head, and Major held the straw close to Troy's mouth. Troy took two more sips than lay back on his pillows.

"Tell me about Brandon, Major."

"My favorite Brandon story is right after the tornado when Brandon found a handheld ham radio in the field, he used it to call for help, and Stuart answered him. Stuart asked him if there was a road sign, and Brandon walked to the closest sign he could see, but he made sure that he and Henry, a younger boy who also survived the tornado, stayed together. He sounded like a kid on the radio, but he was a man, taking care of a younger boy."

Troy relaxed. "Tell me another Brandon story."

Major smiled. *This is exactly what he needed to relax. Brandon stories. Even lame stories from a bad storyteller.*

"You probably already know this, but Brandon is big on rules, at least the ones he likes. One of his favorite farm rules where he is staying is bath, snack, bed. You wouldn't think a boy would be excited about a bath or going to bed, would you? The kids have chores and work hard and play hard. A bath is a luxury these days, as you know, and Sandra's snacks are amazing. There isn't much on the farm, but she always comes up with something the kids love. When the kids come in from the cold, she gives them hot tea with honey. As far as going to bed, everyone goes to bed not long after the sun goes down and sleeps soundly and wakes up at dawn for a delicious breakfast and another busy day."

Major offered Troy another sip of water, and Troy took three long sips.

"What are some other rules?"

"There is one rule that the boys make a point to break every chance they can. The old farmhouse has two stories and a grand staircase with a banister."

Troy smiled. "No sliding down the banister, right?"

"You got it. The first time I saw Brandon slide down the banister then check to be sure no one saw him, I had to return to my room to keep from giving myself away."

"I did the same thing when I was a kid. Must be genetic."

"Brandon said you build houses."

"I do. Brandon and I have built birdhouses together since he was barely able to walk. Thank you, Major. My leg still hurts, but you've given me the best possible medicine. I can't tell you how worried I've been about my son."

"What about Peyton?"

"It's complicated. I'll take some more water."

Troy sipped on the water while Major held the glass for him.

"Right in here, Dr. Jody," Mr. Young said.

Jody stepped into the camper. Even though she was nearing retirement age, her black curly hair under her bandana still glistened, and her slender body hid her strength that had served her well over the years to deliver a calf or calm a horse.

"I'm Jody," she said. "With your permission, I'm here to assess you. I'm a veterinarian, but in these times, we all make do, don't we?" She frowned as she glanced at Troy's leg. "Nasty wound." She knelt next to him and examined it closely. "Looks like a snake bite. When did it happen?"

"I'm not sure, but I think it was yesterday morning. I had walked all night and decided it was quicker to walk through the swamp rather than find a way around it. I fell more than once, but one time, I slipped on the bank. I thought I'd hit my calf on a stick or cypress knee when I went down. Later in the day, I had pain in my leg but kept moving."

Dr. Jody nodded. "So, this is day two." She rose. "You sat him up, didn't you, Major? Well done. It's best to keep his heart above the wound. Days three and four are the roughest, at least typically, for humans. The biggest thing to watch for is compartment syndrome caused by the internal swelling and bleeding which can cut off the blood supply to the rest of the leg, and the tissues die. Send for me if his foot turns cold. I need a marker."

Mr. Young pulled a permanent marker out of a drawer and handed it to her.

"I need to mark the progress." She drew a circle around the deep, dark purple that surrounded the puncture wound. "This is where the worst of the bleeding is. Mark it this same time tomorrow. Let me know if it turns red or hot."

"Troy, the best medicine for you until the pain subsides and the swelling starts going down is distraction because you're stuck. You have to rest and sleep sitting up. You'll need to keep up your liquids, and time on your feet must be kept at a minimum. Ten minutes a day total. That gives you a chance to go to the bathroom, and that's about it. Let Major know if your foot feels cold."

Jody stopped after Mr. Young closed the camper door behind them. "Major, I'd recommend moving Troy into the house so that Molly can keep a close eye on him. As far as distractions, the farm family is definitely the best."

Annie waited for Jody on the path to the house, and Jody grinned. "We'll meet you at Number 48 in fifteen minutes, Mr. Young. I need to look at Annie's greenhouse."

"Sounds like you've got your camper back, Mr. Young. Where do we put Troy?" Major asked.

"That's easy. Ask Molly. I'm going to the greenhouse."

When Major went into the house, Molly was in the kitchen. "Troy was most likely bitten by a snake. My guess is a cottonmouth, but Jody didn't say. He needs to stay off his feet with his heart higher than his feet. Jody wants him in the house because it will be more convenient for you to keep an eye on him, and she said the best medicine for him was distraction because the next two days will most likely be the worst. Where do you suggest?"

"Why don't we rearrange the furniture a bit, and put the rollaway bed next to the window in the den that looks out on the back porch? I think I saw a trifold screen in the storage room. That would give Troy a little privacy, but he'll definitely have distractions."

"Seems to be exactly what Jody had in mind."

While Major set up the rollaway bed, Molly searched the storage room. She called out from upstairs. "Need some help, Major."

When Major reached the bottom of the stairs, she said, "Would you carry this downstairs? It's heavier than I remembered."

"Will do." He took the stairs two at a time. "I set up the bed. We need sheets and a couple of pillows to keep Troy propped up."

"If I throw the pillows down the stairs, will you promise not to tell on me."

"Sounds smart to me, including the part where you don't want the kids copying your method to get something downstairs with maximum efficiency and minimal effort."

"Good. I'll carry down the sheets."

"As soon as we get the bed made, I'll bring Troy inside."

Major carried the screen to the kitchen and narrowly missed being hit by pillows flying down the stairs.

"Sorry I missed." Molly chortled as she made up the bed while Major gathered the pillows.

"Should have known it would be an ambush. Ready for me to bring Troy to the house?" he asked.

"Will be by the time you get here."

When Major reached the camper, Troy asked, "What's the verdict?"

"Molly fixed up a not-so-private suite for you in the den. You're next to the window that looks out back, and you'll have distractions galore. She found a screen to put up so you have a semblance of a room, except it's more like a cubicle. I guarantee you won't be bored."

Major helped Troy to the house and left when Molly took over. Jody and Mr. Young waited for him by the barn.

"Major, Troy's condition may deteriorate in the next few days. If you have any antibiotics, I'd suggest starting a course of five days with a double dose now. There's a ten percent fatality rate, but those statistics are from the days of early medical intervention. The three things to watch for are compartment syndrome, signs of infection, and difficulty breathing. Not much we can do other than give him antibiotics and keep him calm, but send for me anytime."

"Would antivenom made a difference?" Major asked.

"Maybe. Maybe not. Antivenom is tricky with humans because of serum reactions. It's definitely a case of the cure is worse than the bite for some people. We'll never know even if we had any because twenty-four hours is way too late."

CHAPTER THREE

As they entered Plainview, Rosalie asked, "Do we need to pull over to see who snuck into the pickup bed?"

Stuart snickered. "My money would be on Annie. What do you think?"

"I would have said Annie," Rosalie said. "Maybe Josh. He'd be up for an adventure."

After they cruised through Plainview and were on the highway going north, Aimee Louise said, "Mr. Young."

"He is the most versatile," Stuart said. "He's quiet and keeps busy. He could be gone for most of the day, and no one would notice."

"Let's wait to check the pickup bed until we're too far away to turn back," Rosalie said. "We could use someone sneaky. I've got something for us to think about. Did anyone see Penny before we left?"

Stuart snorted then leaned forward and scanned the road ahead. Rosalie scoured the roadside, and Aimee Louise glanced at her side mirrors for any traffic coming up on them from the rear.

"Road block ahead. Can't tell if it's staffed." Stuart pulled the binoculars out of the console as Aimee Louise lowered her speed.

"I'll hand you the map for the county then hop into the pickup bed," Rosalie said.

Rosalie handed the county map to Stuart before she slid open the window that separated the cab from the back. After she slipped through with her rifle, Aimee Louise cringed at the metal-on-metal screech as Rosalie opened the topper's side windows.

"Jarring noise," Stuart said.

Aimee Louise shuddered. "Jarring is a good word."

"Windows are open," Rosalie said.

"Still don't see anyone at the blockade." Stuart examined the roadblock with the binoculars. "We may be able to get past it on the right shoulder."

"Trick." Aimee Louise slammed on the brakes and threw the truck into a controlled spin. She accelerated as the truck completed its one hundred eighty degree turn and sped south on the highway. Angry shouts then shots rang out from the barricade.

"How did you know?" Stuart asked as he examined the county map.

"A gust of wind blew the barrier, and it swayed until a hand steadied it. Most likely cardboard."

"There's a side road coming up that leads to the back roads headed north," Stuart said.

"Tell me when to turn."

Stuart focused on the righthand side of the road. "Not far. Coming up on the right."

Aimee Louise slowed. "Good timing. There's another makeshift roadblock ahead."

Stuart narrowed his eyes as he peered at the barrier across the road. "We came through here not more than five minutes ago. Sure am glad we have these maps. We're going to have to stay away from major roads too."

Aimee Louise drove onto the shoulder before she turned on the dirt road.

Rosalie asked, "Why did you move off the road before your turn?"

"The trees along the side of the road gave us a little cover, so our side exposure during the turn was limited."

"According to the map, our side road will parallel the highway," Stuart said. "We can cut back over to the highway close to where Phil's group was."

Rosalie climbed back into the cab of the truck. "Show me."

Stuart pointed. "We have two options."

Rosalie examined the map. "The first one goes straight to the highway. The second one looks like it goes through a small community. First one looks better to me."

Stuart nodded and peered out Aimee Louise's window. "It's looking dark in the west. We might have some rain coming."

Rosalie lowered her window and sniffed. "Smells tropical. No one said anything about a storm in the Gulf on the radio this morning."

"We're a lot closer to the Gulf," Stuart said. "The water in the Gulf is warmer and saltier than the ocean, and a wind from the west would carry the saltiness. That may be the tropical air you're smelling."

A low rumble of thunder sounded in the distance as Rosalie raised her window. "I'll bet our highway robbers are closing up shop. Their cardboard barriers wouldn't do well in a rainstorm, which reminds me, I'll close the side windows in the topper."

Rosalie climbed through the pass-through window to the pickup bed. The windows screeched as she closed them. When Rosalie returned to the cab, she said, "I need to oil those windows. That scraping sound reminds me of fingernails on a blackboard."

"Is that our turn coming up?" Aimee Louise asked.

Stuart squinted at the map. "It's a little early, but we may want to cut over. Some of the back roads flood easily during a storm or just turn to mud."

Aimee Louise turned onto the narrow dirt road.

Stuart frowned. "This is a single-lane road."

"If a vehicle comes from the other direction, I'll find a good place to pull over so they can pass, and Rosalie can take her position in the pickup bed."

"There's a garden." Rosalie pointed to the right. "First sign of active habitation that we've seen in a while."

"There may have been other gardens not visible from the road along the way. These folks must feel relatively safe and remote." Stuart examined the homestead as they drove past. "They are smart. Did you notice the weeds in the front yard? They aren't advertising they are here."

Aimee Louise sped up, and Stuart peered into the side mirror. "Sky's darkening behind us, but our road's dry so far. Doesn't hurt to stay ahead of the storm."

A gust of wind rushed from the west, and the trees alongside the road swayed and dropped leaves and small branches as a wall of rain slammed the truck. Aimee Louise turned on the windshield wipers and maintained a steady speed.

"Just ahead," Stuart said. "We're coming to the highway."

The truck lost traction on the slippery road and slid toward the ditch, but Aimee Louise maintained control as she slowed to a stop.

"Hard to see, but I don't see anything on the road either way," Stuart said.

Aimee Louise eased out onto the highway and headed north.

"I see an open roadblock ahead. The barriers are on the side of the road," Stuart said.

When they reached the barriers, Aimee Louise slowed then pulled near a truck that was parked alongside the road and lowered her window. The wind and rain blew into the truck, and water trickled down her face.

When the driver of the other truck lowered his window, she waved. "Is Phil around?"

"Who wants to know?" the man asked.

"You can tell him his angel is looking for him. He'll know who I am."

"You're his angel? He talks about you all the time. I thought he'd got knocked loopy in the head in that crash. Is Major with you? Phil's out at his place. Do you know where that is?"

"Major couldn't make it, but Deputy Stuart came with me."

"What about that redhead? Phil couldn't shut up about his angel and the redhead. Is she real?"

Rosalie lowered her window and grinned. "About as real as you are."

The man guffawed. "This is like meeting celebrities. Follow me to Phil's. I want to be there when he sees y'all. Sometimes I think even he wonders if you are real. That was one rough night. Seriously, you all had quite an impact on our little community when you saved Phil. Follow me."

The man pulled in front of Major's truck, and Aimee Louise followed him.

"Dang," Stuart said. "I've been hanging out with celebrities."

"Don't start," Rosalie said, and Aimee Louise smacked his arm.

"Ow." Stuart grinned. "You celebrities are sensitive, aren't you?"

"Keep it up," Aimee Louise growled. When Stuart pursed his lips and zipped his thumb and finger in front of his mouth, Rosalie snorted.

When the rain became a deluge, Aimee Louise turned her wipers on high. The truck in front of them slowed then turned in at a driveway, and Aimee Louise followed. After he parked near the house, the man jumped out of his truck and shouted over the rain and thunder, "Stay put. I'll make sure Phil's home then we'll wave you in."

He dashed to the house, but was soaked before he reached the porch. Rosalie climbed into the pickup bed and returned with their rain jackets. "Put these on."

The man knocked on the door, and when Phil opened it, the man turned and waved. The three jumped out of the truck and hurried to the house.

"It's my angel." Phil hugged Aimee Louise; Rosalie grinned as Stuart glowered.

"And here's Red. I didn't make you up after all." Phil hugged Rosalie then held out his hand, and he and Stuart shook. "Nice to see you again, Deputy. No Shadow?"

"We left Shadow to guard the homestead," Stuart said.

"Well, come on in. My wife will be tickled to meet you all. You traveling?"

"We are," Stuart said. "We're looking for that team that was ambushed."

They stepped inside a large room with a magnificent river rock fireplace at one end. A row of four burning candles inside pint-sized canning jars on the fireplace mantle lightened the room made dark by the storm. A large sectional sofa, a three-cushioned sofa, and two recliners faced the fireplace. A homemade, plank coffee table sat in front of the sofa. A hand-hewn dining table surrounded by eight chairs was at the other end of the room. The tantalizing fragrance of chicken and herbs added to the warmth and welcoming atmosphere of the home.

A slender woman with short gray hair joined Phil. "I'm Deana. It's so nice to finally meet you all. You're staying for supper, right? I've got a big pot of soup on top of the stove and rolls ready to pop into the oven."

"Is there anything I can do?" Rosalie asked.

"I never turn down a little help." Deana put her arm around Rosalie's shoulders as they strolled to the kitchen. "Do you mind being called Red?"

"Fine with me," Rosalie said. "I'm not sure Mr. Phil would recognize me by any other name."

"Isn't that the truth?" Deana chuckled.

"Please have a seat." Phil waved at the comfortable, inviting furniture. "You're looking for the team that was ambushed? Our son, Scooter, took off work to help manage their care. They were in bad shape. Scooter returned to work after they were stable and left the three of them under the expert care of a retired nurse. I can take you there in the morning. It's too nasty to go anywhere tonight, especially on these country roads. Deana will want you to stay with us."

"We think we know the team. Two women and a man, right?" Aimee Louise said.

"You're right, Angel. A married couple and a woman. Let me see if I can remember their names." Phil furrowed his brow and scratched his head. "I'm not so good at names, but if you told me— "

"Peyton, Nate, and Charo?" Stuart asked.

"That's it. Two men were at the town roadblock day before yesterday and were asking about them. Wasn't any of their business as far as we could tell. We said we hadn't heard about any ambush. In fact, one of our guys tried to pump them for information, nosy-like. They told him it was confidential business and left in a huff. Best brush-off I've ever seen." Phil smacked his knee and chortled, and Stuart chuckled.

"I'll have to remember that," Stuart said. "Genius."

"It was, wasn't it?" Phil said. "One of the women on the injured team told Scooter she had to leave to get her son. He wasn't sure if she was delirious from the pain or not. Was she? The other woman mumbled about her dolly. Scooter was worried about her for a while. She was in the worst shape. I'd love to have just three minutes with those cowards that ambushed those folks. Scooter was sure they thought they'd left her dead. She was close to it. Who beats a woman near to death like that?"

Stuart shook his head. "Peyton's son is at my father's farm in Georgia. Charo and Nate's daughter is named Dolly. She's at the farm too. The three of them were on their way to reunite with their children. Do you remember the truck crash north of here?"

"Who could forget? That was horrible. Shook everyone up."

"Dolly, Nate's father, Peyton's son, and another young boy survived the crash. We took them to my father's farm with us. Dad was recovering from an injury, and we were on our way there to help Mom with the farm. At the time, we didn't know about the kids' parents, and my folks had plenty of room. We still haven't heard anything about the younger boy's mother or father, but he's got a home and family until they show up."

"Glad you found me. I'll get you to your team tomorrow. They may not be quite ready to travel, but maybe you three can help out on the farm. There may be a few critical farm chores that were set aside to take care of the injured folks."

"We're the right crew for farm chores." Stuart chuckled.

"Ms. Deana said their well pump is solar and battery powered. Isn't that brilliant? Angel, I'll show you where you can wash," Rosalie said with a twinkle in her eye.

"Thanks, Red." Aimee Louise elbowed Rosalie, and Stuart rolled his eyes.

"Solar power for your well? That's a great idea, Phil."

"I can't take the credit. Our son bought the solar panel and battery banks long before the big power outage. He said we needed to be sure we had a reliable water supply. Who knew doctors were so smart?" Phil waggled his eyebrows, and Stuart chuckled.

"What about your candles? Does Deana make them?"

"Deana and her friends do. When a neighbor has a pig or cow ready to harvest, we help with the work then each family takes home some meat to can or dry and fat to render into lard or tallow. The group of women who make candles get together and socialize while they render the fat. Candles make a good trading commodity, but most of us use them at home. I don't think anybody has much kerosene oil for lanterns left. Most of us rely on natural sunlight for the majority of our day; we get up before dawn and go to bed not long after it's dark."

"I'll bet Aimee Louise and Rosalie will know how to make candles by the time we leave," Stuart said.

"Those two girls are really something," Phil said.

"Yes, they are," Stuart said. *What are you leading up to?*

"But Angel is your girl, isn't she?"

Stuart's eyes widened, and he felt his cheeks grow warm. "Does it show?"

Phil chuckled. "I saw it the first time I met you two. She's a talented girl. Unique."

"Yes, she is. She's not as fragile as she appears, though. She's formidable."

"Yep, she's your girl. You know she feels the same about you, right?"

"Interesting. I'm not so sure about that."

"I'll show you where you can wash up." Phil rose. "Doesn't hurt to be patient. I noticed right off that the two of you are closer friends than most young couples I've seen. I can tell you from experience—being friends is the key."

"Thanks. I'm counting on it."

After Stuart washed his hands, Phil was waiting for him in the hallway. "We're eating in the kitchen."

When they strolled into the kitchen, the flames on the candles on the table and the sideboard flickered and danced. Aimee Louise said, "Ms. Deana invited us to stay with them tonight."

Phil elbowed Stuart. "Told you."

Stuart covered his smile with his fingers. "Where do I sit?"

Phil sat at the head of the table. "Sit next to me."

Aimee Louise sat next to Stuart, and Rosalie sat across from Aimee Louise. Deana lifted the large soup pot and placed it on the table before she sat between the two girls.

Phil said a quick blessing then Deana said, "Pass the rolls and butter around while I fill the bowls with soup and pass them."

While the soup in the bowls cooled enough to eat, everyone ate their first roll then Phil passed the rolls around again. After Phil slurped a spoonful of soup, Stuart spooned up chicken and vegetables. "Mmm. This is good, Ms. Deana."

She beamed. "There's more than enough for seconds or thirds, and we have another batch of rolls in the oven."

Rosalie and Aimee Louise sipped their soup.

"What will you do with all the leftovers?" Rosalie asked.

"I'll can the soup. If there are any leftover rolls, we'll have them with our eggs in the morning. I've got my canner all set up on my back deck. The deck is covered, so a little rain won't slow me down."

"We can help," Aimee Louise said.

"That would be nice," Deana said. "I've got the jars ready to go. We'll set up an assembly line."

After everyone had eaten their fill of soup and rolls, Deana said, "We have apple pie for dessert." Deana brought the pie to the table and placed slices on dessert plates, and the girls passed the plates.

"Excellent, as usual," Phil said.

"I'll pack the leftovers for your lunch tomorrow. Ready to can?" Deana asked.

"I could use a little help myself," Phil said. "Grab your raingear, Stuart. We're going out to the barn."

After they dashed through the rain to the barn, Phil said, "I need help repairing these stalls. Don't know if you remember my buddy, Fred. He was really sick the last time you all came through here. He's recovering, but it's slow, and he's still bedridden. His brother is helping out at Fred's farm, but the barn is a hazard. The brother wants to move the two cows here. He'll provide their feed, and I told him I would milk them. There is no time to rebuild Fred's barn with all the other work that needs to be done."

Stuart examined the stalls. "Wouldn't take much to fix these up. You have any lumber?"

"I've got lumber, tools, and nails in my equipment shed. Let's go look."

They loaded the lumber, tools, and supplies they'd need onto a trailer then Phil pulled the trailer to the barn with his tractor.

Stuart laid out the lumber for repairs then held each board in place as Phil secured it. After an hour, Phil sat on a square hay bale. "Looks good. It would have taken more than half a day for me to do this by myself. Thanks for the help, Stuart."

Stuart loaded the tools, extra lumber, and supplies back onto the trailer, and Phil drove the tractor to the equipment shed. Stuart jogged along behind the trailer then put the lumber and supplies away while Phil parked the tractor. As they strolled to the house, the rain slowed to a drizzle.

"Deana and I get up at four. I assume you all want an early start."

"Four sounds good. Can you give us directions?"

"It's not that far, and Deana would never forgive me if I didn't make sure the girls were safe. Fred's place is on the way, and we could make a fast stop there to check on Fred's brother before we continue on."

When the men reached the house, Aimee Louise and Rosalie were pulling gear out of the truck.

"We already took all three go-bags into the house," Rosalie said. "We have my spare rifle and our extra ammo and the maps. Is there anything else you'd like us to take in?"

"I'll help carry. I have another ammo box and rifle in the back wrapped in a blanket. I'll check to see if anything got wet, but I doubt I'll find anything. I'm glad you closed the windows before the storm hit; otherwise, we'd be spending most of the night drying out everything we had in the pickup bed."

After Stuart checked the bed, he hopped out and closed the tailgate. "We had a small leak at the back where the tailgate and window lost their tight seal, but only the tailgate was wet on the inside."

Deana met them when they entered the house. "The girls have already seen their room. Phil, will you show Stuart where he's sleeping tonight?"

"I fought for bunkbeds in the room you're sleeping in, Stuart, but I got overruled." He led Stuart to the room. "Deana said I could have bunkbeds if I changed the sheets on the top bunk. When I suggested I could just throw a sleeping bag up there, she informed me the discussion was over. I apologize for the lack of bunkbeds and the flowered bedspread. Deana says it's a coverlet. I figured saying the flower part was bad enough."

Stuart chuckled. "Are you planning to build a bunkhouse?"

Phil frowned as he whispered, "Don't let Deana hear you. I found the perfect spot and have been clearing trees when I've had the chance for the past ten years. How did you know?"

"Mom told Dad the same thing. He's still hunting for his perfect spot."

"I like your dad already. The bathroom's down the hall. The girls' room has its own powder room, at least that's what Deana calls it. She was fancy when I married her. I told her I'd never be fancy like her, and she said that was okay because she could be fancy enough for both of us. See you in the morning." Phil closed the door as he left.

Someone tapped on his door then Aimee Louise and Rosalie came in. "Did Phil say anything?" Rosalie asked.

"About what? He said they get up at four, and he'll lead us to the farm where the team is."

Rosalie nodded. "Deana told us he'd say that, but she doesn't think he'll get away from Fred's as fast as he does. She said Fred's brother is a hard worker with a big heart, but he's not an experienced farmer."

Stuart furrowed his brow. "I hate to hurt Phil's feelings—"

"That's okay. We've got Red," Aimee Louise said.

Rosalie snickered. "And I've got Angel for backup. We're just giving you a heads up. That's why we brought the maps in. Phil can show us the best route, and maybe he can help us spot alternatives in case things turn sour."

Aimee Louise and Rosalie headed to the door. Aimee Louise paused, "Goodnight, Stuart."

The girls slipped out and eased the door shut behind them.

After Stuart blew out the small candle on the dresser and climbed into bed, he pulled up the flowered bedspread and closed his eyes. *Do I need a bunkhouse?*

CHAPTER FOUR

Stuart jerked when he heard Aimee Louise whisper, "Stuart." He rolled over and sighed. *Nice dream.*

"You said it too quiet," Rosalie said. "Stuart. Get up."

Stuart opened his eyes. Aimee Louise and Rosalie were in his room, and Rosalie held a small candle.

"Breakfast is almost ready." Before they left, Aimee Louise lit Stuart's candle with the one Rosalie carried.

After Stuart dressed, he opened his bedroom door, and the aroma of coffee lured him to the kitchen.

Deana dished up oatmeal into bowls and fried eggs. Aimee Louise poured Stuart a cup of coffee and handed it to him.

Rosalie placed a bowl of oatmeal and a plate with two fried eggs and two rolls in front of him. Aimee Louise had a bowl of oatmeal and a plate with one fried egg and a roll in front of her. Rosalie carried her plate to the table and sat.

"Eat your breakfast while it's hot." After Deana cooked her egg, she joined them at the table. "Phil left a little over an hour ago. Fred's brother showed up, and he was frantic. He said one of the cows was sick. From his description of how she was acting, I think she's calving. It's her first time if she is, so it may be quite a while before she delivers. I suspect Phil might try to get her here if she can travel because she and a newborn calf would be much better off in a dry barn. I think it's about three now. Maybe three thirty."

Deana pointed to the maps that were on the table at Phil's seat. "Phil and I went over the maps before he left, and I took notes. He was really sorry that he had to leave, but he told me you'd understand, Stuart. We'll go over them after your breakfast."

After they ate, Stuart and Rosalie cleared the table while Deana pulled out her notes, and Aimee Louise spread out the maps. Rosalie moved one of the candles from the counter to the table then pulled out her notebook to take notes.

Deana handed Rosalie her notes before she pointed to the penciled Xs at different points on the map. "Phil marked his recommended travel route with Xs along the way. Stuart, he wasn't exactly sure where your parents' farm is, but he said you'd know the best way to get there after you checked on the team at Keith's farm. The circles with a minus inside are what Phil considers as potential trouble spots. He said you might want to approach them with the idea to divert if needed."

Rosalie glanced at the map. "Your notes say the circles with a plus inside are good places to shift to a different road."

Deana, Aimee Louise, and Stuart examined the map.

"Looks like each trouble spot has a circle with a plus inside on each side of it," Stuart said.

"Yes," Deana said. "He said if you don't run into any trouble, you'll be at Keith's farm in an hour. The safer routes have you backtracking and could add an extra hour or even two, depending on the condition of the road."

After Rosalie copied Deana's notes, she asked, "Do you have any oil or grease? The side windows on the topper scream like banshees when I open or close them."

Deana chuckled. "I've got some bacon grease on the back of the stove. Help yourself, but stay away from bear country. The odor will linger, and you'll smell tasty."

Stuart straightened his back. "We'll add bears to our Do Avoid list."

"Done," Rosalie said as she dipped some bacon grease into a small bowl.

"Are you thinking you'll be moving the injured folks to your dad's farm?" Deana asked.

"I hadn't really thought about it," Stuart said. "I thought we might stay and help with the farm and not move them. I thought we'd take them back to Florida when they were stronger, but it makes more sense to take them to my dad's farm where their families are. There's room for them, and Mom and Nate's dad could share the work of taking care of them."

"Another option is that you could bring them here. I pulled a few things together that may make it more comfortable for them to travel. I have two large boxes. I'll put them on the dining table."

While Rosalie greased the topper windows, Aimee Louise and Stuart finished packing up their bags, and Aimee Louise carried them out.

Stuart carried out the first large box. "Deana packed two boxes of extra supplies for us. Be right back."

While Stuart brought out the second box, Rosalie slid the windows open and closed in silence.

"Success." She climbed out of the pickup bed while Aimee Louise handed Stuart the bags and boxes that went into the back. Rosalie carried the go-bags to the cab.

Aimee Louise gazed at the sky. "No stars or moon. We'll have cloud cover through the morning."

"Would have been nice to have a little moonlight," Rosalie said.

Deana carried a tote bag to the truck. "Here, Red. I packed lunch and some snacks for y'all. I added a candle and matches for the road and three small candles for trade if you need them. Candles are gold around here. We hear there are some roadblocks set up to charge what they call a toll, but I don't know how to tell if you've got murdering thugs or just plain highway robbers at a roadblock. When in doubt, shoot your way out. Is that a saying?"

Rosalie chuckled. "Is now."

Deana snorted. "I've got a friend who loves to do cross-stitch. I might have a pillow for you when you come back through. Which reminds me: plan on stopping here, no matter what the time of day or night, on your way back. You can eat, rest, or sleep. Whatever you need. Doesn't matter how many you have with you either. We've got cots for extra folks. I like to be prepared for contingencies."

Deana hugged Rosalie, Aimee Louise, and Stuart. "It's good luck when a farm wife hugs you. Phil told me that when we were first married."

As Aimee Louise drove away from the house, Rosalie slid open the window to the pickup bed. "I'm glad we stopped. Deana and Phil are amazing. I added stop at Phil and Deana's on our list." She climbed through the window. "I opened both windows. We have a win for bacon grease. Watch for bears."

"Headlights or no?" Aimee Louise asked when they reached the highway.

Stuart furrowed his brow. "Yes. Given the time of year, deer are most likely moving. I realize we'll be seen too, but we can reassess at our first safe turn." He waited then smiled. *Aimee Louise agrees; if she didn't, she'd argue.*

After half an hour, Rosalie called out from the back, "Pull over. I hear something."

Aimee Louise eased off the road and turned off the headlights. She and Stuart lowered their windows as she turned off the ignition.

Rosalie stuck her head through the opening. "You hear it? A rumble behind us. Reminded me of the truckload of kids."

"We need to find a place to pull off the road," Stuart said.

Aimee Louise started the engine then increased her speed as Stuart leaned out the window. "About a hundred yards ahead on the right is a grove of trees. If the ditch is still shallow, drive into the trees."

"Shine a flashlight on the shoulder," Aimee Louise said.

Stuart grabbed their flashlight out of the glove compartment and held the light on the shoulder as Aimee Louise jammed her foot on the accelerator to speed to the trees.

"Good place ahead to turn," he said.

Aimee Louise hit the brakes. "Got it." She took the ditch at an angle and accelerated through the field to the trees. She nosed the truck in between the trees and behind a thicket so that it was not exposed to the traffic from the south and turned off the engine.

"It's getting closer," Rosalie said.

Aimee Louise jumped out of the truck and raced to the edge of the road. Rosalie tumbled into the cab as Stuart grabbed his rifle then jumped out.

"I've got your back," Rosalie called as Stuart chased after Aimee Louise.

Stuart almost stepped on Aimee Louise who had lain down in a depression in the high grass. He crawled away from her and found another depression with high grass. He lay flat as the rumble of the truck neared.

When the truck's headlights came up over the rise, the truck slowed. Stuart assumed a prone shooting position and aimed at the truck as the passenger peered out the side window.

Binoculars?

He flattened. "Night vision. Stay low, Aimee Louise."

Aimee Louise called out, "Inside."

Brilliant.

The truck sped up before it came to their position and continued north. Stuart narrowed his eyes as it hurled past them. *Looks exactly like the truck that crashed.* He crawled to Aimee Louise, but she wasn't there.

His heart pounded as he whistled the cardinal call, and she answered. *She moved closer to the road.*

Stuart crawled to the road and whistled again.

"Here," she said.

He reached to his right and touched her foot. After he crawled next to her, he said, "You scared me when I couldn't find you. What did you see?"

"The truck wasn't empty."

"Are you sure? It was dark."

"The flap was pulled to the side. Someone in the back had a flashlight on. I saw at least four men but no children."

"Coming in," Stuart called.

"Heard ya," Rosalie replied.

When the three of them were together at the truck, Rosalie asked, "What do we do now? Follow them north or divert? I vote follow them. They can run our front door, as the truckers say."

Aimee Louise tilted her head.

"She means they'll be in front of us and come across any roadblocks or problems before we do," Stuart said. "Or as Josh would say, they'll run interference for the pizza express."

"I'm wondering now how Sara would explain trucker-talk, but back to our question," Rosalie said.

"The only reason to divert is if there is another truck behind them traveling just as fast as they were," Stuart said.

"We listen for it," Aimee Louise said.

Stuart nodded. "Rosalie heard the first one. Let's continue north. I think we're less than a half hour from the farm where the team is."

After they climbed back in, Aimee Louise headed the truck through the grass to the road.

Before Rosalie hopped into the back, Stuart asked, "What did you do when Aimee Louise called inside?"

"Rolled under the truck. Seemed like the quickest inside I could do then I thought about fire ants. I wouldn't do that again."

"When the rumbling truck slowed, the passenger scanned the field with night vision binoculars. I'm not sure what he was looking for, but he didn't find it because the truck resumed its speed before it got to us."

"Should we check to see if there's someone hiding from the truck like Brandon and Henry did?" Aimee Louise asked.

"Didn't think about that." Stuart frowned. "The idea worries me, but if someone is hiding from the truck, they'd hide from us too. Let's continue north. I'll turn on the ham radio, though, to see if we can pick up anything." When Stuart turned on the radio, he set it to scan the standard simplex channel, but it was quiet.

Aimee Louise pulled onto the road and headed north with her headlights on. Stuart put down his window and scanned the road ahead.

After twenty minutes, Aimee Louise asked, "Are you holding your breath?"

Stuart chuckled. "I think I've been holding it since we left Phil's."

"Is there any reason for us to go to South Carolina?" Aimee Louise asked.

"I'm not sure there is, but we need to relieve the farm folks of the burden of taking care of the team."

"If they can travel, could we take them to your dad's farm, or is that too much of an imposition?"

Stuart stared at Aimee Louise. "Deana and I talked about taking the team to Dad's farm. She'd already packed what we'd need for makeshift beds for them. Did you and Deana talk?"

"I asked her for her opinion. I think about everything. Don't you?"

Thought I did.

"Not as good as you do," he said. "Could you pull over? I want to check the map one more time but don't want to take away your night vision."

After Aimee Louise eased to the shoulder and parked, Stuart hopped out of the truck with the map. He held the map near the headlight then climbed back in. "Okay, let's go."

"Everything okay?" Rosalie asked from the back.

"Just double-checked the map. We're closer than I thought. Our turn is the next one on the left. Less than two miles."

Aimee Louise turned on her headlights and resumed a steady speed. After a mile, she slowed, and Stuart moved closer to her and breathed in as he peered at the roadside on the left. *Aimee Louise always smells nice.*

"There it is," he pointed to a side road a few yards ahead.

As Aimee Louise turned onto the paved road, Rosalie stuck her head through the opening. "Another rumble behind us. Do we wait to see what it is?"

"Let's keep going. I don't know what good it would do to watch another truck," Stuart said.

Aimee Louise picked up speed.

"I closed the side windows," Rosalie said. "According to Deana's notes, we turn right in three miles then the farm is on the left two miles down that road. I'm moving to the cab. I can always hop back."

"Three miles coming up," Aimee Louise said.

Stuart and Rosalie peered out their windows.

"Road coming up on the right."

As they neared the road, Stuart said, "Have you noticed there aren't any road or street signs anymore?"

"Scavenged for repairs," Aimee Louise said. "That's what I'd do with them."

"The people who live on the road could have taken them down, so strangers wouldn't turn down the road looking for houses to rob," Rosalie said.

"Did you hear that? Barred owl," Stuart said. "It's checking in with its mate and hunting."

Rosalie lowered her window. "She answered."

"Two miles down the road then on the left," Aimee Louise said.

Aimee Louise slowed after the first mile, and Rosalie lowered her window then raised it when the mosquitos swarmed her.

"I'm guessing there's a pond nearby," Rosalie said. "I'm climbing into the back and pulling out our spray."

She spritzed herself and the back of Aimee Louise's neck before she handed the bottle to Stuart. Stuart sprayed his arms and rubbed some of the spray on his forehead and neck.

"There's the barn," Aimee Louise said.

"Talk about bare bones. That poor building is ready to fall. I thought Fred's barn was the one about to collapse," Rosalie said. "Would that be our first project?"

"We could stay and help, but I think the best thing we could do is to relieve them of the burden of caring for three injured people," Stuart said. "Rosalie, would we be able to make two beds for seriously injured people in the back of the pickup?"

"I peeked in the large boxes. Deana packed what we'd need for two comfortable pallets. We can flatten the boxes for the foundations. I suspect you could rearrange everything so we'd have plenty of room."

"If all three are injured, the backseat can be a bed for the least injured person, but Rosalie would be stuck in the pickup bed by herself to care for two injured people," Stuart said. "Am I overthinking?"

"Yes." Aimee Louise stopped at the gate that led to the house. "I see a light." She tapped the horn twice.

A woman came out of the side door. "That you, Phil?"

"Phil had to go help Fred. It's Deputy Stuart, Angel, and Red," Stuart said.

"You have Angel and Red with you? Come on in. I just put the coffee on, and Peyton heard me in the kitchen. We're waiting for the coffee to finish perking. Keith's feeding the goats and chickens down at the barn."

Stuart handed Aimee Louise the spray. "Spray yourself. It's buggy here. Did you catch that Peyton's well enough to get to the kitchen on her own?"

When they reached the door, Peyton grinned and one-arm hugged each one. "I've heard all about Angel, Red, and Deputy Stuart."

Peyton's face was bruised, her lip was split, and her knuckles had open cuts and abrasions. Her left forearm was wrapped with gauze, and a sling supported her arm.

A single candle on the table provided light for the kitchen.

"Y'all sit. I'm Leslie. I almost forgot my manners in all the excitement. Coffee?"

"I'll take care of the coffee, Ms. Leslie. You go ahead and sit," Rosalie said.

"Thank you, Red. I don't mind getting off my feet for a bit." Leslie sat next to Peyton, who smiled and patted her hand.

Rosalie poured coffee for Stuart, Peyton, and Leslie. She sat on the other side of Peyton.

"How are your patients?" Aimee Louise asked.

"You can see Peyton. She has a bad laceration on her arm from a knife, but there have been no signs of infection. The rest of her injuries just need healing time."

"What about Charo?" Rosalie asked.

"Charo has the worst physical injuries. They broke her arms and her left ankle, but they mostly concentrated on her face, and it is still bad. Doc Scooter said her jaw isn't broken, but I feel awful that I didn't have any ice to keep the swelling down. It's gotten difficult for her to talk the past few days; I'm grateful she didn't lose any teeth. Doc said he didn't think she'll lose her eye, but her sight may be wonky for a long time, and she may have some facial nerve damage. Doc said he couldn't find any signs of brain damage or internal injuries."

Peyton cleared her throat. "Charo kept taunting them to draw them away from me and Nate. She's a real hero, and as soon as she's well, I intend to give her a time out."

Rosalie snickered. "What about moving her? Could she take three or four hours of travel? Her family is at Deputy Stuart's family farm."

"Dolly's there?" Leslie's eyes widened. "Being around Dolly is the best medicine she could have right now. Medically speaking, she's still fragile, but it would do her a world of good to see Dolly. Is that your plan? We'd have to pad her like crazy to stabilize those bones and keep her comfortable. Doc left her some powerful pain pills, but I've held off because she's holding her own. They could definitely help her for three or four hours of travel."

"What about Nate?"

Leslie gazed at Peyton, and Peyton stared at the table. Leslie shook her head. "Nate's injuries are the worst of all. He has a black eye and abrasions on his wrists, neck, and ankles from trying to get loose. He has cigarette burns on his face and neck, but his real injuries are in his heart."

"They tied him to a chair while they beat me then worked over Charo," Peyton said. "He won't talk. He's a shell of himself. They destroyed him."

"Doc Scooter said Nate needs time, but Scooter also warned us he knows nothing about how to manage the intense emotional shock Nate suffered." Leslie's sorrow lined her face. "We're gentle with Nate. He'll do as he's told, but he understands only simple statements. If you tell him to wash his hands and come to the table, he freezes. He doesn't know what to do."

"It's hard for me to remember the simple statements," Peyton said. "I worked for so long with the old Nate that I have trouble dealing with the new Nate. I'm glad he wasn't hurt any worse physically, but I don't do well with him. I think because I miss the old Nate so much. I can sit next to him and pat his hand, but he responds to Leslie."

"Does he do best with only one person telling him what to do?" Rosalie asked.

"I think that does work best for him," Leslie said.

"You drive, Stuart. I'll help Nate," Aimee Louise said. "We'll need to keep the distractions at a minimum, so we don't confuse him."

Leslie stared at Aimee Louise. "I think you're right. I'll introduce you when I get Nate up. Maybe we can make it an easy transition."

"I can take care of Charo," Peyton said. "That leaves you free, Red, to back up Stuart, but I need a pistol and a holster. I've felt naked without one."

"We have one we can give you," Rosalie said.

"I'll get it." Stuart left then returned with a firearm and holster.

"That's perfect. Leslie gave me a belt so I'm set." Peyton examined the pistol then slipped the holster onto her belt. "There. All dressed."

Leslie rose at the sound of feet stomping and scraping on the back porch. "Keith's back from the barn."

Keith came into the house. He'd removed his muddy boots and left them on the porch.

"There you are, Keith." Leslie rose. "I'll pour you some coffee."

Keith smiled. "Deputy Stuart, Angel, and Red. Welcome. You're famous in these parts."

Stuart rose, and the two men shook hands.

"We're talking about leaving this morning and going to Deputy Stuart's family farm. That's where our children are," Peyton said.

Keith narrowed his eyes. "What about Charo? Can she travel?"

"It's a three-hour trip, and her daughter Dolly is there," Leslie said. "All she needs to heal is time. We can stabilize her arms and ankle and make her comfortable for the trip. Peyton can take care of her."

"What about Nate? Shouldn't he stay here with you?"

Leslie shook her head. "Nate's tricky. We'll try to transition from me to Aimee Louise."

Keith nodded. "Might work. She's exactly what he needs right now—an angel."

"Everybody ready for breakfast? I've got biscuits ready for the oven, and I'll scramble up a mess of eggs. Ever had goat butter?"

"I'll set the table," Peyton said.

Rosalie poured a cup of coffee for Keith and refilled Stuart's cup. Aimee Louise cracked eggs into the bowl Leslie had set on the counter while Leslie popped the biscuits into the oven.

"Y'all are really special." Leslie poured the bowlful of beaten eggs into her large cast iron skillet. "I could easily get spoiled by all this good help."

After everyone ate, Peyton said, "Angel and I will take care of the dishes, Leslie, if you and Red would like to check on Charo."

"I'd like that. We can pack up Charo's things too." Leslie turned on the burner under the large pot of water on the stove.

"I'll set up a space for the bed in the pickup," Stuart said.

On his way out the door, Keith said, "I'll be at the chicken coop if you need me. I found a place where a critter could get in when one of the chickens got out yesterday. I blocked it last night, but I need to make a more permanent repair."

"Do you want me to help you?" Stuart asked.

"No, but thanks anyway. It's a quick repair. I just didn't want to tackle it last night."

Aimee Louise cleared the table while Peyton checked the water on the stove. Peyton poured half the hot water into the dishwashing sink and half in the other sink to rinse before Aimee Louise poured soapy solution into the first sink and slipped silverware and dishes into the water. Aimee Louise washed and rinsed; Peyton dried and put away the dishes and silverware.

"Aimee Louise, does it bother you when people call you Angel?"

"No. Mr. Phil called me Angel the first time he met me. I like Mr. Phil."

Peyton nodded. "I thought it was a charming nickname for you, and Red is perfect for Rosalie, also known as Dead-Eye Red. Isn't that what Josh called her?"

"Josh is good at coming up with names."

As they put away the last dish, Leslie came into the kitchen. "You've got the dishes washed and put away already. You two are efficient. I checked on Charo, and she is awake. It's still hard for her to talk. I told her y'all were here and were planning to take her to

Stuart's farm. She really brightened up. She's looking forward to seeing Dolly."

Peyton said, "I'll be outside if you need me. I want to see what Stuart has planned for a bed in the back of the pickup."

Leslie bit her lip. "Angel, I'll bring Nate to the kitchen. We'll see how he does. Might be best if you sit at the table, so he can see you when we come in."

Leslie hurried down the hall as Aimee Louise sat at the table and folded her hands in her lap.

"This way, Nate. We're going to the kitchen," Leslie said. When Leslie and Nate reached the kitchen, Aimee Louise stared at her hands in her lap.

"Do you remember Aimee Louise?" Leslie asked.

Aimee Louise shifted her gaze to Keith's chair on her right and noticed in her periphery that Nate stood motionless in the doorway.

"No." Nate's voice was flat.

"It's okay. I can remind you that she was at the farm in Florida."

"Oh."

He's trying to be polite. He doesn't remember the farm, but he doesn't want to be rude.

"Come sit with me at the table," Leslie said softly.

"No, thank you."

He's responding to Ms. Leslie. He needs to stay here.

"You did good. We can go to your room if you want."

Nate turned to the hallway, and Leslie walked along with him to his room.

In a few minutes, she returned to the kitchen. "What do you think, Angel? Should we try again in a bit?"

"He tried to be polite. Is that new?"

Leslie sat at the table. "Now that you mention it, that is new."

"He is trying to reach out to you. I think right now, he can work on only one person at a time. It may not be long until he reaches out to Mr. Keith."

"Really? That's very encouraging, and I agree with you. He's welcome here until he's able to leave, however long it takes. For now, he stays, right?"

"Yes. We'll stop on our way back to Florida, but we're not sure when that will be."

"It doesn't matter. I'm sure Nate will be stronger."

"Is it okay if I say hello to Charo?"

"Excellent idea. Let's go to her room. I'll tell her you're here then you can come in. I like to do things slowly."

"I appreciate that."

Leslie led the way to Charo's room and tapped on the door before she stepped inside.

"Charo, Aimee Louise is here. Is it okay if she comes in?"

Leslie waved Aimee Louise into the bedroom. Charo's mouth curved into a one-sided smile as Aimee Louise sat on the chair next to her.

Aimee Louise said, "Stuart and Peyton are working on a comfortable place for you to travel in the back of the pickup. Do you feel up to a long drive?"

Charo winked with her good eye.

"I'll be driving. I'll take it as easy as I can."

Charo wiggled the fingers on her right hand, and Aimee Louise patted her hand then left her hand near Charo's fingers. Charo patted Aimee Louise's hand.

"We'll be ready to put you in the truck soon."

Before Aimee Louise rose, Charo patted her hand again.

"Thank you," Aimee Louise said. "You'll do great."

When Aimee Louise strolled into the kitchen, Leslie stood at the stove. "I'm heating some broth for Charo."

"Who do you think attacked them?" Aimee Louise asked.

"I don't know, but I don't think it was random. Sometimes I have the feeling that Peyton knows. As friendly as Peyton is, she's obviously FBI and not prone to share information except on a need-to-know basis."

"Interesting."

Stuart came inside. "What's interesting?"

"We agree that Nate needs to stay here for a while. It's a bit too early to change his environment," Leslie said.

"That's too bad, but I think we all want to do what's best for Nate. Would you two come check the bed in the back of the truck?"

"Sure will." Leslie headed outside.

Aimee Louise followed Leslie, but Stuart touched her shoulder before she reached the door. "Can I talk to you a second?"

She tilted her head. "Yes."

He cleared his throat. "Do you agree with leaving Nate here and taking Charo to the folks' farm?"

"Yes. Don't you?"

Stuart shrugged. "I wasn't sure about splitting up Nate and Charo. It didn't seem right."

Aimee Louise looped her arm through Stuart's. "Both of them need time to heal in their own ways. Nate will heal better here as he learns to trust people and himself again. Charo will heal better under the care of your mother and the judge, and she won't be lonely. Dolly will make sure of that. Leslie can't properly take care of both Nate and Charo, and Nate can't leave here quite yet. He feels safe here."

"Thanks," Stuart said as they walked together to the truck. "I was worried."

"I know," Aimee Louise said.

CHAPTER FIVE

When they reached the truck, Leslie said, "Angel, come look. We think we've made the bed comfortable and safe. We rolled quilts to make bumpers on the sides so Charo won't accidently roll. Can you think of anything else we can do?"

"Where will Peyton sit?"

"I'll sit next to her." Peyton peered at the back. "We might have to move a few boxes or something."

"You'll need a seat with a back and a little room for you to stretch out," Leslie said.

"I'll have to have access to the window between the cab and the back too," Rosalie said. "You've tossed us back to the drawing board, Angel. Good eye."

"Give me a second," Stuart said. "I can move a few things for you." Stuart climbed into the back and moved boxes away from both side windows and the window between the cab and back. "Toss me a quilt, and you'll see what I have in mind."

Rosalie folded a quilt and handed it to Stuart who placed it on the opposite side of the truck bed across from Charo's bed. "What do you think?"

Peyton climbed into the truck and sat on the quilt. "We can open the side windows for air flow. Not sure we thought about that. Might use a second quilt for padding and a pillow for my back, but I think this is perfect. Do you have enough room to go from the front to the back, Red?"

"Plenty of room. Well done, Deputy Stuart," Rosalie said.

"No reason for me to stand here and watch you all work," Leslie said. "I'm going inside to help Charo with her soup and to pack a few extra things while you figure out how to move her to the truck."

Stuart untied the fuel can that rode on the back bumper and carried it to the side of the truck to fill the tank. While Peyton and Rosalie discussed different ways to create a makeshift stretcher, Aimee Louise hurried into the house.

"Ms. Leslie, do you happen to have an old wheelchair?" she asked.

"I like how you think, Angel. Of course, an old nurse would have a wheelchair stuck back. I didn't even think of that. Go look in that back bedroom closet. I think that's where it is. I'll be in Charo's room."

Aimee Louise hurried to the bedroom and opened the closet but didn't see a wheelchair. She searched behind the clothes and stacked boxes but found nothing. She frowned as she scanned the room then dropped to her hands and knees to peer under the bed.

Bet that's the wheelchair wrapped in a sheet.

She slid it out and pulled off the sheet then spread the wheels apart and locked it open. She found the foot rests wrapped in another sheet.

After she folded the sheets and set them in the closet, she rolled the wheelchair to Charo's room. "Here we are."

"That is super. I set a small box next to the back door. You want to let the folks outside know we have a wheelchair?" Leslie asked.

When Aimee Louise approached the truck, Peyton was sitting on the tailgate while Rosalie paced and waved her arms in an animated, one-way discussion. Stuart and Keith had the truck's hood open but were involved in a quiet conversation.

Stuart noticed her first. "Angel. You disappeared."

"We have a wheelchair for Charo," she said.

"What?" Rosalie asked. "Where did you find a wheelchair?"

"Under the bed."

Rosalie shrugged. "I did ask where."

"Does that mean we're ready to leave?" Peyton jumped off the tailgate.

"We need to check to be sure we're not leaving anything." Stuart stepped back from the hood, and Keith slammed it shut.

"Ms. Leslie has a box next to the back door, and we need to load Charo's things then that's it," Aimee Louise said.

"Do we know how we're going to lift Charo from the wheelchair to the back of the pickup then to her bed?" Stuart whispered to Aimee Louise as Peyton and Rosalie rushed to the house. "Let me guess. Two person lift then blanket drag. Am I close?"

"Perfect."

"Thanks."

"You all about ready to load up Charo?" Keith asked. "Leslie told me about the wheelchair. I figured you and I could do a two-person lift to put her in the wheelchair then take her out at the truck, Stuart. Does that fall in line with your plan?"

"Sure does."

"We'll wait inside until you let us know you're ready, Aimee Louise," Stuart said.

Aimee Louise trotted to the truck. "Anything we need to do besides load Charo?"

"Just Charo," Rosalie said.

"Stuart and Keith will bring her out on the wheelchair."

"We've got our transfer blanket in place, and we tested its ability to slide," Peyton said.

"I'll let them know we're ready." Aimee Louise hurried to Charo's room. Leslie had fixed the left leg rest in a horizontal position to support Charo's ankle.

"Ready to go," Aimee Louise said, and Charo wiggled her fingers in a finger dance.

Stuart and Keith lifted Charo while Leslie provided support for Charo's injured leg. The men transferred Charo to the wheelchair in a slow, smooth motion. Aimee Louise took over the support of the injured leg while Leslie placed a pillow under Charo's ankle on the foot rest.

"How are you doing?" Keith knelt next to Charo, and she raised a thumb.

Leslie placed a small, lightweight blanket over Charo's lap and legs. "Ready to go."

Aimee Louise rushed down the hallway and was surprised by Nate, who stood in the kitchen. When Charo was wheeled into the kitchen, he approached the wheelchair and kissed Charo on the forehead.

"Take care of her, Angel," he said.

Leslie's eyes widened before she hurried to the door to hold it open.

"Do you want to go too?" Aimee Louise asked.

"Next time." Nate shuffled down the hallway to his room.

After Aimee Louise joined Leslie outside, Leslie grabbed her arm. "What did he say?"

"I asked him if he wanted to go too, and he said, next time."

Tears slipped down Leslie's face. "I never expected him to even notice that Charo was leaving, and I was surprised to hear him call you Angel. I told him you were Aimee Louise when I brought him into the kitchen."

Aimee Louise hugged her. "He hears and understands more than we thought."

Leslie nodded. "You're right. Let's get you all on the road."

A tear had stained Charo's cheek. Aimee Louise knelt next to her and held her fingers lightly. "When I asked him if he wanted to go too, he said, next time. He wants to get well. That is exciting news."

One side of Charo's mouth quivered, and she wiggled her fingers.

* * *

Stuart and Keith half-rolled and half-carried the wheelchair across the bumpy yard to the truck. After they positioned Charo next to the tailgate, Stuart said, "We'll lift you onto the blanket then Rosalie and Peyton will slide you to your travel bed. Sound good to you, Charo?"

Charo held up one thumb.

"We've got the Charo seal of approval; let's do this," Rosalie said.

"Now the easy part," Keith said. "Jump on up into the truck, Charo."

Charo snorted.

"You told him, Charo." Peyton laughed.

As Stuart and Keith lifted Charo to the back of the pickup, Aimee Louise provided support for her legs. When Charo was solidly situated on the blanket, Rosalie and Peyton slid her to the front of the pickup bed then Stuart jumped into the truck to help lift Charo onto her pallet of soft quilts. Peyton and Rosalie rearranged the blankets and quilts around Charo until she grunted and wiggled her fingers at them.

"We can take a hint. We're done," Peyton said.

Beads of sweat had stuck Rosalie's red hair to her forehead. She wiped her face with the carry blanket before she folded it and placed it on the floor next to Charo.

Peyton snickered. "Your damp, red hair makes sword slices across your forehead. You're a swashbuckling pirate."

Rosalie grinned as she jumped out of the truck. "Aye, matey."

Leslie approached Stuart as the team headed to their seats for the trip. "Nate's at the back door; he'd like to see Charo before you leave."

Aimee Louise and Rosalie climbed into the truck to give Nate space. Stuart stayed near the back to close the tailgate as Peyton propped up Charo with another pillow then sat in her out-of-the-way spot. Keith waited at the back door for Nate then followed him as Nate made his way across the yard with cautious steps.

When Nate reached the back of the truck, he smiled at Charo. "You'll be safe. See you soon."

Charo wiggled her fingers then made a heart.

Stuart walked alongside Nate as he returned to the house. When Nate stumbled on the stoop, Stuart caught his elbow, and spoke in a soft voice, "I would feel the same way you do if it had been Aimee Louise."

Nate stared at Stuart then nodded. Keith opened the door, and Nate went inside. Stuart hurried back to the truck and closed the tailgate before he jumped into the passenger's seat. After he buckled up, Aimee Louise drove the truck down the driveway.

"I was holding my breath from the time Leslie told us Nate wanted to see Charo until he made it back to the house," Rosalie said.

Peyton called from the back, "Charo and I were too."

Stuart studied the maps. "Turn left when we get to the road. We'll try a different route. If there are too many roadblocks, it won't be hard to get back to our road that we've traveled before. I don't think it will cost us any extra time, and it's paved."

At the end of the driveway, Aimee Louise turned left. After an hour of silence as they continued north on the road, Stuart pointed to an upcoming driveway. "There's another driveway blocked by a downed tree. Could have been a storm, but looks more intentional."

"There aren't any other trees down alongside the road, either," Aimee Louise said.

Rosalie peered into the back. "Peyton and Charo are asleep. The drone of the truck tires almost put me out too."

Stuart consulted the map. "About five miles ahead, we turn right. It's about two miles south of a small town. Watch for a roadblock, but I don't expect there to be one that far out of town."

"Should I wake Peyton when we get close?" Rosalie asked.

"Good idea," Stuart said. "She'd need to be alert if we came across anything, and she could watch the back."

Rosalie leaned through the opening. "Peyton?"

"I dozed off. I'm awake," she said.

"We'll be close to a town in about five miles. Stuart thought you could watch our back."

"Will do."

"I heard." Stuart narrowed his eyes. "Is that a car or truck alongside the road ahead?"

"They'd expect us to slow down," Aimee Louise said. "I'll maintain our speed."

When they were closer to the car, Rosalie said, "A woman's waving. Is there someone lying in the ditch?"

As they neared the car, Aimee Louise sped up. "Trap. Hang on."

"I've got the right side." Stuart lowered his window and aimed his rifle at the car.

Rosalie lowered the window on the driver's side.

"I've slid open the side windows," Peyton said.

When they reached the car, the woman shouted, "Help! Stop!"

When the man in the ditch jumped up and opened fire at the truck, he hit the lower part of the truck body on the passenger's side. Stuart returned his fire, and the man dropped. Two other men stepped out on the other side of the road ahead of them and fired shots. Rosalie shot back, and one man collapsed then the second man fell when Peyton returned his fire.

After they passed the car, the woman stepped into the road and fired a shotgun at them, but the truck was out of range.

When the car was out of sight, Peyton leaned into the cab. "Why did we speed up? What gave them away?"

"Aimee Louise sees things other people miss. It was her call," Stuart said.

"Not surprised. I've always known there was something special about Aimee Louise. Charo's awake. I'll give her some water, but it's too bad Sara's not here to tell her what she missed. My story's going to be dull," Peyton said.

"Mention the fairies," Rosalie said. "That will help."

"I will." Peyton snickered.

"Turn coming up ahead," Stuart said.

Aimee Louise slowed her speed, and Rosalie leaned over the front seat as she peered out the windshield. "I don't see anything between us and the turn."

"Be ready, just in case," Stuart said.

Rosalie called out to Peyton, "Right turn coming up. I've got the left side."

"Got it. I'll watch the rear."

"Stuart." Aimee Louise pointed to the field where they would turn.

"Expect Aimee Louise to make a sharp right turn, and watch the left side," Stuart said. "There's a tractor in the field."

"I'll keep Charo from being jostled by the turn," Peyton said.

Aimee Louise slammed on the brakes when the truck reached the turn and accelerated out of the skid. As the truck sped past the tractor, Peyton said, "Man at the tractor with a pistol, but we're out of range. How did you know?"

Aimee Louise said, "No farmer would leave a tractor alone in a field near a road like that."

"Was it an ambush?" Rosalie asked.

"I wouldn't put my newest tractor in the line of fire, but no reason to hang around and find out," Stuart said.

Aimee Louise slowed to a normal speed. "When's our next turn?"

"We can either go through town or go around to get to the farm. I'd rather avoid town, but it's an extra ten or fifteen minutes."

"Bypass," Aimee Louise said.

"Our turn is in four miles."

"Hey, don't I get a vote?" Rosalie asked.

"No," Aimee Louise said.

"What if Peyton and Charo agree with me?" Rosalie asked.

Stuart shrugged, and Peyton tittered.

When they reached the turn, Rosalie said, "It's a dirt road."

"I'll sit close to Charo," Peyton said. "We'll be fine."

After Aimee Louise turned, she slowed her speed to avoid the deep ruts in the road.

"No tire tracks since last rain," Stuart said. "That's good."

"When's our next turn?" Aimee Louise asked.

"Three miles. We'll turn left onto another dirt road. When we get to the paved road, we turn left."

After they turned onto the paved road, the sky at the horizon to the west deepened from pinks and blues to a blaze of orange. When the colors of the horizon slipped from dark orange to deep red, Stuart said, "Two curves then we'll come to the driveway."

"I remember," Aimee Louise said. "Driveway's across from the mailbox. Do I park in the trees near the road?"

"We can park in the grove of trees closer to the house," Stuart said. "I'll approach the house. Follow me and let me know if you see any danger. Rosalie, stay near the front of the truck for backup."

"Barred owl?" Aimee Louise asked.

"Yes, warn me with the barred owl hoot," Stuart said.

Rosalie told Peyton the plan. When Aimee Louise turned at the Newton's farm, Peyton whooped. "Charo and I are excited."

Aimee Louise turned off the headlights and eased down the driveway to the grove of trees then backed in to park.

Stuart, Aimee Louise, and Rosalie climbed out of the truck and eased their doors closed. Stuart slipped toward the house, and Aimee Louise followed him.

Brandon and Stuart's dad walked toward the house from the garden. When Stuart cleared his throat, his dad moved Brandon behind him then Stuart called out, "Dad, it's me."

"You alone, Stuart?" Scott asked.

"Nope. I brought girls with me." Stuart strode to his father, and they hugged.

"Any problems, Dad?"

"None."

"You doing okay, Brandon?" Stuart asked.

"Yep. No, I'm hungry, Deputy Stuart. Does that count?"

Stuart chuckled. "I'd guess you've been working hard. Dad, do you still have your old wheelchair?"

"Sure do. What's going on?"

"We brought company." Stuart called out, "Rosalie, would you go inside with Brandon?"

"Red is here? That's awesome," Brandon said.

When Rosalie reached Stuart, he said, "Rosalie, ask the judge to come out here for a minute, and keep everyone else inside; we'll be in as quick as we can."

As Rosalie and Brandon went inside, Stuart said, "Aimee Louise, would you move the truck close to the house?"

Stuart and Scott sauntered to the house; after the judge joined them, Scott asked, "What's going on?"

"I wanted to tell you two first. We brought Charo and Brandon's mom, Peyton, with us."

The judge swayed and Scott steadied him. "Charo's here?"

"Yes. She was badly injured. She's alert but can't talk because of her injuries. I'll tell you all about it later."

"What about Nate?" the judge asked.

"Nate is okay physically, but he's not quite strong enough to travel. He's getting good care."

"Where's Charo?"

"She's in the back of the pickup. We need a wheelchair, Dad, to get her to the house. Could you bring yours out?"

Scott hurried to the house. After Aimee Louise parked, Stuart and the judge walked to the back of the pickup. "Remember, Judge. She was badly injured and looks it, but her spirits are good. We're convinced Dolly will help her heal."

When Stuart lowered the tailgate, the judge peered inside.

"Charo, darling. You're a beautiful sight for these old eyes." He glanced at the house. "Scott's gone to get his wheelchair for your short ride to the house. Brace yourself for Dolly squeals."

Charo raised two thumbs and wiggled her fingers. The judge chuckled. "I can read your excitement in your fingers."

Scott brought his wheelchair to the back of the pickup. "What's the plan?"

"Peyton and I will slide Charo to the edge of the tailgate then you and I can move her to the wheelchair with a two-person lift." Stuart hopped into the back.

"I'll hold the wheelchair steady," Judge said.

Stuart and Peyton lifted Charo from her makeshift bed to the quilt then slid her to the tailgate. After Stuart hopped down, he and Scott lifted her to the wheelchair.

Judge kissed her forehead. "Welcome to the Newton Farm. We're famous for our healing skills."

Peyton and Scott lifted the wheelchair over the bumps as Judge pushed. Stuart grabbed bags out of the back of the truck and hurried ahead to open the door to the kitchen. When he set the bags inside, Rosalie, Brandon, Henry, and Dolly sat at the table.

Sandra said, "Rosalie said you've brought company. We're having soup and rolls for supper; you all are just in time."

When Peyton and the judge rolled Charo into the kitchen, Dolly squealed. Before she could hop onto Charo's lap, Rosalie caught her then handed Dolly to the judge.

"Maybe Mama Sandra can show us where your Mommy's room is," Judge said.

"I sure can. Come this way," Sandra said. "I might need a little help, Rosalie."

Judge followed Sandra as Scott pushed the wheelchair, and Dolly skipped alongside. "You'll like it here, Mommy. You'll get all better, and you can come to the garden and watch me weed. I weed better than anybody. I can teach you how to weed."

Rosalie grinned as she brought up the rear.

Brandon's eyes were wide. "Mommy?"

Peyton ran to him and grabbed him in a hug. She snuggled him and cooed.

Stuart rushed to Henry. "How you doing, man?"

After they fist-bumped, Stuart hugged Henry. "Missed you, Henry."

"I missed you too, Deputy Stuart, and so did Mama Sandra. Did Ms. Aimee Louise come with you? Does she remember me?"

"Aimee Louise is here, and she loved the picture you made for her. She'll be happy to see you."

"Ms. Aimee Louise is special."

"She is, Henry. Not everybody sees that. You are very wise, my friend."

Aimee Louise carried bags into the house. When she saw Henry, she dropped the bags and hurried to Henry. "I look at my picture you drew for me all the time. Did you remember me?"

Stuart grinned as Henry giggled. "I remembered you. I drew you another picture."

"Show me," Aimee Louise said.

Henry took her hand, and they headed upstairs.

"I'll be up in a few minutes. I need to talk to my dad first," Stuart said.

When Scott returned to the kitchen, Stuart said, "Can we go for a walk?"

The two men strolled to the barn. "Dad, I'll tell you about the attack. Aimee Louise and I don't think it was random." Stuart explained the brutal injuries Charo suffered, and Nate's condition in response to them.

"I told Nate I understood his reaction. I'd be in the same shape he is if the attack had happened to Aimee Louise and me. I can imagine how helpless he felt."

"Are you and Aimee Louise getting serious?" Scott asked.

"Dad, I've been serious since forever. Aimee Louise is moving at her own speed, and I'm okay with that because I am encouraged every day."

"Whenever you're ready to settle down, the farm is yours, if you're interested. Your mother and I would love to retire. Just letting you know."

"Might be a while, Dad."

As they strode to the house, Scott said, "We've heard rumors of raids on farms south of us. Any truth to it that you know of?"

"As we came north, we saw driveways with access blocked by felled trees. Fields close to the road were in weeds. Might not be just a rumor."

"I've been thinking about what we could do to be less of a target. No reason to leave the mailbox up; we haven't had any mail delivery in over a year. That's a start. I didn't think about not mowing the field near the road. Makes sense."

"Let's check the trees close to the road in the morning. Wouldn't take much to drop one or two."

Before they went inside, Scott said, "Your mother wants to introduce Rosalie to her friend's nephew. I plan to stay pretty scarce. You're welcome to help me in the fields anytime."

Stuart chuckled. "Thanks for the warning, Dad. I might take you up on the offer."

When they went into the house, Sandra was heading to Charo's room with a bowl of soup. "Our supper is ready, but I put it on a slow simmer while I made carrot soup for Charo. Dolly said her mommy's eye would get better if she ate carrots. Who am I to argue with the expert?" She chuckled as she continued down the hallway.

Stuart took the stairs two at a time to join Aimee Louise and Henry upstairs. When he burst into the room, the two of them were sitting on the floor, and Henry was reading a book to Aimee Louise.

"Hello, Deputy Stuart," Henry said. "I'm reading my favorite book to Ms. Aimee Louise."

Aimee Louise glanced at Stuart and smiled. His eyes widened as he sat next to her. *Aimee Louise never smiles.*

"We like you a lot, Deputy Stuart," Henry said.

"Thank you. I like you and Aimee Louise more than anyone else I know."

Henry nodded. "Did you know Ms. Aimee Louise's other name is Angel?" Henry turned to Aimee Louise. "Ms. Rosalie told me I can call you Angel if I want to. I think I want to. Is that okay?"

Aimee Louise hugged Henry. "It's wonderful."

Sandra shouted from the bottom of the stairs. "Supper's on the table."

Henry led the way to the stairs and craned his neck to see if anyone was watching then slid down the banister. He scanned the hall before he sauntered to the kitchen.

Stuart chuckled as he and Aimee Louise descended the stairs. "Mom's number one rule is to stay off the banister. I'll bet Henry and Brandon break that rule as often as I did when I was a kid."

"I'll have to try it," Aimee Louise said. "I missed out on banisters when I was growing up. Our apartment had an elevator."

"I could teach you, and Henry would make a great lookout." Stuart smiled.

Aimee Louise linked her arm through Stuart's as they strolled together into the kitchen. "Is that what they call partners in crime?" she asked.

They took their seats at the kitchen table as Sandra dished up soup, and Rosalie buttered a roll for Dolly.

"Mama Sandra made carrot soup for my mommy," Dolly said.

"Peyton and Brandon are helping Charo sip her soup and will come to the table in a bit," Sandra added. "Peyton and Brandon may be inseparable for a while."

When Peyton and Brandon came to the table, Rosalie dished up their soup.

"I'm finished. Can I go see my mommy?" Dolly asked.

The judge rose and picked up his bowl and spoon. "We can go together. Let's clear our dishes first."

After their dishes were cleared, Dolly grabbed the judge's hand, and they hurried down the hallway to Charo's room.

"You cooked, Mom," Stuart said. "We'll take care of the dishes."

Rosalie turned up the burner under the pot of water on the stove, and Aimee Louise and Henry carried bowls and spoons to the counter near the sink.

"I'll fix you a cup of hot tea if you'll turn on the lantern in the living room," Scott said.

"Why do I think you all are up to something?" Sandra chuckled as she left the kitchen.

Peyton put her arm around Brandon. "What do you think? Are they up to something?"

"No. Deputy Stuart is in charge."

"Good answer," Rosalie said as she poured the hot water into the sink.

After the dishes were clean and put away, Stuart said, "I'm going out for a perimeter check."

"We're coming too," Rosalie said as Henry took Aimee Louise's hand.

When they stepped outside, Henry said, "I didn't know the moon gets bright in Georgia just like it does in Florida. We don't even need a flashlight."

CHAPTER SIX

As they strolled past the truck on their way to the driveway, Aimee Louise said, "I picked up the end of a radio transmission from a South Carolina repeater. I'll check it in the morning."

"That's exciting," Rosalie said. "What did you hear?"

"Not much, except it sounded like a group that meets regularly from the way they signed off. I'll come out before sunrise."

Stuart nodded as they continued up the driveway. *No surprise. She rarely misses watching sunrise.*

"Tap on my door; I'll come out with you," he said.

"I like to see the sun come up too," Henry said as he swung Aimee Louise's hand.

"We'll get you up too, Henry, but you and I might need a nap in the afternoon," Stuart said.

After they reached the road, Stuart faced the house. "Look, Henry. We can see the lights from the kitchen from the road. What can we do about that?"

"I would ask Angel."

"Excellent answer. What do you suggest, Angel?" Stuart asked.

"Let's walk in the field along the road until we can't see lights."

Henry set the pace as they ran to the gate that opened to the field then along the inside of the fence back to the road.

"Good run, Henry," Rosalie said.

"I been practicing."

"Ready to run to the other side of the field?" she asked, and Henry raced ahead while they followed.

When they reached the opposite side, Stuart said, "I needed that run. Let's walk until we see lights at the house."

They crept along as they peered in the direction of the house.

"Stop." Henry held up his hand. "I see a light."

Stuart peered at the house. "I don't see anything."

"Want to mark it?" Rosalie asked. "I have a long piece of string in my pocket."

"Ms. Rosalie has everything," Henry said. "That's what Dolly said."

"She sure does," Stuart said. "Tie it to the lowest wire on the fence so we can find our first point tomorrow morning, Rosalie. I'll cut it with my pocket knife." Stuart took a step away from Henry and closer to the driveway. "Now I see it."

"Let's check for more than one light," Aimee Louise said.

They continued at the same slow pace as Henry led the way. "Stop," Henry said. "I see two lights."

Stuart stared at the house then stepped on the other side of Henry. "You have really good eyes, Henry; I can barely see two lights from here. I'm glad you came with us."

Rosalie tied another string on the lowest wire. "Ready to cut."

After Stuart cut the string, Henry asked, "Do we look for more lights?"

"Yes, and watch for the two lights to be much brighter."

Henry and Rosalie took the lead with Henry as the spotter and Rosalie as the marker.

When they reached the driveway, Henry asked, "What do we do next, Angel?"

"We wait until morning to find the string to decide how to make the lights not visible from the road."

"Invisible lights," Henry said as they sauntered to the house. "That's tricky."

When they went into the kitchen Peyton asked, "Henry, I've heated up some water. Ready for a bath?"

"Is it time?" Henry asked.

"I had my bath." Dolly was sitting at the kitchen table. "I'm waiting for you."

"Yes, it's time for your baths, and Mama Sandra told me about the farm rule." Peyton ushered Brandon and Henry to the guest bathroom where Dolly had taken her bath. The judge carried the pot of water from the stove to warm up the water for the boys.

"Do I know the farm rule?" Rosalie asked.

Dolly jumped up from her seat and twirled as she sang. "Bath, snack, bed."

"Mom told me when I was in high school that she wanted one rule that is never broken." Stuart grinned.

After snack, the children said their good nights before they trudged off to bed.

* * *

A tap on his door woke Stuart before daylight. He lightly touched Henry on the shoulder and whispered, "Ready to get up, Henry?"

As Stuart rushed to dress, Henry stumbled to the door with his shoes in his hand. *That little sneak slept in his clothes.*

Stuart and Henry crept down the stairs then tiptoed out the kitchen door. When Henry shivered, Aimee Louise handed him his jacket.

"Thank you, Angel."

"I didn't expect it to be so chilly this morning," Rosalie said. "How did you happen to have Henry's coat?"

"He asked me last night to have it for him," Aimee Louise said.

Stuart shook his head. "Little kids are smart these days."

Henry giggled. "Mama Sandra told me it would be cold. She said Angel would bring my jacket if I asked her."

"She was right," Rosalie said. "But you're still smart."

"Dad said he built a bench near the garden for the judge so he could keep an eye on Dolly while she weeded. It might be the perfect spot to wait for sunrise."

On the way to the garden, Henry said, "Angel, Ms. Rosalie told me we don't talk while we wait for the sun. I can be very quiet."

"I know you can, Henry."

When they reached the bench, Aimee Louise sat between Stuart and Henry. Rosalie paced to the other side of the garden.

Stuart wrapped his arm around Aimee Louise's shoulders, and she relaxed as she leaned against him. Rosalie's pacing on the other side of the garden rustled leaves with the sound of a sentry. He stared at the horizon, half hoping the sun would delay its ascent.

As the sky lightened, Aimee Louise leaned forward. "Good morning, sun," she said, and Henry cheered.

Aimee Louise and Rosalie raced to the truck. Stuart smiled as the two of them ran in tandem. *They'll always be in tune with each other.*

"Ready to go inside and be warm, Henry?" he asked.

"We can talk now? I liked being quiet. I listened to Angel breathe." Henry jumped off the bench. As they hurried to the house, he said, "Next time, I'll ask for gloves too. My hands were cold until Angel held them."

"There you are." Sandra turned up the burner under the tea kettle. "Was it cold? Ready for your coffee?" She poured a cup for Stuart. "I'll make you some warm tea with honey, Henry. Hang up your coat, so we'll know where it is next time you need it."

Stuart gulped down his coffee while his mom stirred honey into the mug of tea, and Henry hung up his coat.

"What got everybody up so early?" Scott sauntered into the kitchen, poured himself a cup of hot coffee, and refilled Stuart's cup before he sat at the table.

"We watched the sunrise with Angel, Papa Scott," Henry said.

"Sounds like a great way to start the day. What's our plan for today, Stuart?"

"We walked along the road last night and found several points of security weaknesses; I'll show you after breakfast. Also, we talked about taking down trees near the driveway. Aimee Louise and Rosalie are listening to the ham radio in the truck. They'll be in soon with a report of what they heard."

Sandra stirred oatmeal into a large pot. "I'll have breakfast for you in a flash."

After the judge came into the kitchen and poured himself a cup of coffee, Rosalie burst into the kitchen. "Aimee Louise wants you to come listen, Stuart. She caught a good signal from a South Carolina repeater."

Stuart and Rosalie rushed out of the house to the truck. The three of them listened for ten minutes before the signal faded.

"Did you hear it the way I did?" Stuart asked. "Sounded like the North Carolina and Tennessee State Police, sheriff's departments, and a large number of parents who were former military or law enforcement broke up a human trafficking ring in the mountainous regions of western North Carolina and eastern Tennessee. I didn't catch any numbers, though."

"According to one ham, at least twenty camps so far with fifty to a hundred children in each camp. Another ham said the camps were infiltrated by parents in large trucks who removed the children from the camps before the raids were initiated," Aimee Louise said. "The hams discussed some of the North Carolina raids they'd heard about and speculated that the South Carolina and Georgia state police might be planning similar rescues."

"Sure explains why Peyton and Nate were so determined to go to South Carolina," Rosalie said.

"What are you thinking, Aimee Louise?" Stuart asked.

"It's time for us to talk to Peyton."

As they strolled to the house, Stuart said, "I haven't mentioned Troy to Peyton. I'm not convinced the man at the farm is Troy."

"He's Brandon's father," Aimee Louise said.

Stuart stopped. "Why do I have the feeling he isn't Troy?"

Rosalie stopped and stared at Stuart. "Because. I don't know." She rushed to catch up with Aimee Louise. "Is he Peyton's husband?"

"No. He's Brandon's father." Aimee Louise continued to the house.

* * *

While everyone ate, Sandra said, "The judge and I will need Brandon, Henry, and Dolly's help this morning with the garden and chickens. Judge and I will take turns keeping an eye on Charo. The boys and I can let the chickens out to free range while we put fresh hay in their nest boxes and check for eggs. I have seedlings ready to be transplanted, and the boys can haul them in the wagon to the garden for me. The judge, boys, and Dolly can work in the garden while I look after Charo."

"Sounds like we've got a full morning ahead," Judge said.

Henry frowned. "I'm supposed to work with Angel."

"Morning chores first," Aimee Louise said. "We'll work together this afternoon."

"That's a good farm plan." Henry crammed a large bite of biscuit into his mouth.

"I have to stay with Mom." Brandon crossed his arms.

"I'm not going anywhere," Peyton said. "We all have to pitch in at the farm."

Brandon nodded. "That's what we do."

"Peyton, we identified some security issues last night. We need to come up with good solutions," Stuart said.

"My area of expertise," she said.

"We'll show you what we found after breakfast," Stuart said.

Scott and Rosalie cleared the table while Aimee Louise poured hot water into the sink to wash the dishes. As Aimee Louise washed and rinsed the dishes, Stuart dried and put them away while Peyton and Rosalie fetched more water for the large pot on the stove.

After the five of them walked to the edge of the field near the road, Stuart said, "Let's start with our first string and work back to the driveway."

When they reached the first string, Rosalie said, "This is where we, actually our sharp-eyed Henry, got his first glimpse of light from the house."

Peyton peered at the house then crouched as she continued to gaze across the field. "Henry saw a light before the rest of you? Did you see it after he pointed it out?"

"Yes," Stuart said. "Well, no. I didn't see it until I shifted away from him. Then I saw it."

Peyton glanced up at him. "Henry did us a big favor. His view was close to the view of someone crawling through the field. Show me where you were standing when you saw it."

Stuart stepped to a position two feet away from her. "Right about here."

As Peyton rose, Scott said, "A small bush would obscure your view of the house, Peyton." He stepped close to Stuart. "I've got some tall, overgrown bushes near the house that I could move for this view."

Rosalie pulled her notebook out of her back pocket. "After we look at each string, we can line up where we think the bushes go and check the positions this evening."

When they reached the driveway, Scott said, "I was worried we'd have neat rows of bushes, but we can vary their distance to the house to give them a more ragged look."

"You're right, Dad. If you'll show us which bushes we can move, Peyton and I can dig them up while Aimee Louise and Rosalie determine the new spots to place them. After we check them tonight, we can plant them by lantern or wait until tomorrow after breakfast."

"Are we in a hurry to get this done?" Peyton asked as she and Stuart headed to the barn for shovels.

"Yes. The home invasions are getting closer. The best defense seems to be the appearance of a abandoned home."

"The thugs must assume a vacant house has already been looted, and if the house is not vacant, they don't mind hurting people," Peyton said.

"Like your attackers?" Stuart asked.

"Where are the shovels?" Peyton scanned the barn.

"Right here," Stuart said. "Do you know who your attackers were, or who sent them?"

Peyton reached for a shovel then faced Stuart. Only her eyes betrayed her sadness. "No, but I got the distinct impression that Nate did, and he was somehow protecting Charo and me by not cooperating with them, and I don't understand it at all."

"Times are different now, Peyton. What do you know that you're not sharing?"

Peyton's faced reddened, and her eyes flashed. "I don't understand what you're talking about." She stomped out of the barn with her shovel.

When Stuart joined her near the house, he said, "That was dramatic. What's up?"

"You're a real pest, Deputy Stuart. You know that, right?"

Stuart raised his eyebrows and placed his hand on his chest.

"Yes, you," Peyton giggled. "Nate thought someone close to us was leading the Florida kidnappings. For a while, I thought he meant—" Peyton cleared her throat. "Brandon's father, and I quit speaking to Nate. When he brought up the subject later, I refused to discuss it. Now, I feel like a jerk. We were supposed to be partners, and I let him down."

"Is that who ordered the attack on you? The person who led the Florida kidnappings?"

Peyton's shoulders slumped. "I don't know, but I think Nate might." Tears flowed down Peyton's face. "But it's worse; after we were abducted, Charo told them she was me. She had even grabbed my ID out of my bag during the attack and stashed it in her back pocket. When I screamed at them and told them I was Peyton, she laughed and pulled out my ID." She threw down her shovel and ran to the barn.

Scott rounded the corner as she sped past him. "Did you find out what you wanted to know?"

"Yes, but my interrogation skills could use some finesse."

"I'm not sure that's true, Stuart." Scott picked up the shovel that Peyton had thrown down. "Looks like you got some answers that might have never surfaced."

"Thanks, Dad. Did you hear?"

"Sure did. No way was I going to break the mood of your cunning cross-examination."

"And you were as surprised as I was, weren't you?"

"Probably so." Scott pointed with his shovel. "Let's take out these four bushes. I think they're tall enough to work, and I've been worried about bushes so close to the house where an attacker could hide."

While the two men worked, Brandon pulled Henry in the garden wagon to the front of the house. "Mama Sandra told us to bring you the wagon after we were finished with it."

"Then we're supposed to skedaddle," Henry said. "I didn't know what that meant, but Brandon said it meant a fast get-away."

Henry jumped out of the wagon, and the boys raced around the corner toward the garden.

"Your mother's always two steps ahead of me. We should be able to get two of these large bushes into the wagon," Scott said.

When they rolled the first two bushes to the field, Aimee Louise and Rosalie had jammed sticks into the ground as markers.

Rosalie waved. "We think this will block where you saw the single light, Stuart."

After they dropped off the bush at Rosalie's marker, Rosalie followed them to Aimee Louise.

When he reached Aimee Louise's marker, Stuart said. "The tall bush here will block the two lights."

"Wait here," Aimee Louise said. "We have something to show you."

Aimee Louise and Rosalie raced to the driveway then turned toward the house.

"What do you think?" Scott asked.

Stuart shrugged. "No telling."

"Which bush do you like better?" Rosalie asked. "We're speaking in normal voices, not yelling, in case you wondered."

"I'll speak very softly," Aimee Louise said.

"This is a normal tone," Rosalie added.

Aimee Louise whispered. "Can you hear me, Rosalie? She nodded, just to let you know."

Aimee Louise and Rosalie raced back to Stuart and Scott.

"Do they always run in tandem like that?" Scott asked.

"Always."

"We heard everything when you and Peyton were talking. We thought we'd show you. If you said anything here before we started talking, we didn't hear you," Aimee Louise said. "We have a sound vulnerability, but we're pretty sure it's just in front of the house. We'll test it after we place the tall bushes. We know the short bushes are about two feet away from the tall bushes, so we don't have to spend a lot of time with them."

"I was surprised when I heard you talking so clearly in front of the house, Aimee Louise," Scott said. "I imagined attackers lying in the grass listening to every word. Glad you found it. What do we do to fix it?"

"If nothing else, we don't talk when we're in front of the house," Stuart said.

"We could use it to give false information, but that's risky," Aimee Louise said.

"Let's get our other two tall bushes dug up and in place," Scott said.

Rosalie followed Scott and Stuart to the front of the house. Stuart and Rosalie returned with two more tall bushes.

"I heard," Aimee Louise said. "Scott's on his way to the garden."

After they placed the two bushes, Stuart asked, "What did you think about what Peyton said, Aimee Louise? Was she sincere?"

"Yes."

"There's more," Stuart said.

"She didn't say anything that we wouldn't have learned from Charo in a few days. What we want to know is who is Brandon's father because that's the man at the farm. I'll try to contact the farm tonight or at least try to get a message to Mr. Young and Annie. We need to know the condition of the man at the farm before we say anything to Peyton."

"You're right," Rosalie said. "If he died or ran off, we need to know."

Peyton headed toward the field from the driveway. "Sorry, Stuart. I'm not quite myself these days." She examined the bushes. "We still have the four small bushes to dig up, right?"

"Sure do," he said.

"We'll be back later," Aimee Louise said. "Sandra asked us to help her if we had time this morning."

Aimee Louise and Rosalie raced from the field to the driveway and were inside the house before Stuart and Peyton reached the driveway.

"Did Scott pick out the small bushes?" Peyton asked.

"I'll show you," Stuart said.

After they dug up the small bushes, Stuart placed them in the wagon. On the way to the driveway, Peyton said, "Henry told me Brandon found you when he talked on a radio. Is that true?"

"That's true. Did he tell you the two of them survived a tornado in an open field? Brandon was amazing. He took care of Henry and made sure they stayed together."

"I didn't know about that. Brandon's just a little boy."

"You're wrong, Peyton." Stuart stopped and faced her. "Brandon is a hero. He has a kind heart and a strong sense of responsibility. He's the loyal friend every young boy needs at one time or another." Stuart smiled. "Probably genetic."

Peyton nodded her head. "Just like his father."

"Does he know where you were planning to go?"

"I don't know." She frowned. "No, I do know. He'd figure it out. When Brandon disappeared, he was frantic. He wanted to go to South Carolina with me, but I told him I already had a partner. It didn't do any good, though. He always was impervious to insults."

"Would he have tried to find you and Brandon?"

"He'd move heaven and earth to find us. He's very loyal. You were right about genetic. It's just too bad—"

Stuart reached for a small bush then stopped. "What?"

"Brandon's father and I were best friends in college, but we grew into more than just friends. When I discovered I was pregnant, he was ecstatic and wanted to get married right away. I have a tendency to panic sometimes. I was afraid he only wanted to marry me because I was pregnant." Peyton sat on the wagon. "My parents helped me raise Brandon, but his father was always in his life. He took a job out of college close to my parents. He saw Brandon every day. More than I did because I was traveling a lot with my new job. We're still good friends. He dates occasionally but nothing serious. One of my friends who dated him told me once she couldn't compete with me. I thought she was nuts."

Peyton rose. "I married Troy when Brandon was three. Our relationship has always been stormy. Troy wasn't around much. He had other interests. I was in the process of a divorce when Brandon disappeared."

"Did Brandon's father know you were in the process of divorcing Troy?"

"No. I kept it from my parents. If they'd known, they would have told Brandon's father." She smiled. "They've always considered him their real son-in-law and told me so more than once."

"I don't mean to pry, but what is Brandon's father's name?" Stuart matched her smile.

"David. David Griffin. He's a cop. Technically, he's a Fish and Wildlife Conservation Officer, but he's the best cop I've ever known."

"Brandon said his dad builds houses." Stuart furrowed his brow.

Peyton laughed. "He does. He and Brandon build birdhouses, and David gives them to scouting and other groups for wildlife projects. They built a playhouse for a daycare center. They were very proud of it."

"David sounds like a great guy," Stuart said.

"He is." Peyton frowned. "I forgot that for too long. I need to do some serious thinking."

"Sure do."

After they set the small bushes close to the larger ones, they returned the shovels to the barn and the wagon to the garden.

"Mom, come see what we planted," Brandon said. "Henry and I might become farmers. Dolly said she'd weed our garden for us."

"Dolly likes to weed," Henry said. "We promised to save all our weeds for her."

Sandra strolled to the garden. "I can see how much work you all have done. Ready for lunch?"

As the boys and Dolly dashed toward the house, Sandra said, "Remember to wash your hands before you sit at the table."

"I'll supervise." Peyton chased after them.

"Judge, Charo is sitting up and eating soft foods," Sandra said. "It's a big change from yesterday's liquid diet. I promised her a sponge bath after lunch, and Rosalie and Aimee Louise offered to supervise the children if you'd like a little time to nap or read."

The two of them headed for the house arm in arm.

"Guess we'd better head that way, or we'll go hungry," Scott said.

"We'll look at trees after lunch," Stuart said.

When Aimee Louise came out of the house to meet Stuart, Scott continued inside.

"Charo wants Nate here," Aimee Louise said. "It's hard to understand all her words, but I think she claimed he's fine now. I'll see if I can catch Phil's contact on the radio this evening."

"Peyton confirmed that Brandon's dad is not Troy. Brandon's dad's name is David Griffin. I'm sure the man at the farm is David."

"Why would he use the name Troy?" she asked.

"What could he say? My name is David, and I'm really Brandon's father? That would raise too many questions, right? It would have been easier to claim to be Troy. From what Peyton said, there's no way the real Troy would have tried to find her or Brandon."

As they continued their stroll to the house, Stuart frowned. "I'm not sure Peyton believed the real Troy wouldn't try to find her though. It was almost like she was trying to convince herself, not me."

"Sometimes I don't understand people," she said as they went inside.

Neither do I, babe.

CHAPTER SEVEN

When Aimee Louise and Stuart came into the kitchen, Rosalie smiled. "We have our project for this afternoon. When Ms. Sandra asked if we could build a maternity nest for one of the chickens to hatch eggs and raise baby chicks, Mr. Scott said we could use the wood scraps in the barn."

"I know exactly what we need to do for the new mama nest," Dolly said.

"I do too," Henry interrupted.

In their excitement, Brandon, Henry, and Dolly all spoke at once as they blurted out their ideas. Stuart glanced at his dad who beamed at the cacophony of chatter. *What a relief to see Dad happy.*

Sandra clapped her hands twice, and the children stared at her in stunned silence. "If you eat first, you can start on your project."

The kitchen was quiet as the children hurried to finish lunch before they rushed to their afternoon project. Rosalie followed the children while Aimee Louise and Sandra washed dishes and straightened the kitchen. Stuart and Scott headed to the barn for chain saws, the pole saw, and straps.

After they had loaded the equipment onto the trailer, Stuart said, "I'll meet you at the road. I need to check something at the front of the house."

Stuart strode to the front yard then examined the lay of the land. *With the dip of the ditch to drain runoff away from the house, this is a bowl. Perfect set up for a theater to project the sound to the audience in the field. How do I change it?*

Stuart scanned the yard again before he jogged up the driveway to meet his father.

"Look at this old tree, Stuart. It's close to falling without any help." Scott ran his hand down the trunk. "A tightened strap to keep it from going the wrong way, a couple of simple cuts, and it would be down."

Stuart frowned as he paced to the road and back. "How do we get out?"

"Got that covered," Scott said. "I'll show you after we take this old fella down." Scott cut his notch then his felling cut, and the tree dropped where he'd planned. "I'll grab my machete out of my shed and meet you at the front of the house. I'll show you what I had in mind for your escape route."

When Scott joined Stuart, he led his son past the house to the woods. "There's an old barn and a driveway to the road on the land next to us. It's all grown over now, but we can clear a path for your truck. Your mother would say that we should have looked at this before we dropped the tree across our driveway."

Stuart frowned at the overgrown brush in the woods. "Can we even get through there?"

Scott strode to an opening in the brush. "We can cut back the bushes for us to get through, but we may have to take down some small trees for the truck."

After they pushed and cut away the heavy thicket, they came to a cleared path wide enough for two people to walk side by side.

Stuart shook his head. "This is unexpected. I thought we'd have to hack our way to the barn."

When they came to the end of the wide trail, the dilapidated barn was in front of them.

Scott pointed past the barn. "There's a driveway from the house to the road. Lightning struck the house not long after the grid went down, and because there was no way to put out the fire, nothing is left except the chimney. Before Mr. Smith left to live with his daughter in Alabama, he told me that with his wife gone, he didn't have any reason to rebuild. I'd say we were lucky the flames didn't spread to the woods, except Mr. Smith kept the area around his house clear of brush and trees; he called it his defensible space."

After they reached the homesite, they searched for the gravel driveway in the weeds. When their path took a few turns in the high grass and between the trees, Stuart said, "I expected the driveway to go straight to the road, but it meanders like a creek."

"I think the point was to make the house less visible from the road and less inviting for any passersby. Our driveway runs along our property line, so our field is available for crops. This one winds its way to the road, but the large trees made the field less useful for farming."

In spite of the wandering driveway, it wasn't long before they reached the road. Stuart gazed at the field and trees behind them. "There may be a few low-hanging branches to remove for clearance when we bring the truck this way, but overall, there isn't much to do after we get the truck to the barn."

"We've got trees to take down on the sides of our house for the truck," Scott said. "We'll start there. I think we can be done today."

"I might have Aimee Louise drive the truck while I clear in front of it through the woods," Stuart said.

"That's fine," Scott chuckled. "I'm sure your mother has a project for me."

While Stuart took down trees around his parents' house and cut them into manageable pieces, Scott hauled away the branches and tree trunks with the tractor. After they finished clearing the first section of trees, they took a water break in the shade.

"I've been meaning to take down those trees," Scott said. "It would take only one well-placed tornado to rip through here, and we'd have a major catastrophe when a tree crashed through our roof. In fact, I should have remembered Mr. Smith's defensible space for fire and made it a priority to clear the area, but I'm just now getting back on my feet. While you and Aimee Louise make your way through the woods to the barn, I'll cut the trees into firewood size for next year."

As they cleared the last section of trees near the path, Aimee Louise joined them, and Stuart and Scott took a breather.

"The mama nest is built. Brandon and Henry found a partial can of yellow paint in the barn. Is it okay if they use the paint?" she asked.

"I'd forgotten I had that." Scott wiped away the sweat on his face with the bandana he carried in his back pocket. "They're welcome to it."

"After you get them settled, are you available to bring the truck here?" Stuart asked.

"Yes." Aimee Louise raced away.

After they cut down the last tree, Scott hauled it away with the tractor as Aimee Louise drove the truck across the front yard to the edge of the woods.

When she jumped out of the truck, Stuart said, "I'll cut down the small trees and trim back the brush for the truck to get through. I'll show you where we're going first."

As they pushed through the brush then strolled together on the wide path, Stuart said, "It looked more daunting when Dad and I came through the first time."

When they reached the barn, Aimee Louise said, "It wouldn't take much to repair this structure."

Stuart peered at the building. "I'll mention that to Dad. I wonder if Mr. Smith abandoned his property."

They returned to the truck and began the work of clearing brush and trees to make a path wide enough for the truck. When they reached the barn on the other side of the woods, they sat on the back bumper for a break.

Stuart said, "We did the hard part. Won't take long to get to the road from here. I'll take down any low-hanging branches then we're done."

Aimee Louise stopped when they approached the first low branch; Stuart hopped out of the truck and removed it with the pole saw.

"Another one ahead." Stuart took it down and dragged it out of the way.

When they reached the road, Aimee Louise glanced behind them. "We took down five low-hanging branches."

"Wasn't that hard with the pole saw."

They stepped out of the truck and examined the barbed wire across the driveway.

"It's attached to this post." Stuart lifted the post. "It's a gate. We can open then close it when we leave."

After he opened the gate, Aimee Louise walked along the road then returned. "I don't want to disturb the grass any more than necessary. It will recover in a day after we leave. I'll back down the driveway to the house."

Stuart closed the gate. "Never thought about a barbed wire gate before. It blends in with the fence. It would be hard to see at first from the road. Your driving skills are impressive, Aimee Louise."

Aimee Louise stared at Stuart. "Thank you."

On impulse, Stuart asked, "What do you see?"

"Your cloud."

Stuart looked up. "What kind of cloud is it?"

"Special. Nice."

Stuart reached for Aimee Louise's hand, and their fingers intertwined. "You know I want to always be with you."

She squeezed his hand. "That's what your cloud tells me."

"If I could see your cloud, what would I see?"

Aimee Louise raised her eyebrows and looked up. "I can't see my cloud. I'm sure my cloud would be the same as yours." She tilted her head as she gazed at Stuart. "No one ever asked me before."

Stuart hugged her and snuggled her hair, and Aimee Louise buried her face in his chest as she wrapped her arms around him.

Stuart sighed. "Break over."

As Aimee Louise backed down the driveway, Stuart said, "I have a theory. After you park the truck, let's repeat the sound test in front of the house."

"You expect the sound won't carry now because the side trees are gone."

"You're right." Stuart shook his head and smiled. *I have a lifetime ahead of me with the smartest person I know.*

After Aimee Louise backed the truck to the homestead and turned it to head back to the Newton farm, Stuart said, "Let's look at the barn more closely. It's either restorable or a hazard."

They stood back and examined the roof.

"Missing quite a few shingles," Stuart said. "Let's walk around it before we go inside."

After they examined the foundation and the outside walls, Aimee Louise said, "The missing boards on the sides of the building and over the windows and the broken barn doors give it a dilapidated look, but I didn't see anything that has an impact on the integrity of the building."

"I agree. Let's go inside."

After they entered the barn, Aimee Louise pointed up. "That one rafter is split, but the rest look fine."

"Stalls need repair. That's minor." Stuart picked up a ladder that lay on the dirt floor then dropped it. "This must be the ladder to the loft. It's toast."

"The loft doesn't look safe. It needs work."

As Aimee Louise eased the truck back through the new trail, Stuart said, "After our sound test, I'll tell Dad about the barn. It's a big project that I suspect he'll enjoy."

When they reached the house, Aimee Louise parked the truck.

As Stuart reached for the tools to return to the barn, Aimee Louise said, "Did you hear that? Squeals?"

After they dropped off the tools at the equipment shed, they hurried to the side yard. Sandra, Peyton, and a woman stood near the kitchen door while Scott, Rosalie, and a young man who was tall and lanky supervised the children and four puppies.

Peyton smiled at Stuart and Aimee Louise, and rushed to greet them. "The neighbor's dog had puppies. Their mama, Holly, is a collie, and the puppies' father is a yellow lab. I think we'll end up with one or two here, don't you? I always thought Brandon was afraid of dogs, but I guess I was mistaken. Look at them." She nodded her head toward the young man. "That's the neighbor's nephew. Sandra and the neighbor have been trying to get the nephew and Rosalie together. Do you think the mama dog was in on the conspiracy too?" Peyton giggled. "The kids are having a great time. Wonder if they'll try for three?"

Henry ran to Stuart. "We got puppies, Deputy Stuart."

Before Stuart could reply, Henry dashed back. When the judge came out of the house with a bowl of water, Brandon met him then carried the bowl to the puppies.

Scott joined Stuart and Aimee Louise. "I think these folks will be busy for a while. How did it go? Did you get through okay?"

"Worked out great, Dad. We checked Mr. Smith's barn. It's not in bad shape. Wouldn't take much to fix it up."

"That's interesting. I hadn't really looked at it. Mr. Smith signed the deed over to me before he left, so the property is mine. I haven't even thought about it since he left. Not sure what I'd do with a barn." Scott chuckled. "Maybe raise puppies. Just kidding."

"If you put puppies in the barn, that's where the kids would move too," Stuart said.

"You'd have to fix the loft because Brandon and Henry would claim it as theirs," Aimee Louise added.

Stuart smiled. "You understood the joke."

"Did I?"

Stuart hugged her. "The best kind. A joke that is funny because it's nice. And true."

Scott raised his eyebrows. "Let's look at our barn. No work's going to get done around here for a while."

On the way to the barn, Scott said, "Andy told me the Mitchell farm close to town was invaded night before last. All the adults were murdered, and the twin girls are gone—Samantha and Camilla. The grandparents live down the road, and they are distraught. I never thought we'd be facing anything like that. I thought because we are so far from the city, we were safe."

Stuart told his dad about the security precautions at the Major's farm, including always being armed outside, the nighttime security checks, and the call of *Inside* for everyone to run to the house.

"I'll talk to your mom. Both of us have side arms that we like— just didn't think about the risk of not having them handy." Scott rubbed his chin and furrowed his brow. "*Inside*, huh? Sounds like something we need to do here with three kids."

"Rosalie can teach the children," Aimee Louise said.

"We've seen it save the children at the farm more than once, and because the adults act as quickly as the children do and drop whatever they're doing to rush inside, the system works. Aimee Louise and I can teach the adults."

Scott frowned. "You're saying that when someone shouts *inside*, I have to drop what I'm doing and run to the house. Don't I investigate first?"

"Investigate what?" Stuart asked. "If you run to the house, you'll find out why everyone was called in."

Scott narrowed his eyes. "Was that your idea, Aimee Louise?"

"No, Pops thought of it."

"Major Elliott is Aimee Louise's grandfather. The four kids call him Pops because that's what Aimee Louise and Rosalie call him," Stuart said.

"Four kids. And they all run into the house when an adult calls *Inside?*"

"Four kids and eight adults counting Aimee Louise, Rosalie, and me." Stuart chuckled.

"Where do we start?" Scott asked.

"With a family meeting," Aimee Louise said.

"When do we have a family meeting? Who calls it?"

"Have the meeting as soon as the company leaves. As head of the family, you call the first meeting," Aimee Louise said.

"You'll coach me, right?" Scott asked as they continued their walk to the barn.

"We've got your back, Dad," Stuart said.

As they walked around the barn, Scott examined the roof, foundation, and the overall structure. When they went inside, he scanned the rafters, walls, and loft.

"After that one rafter is repaired, the priority is the roof. The rest of the repairs are less critical to saving the barn," Scott said. "I have no idea what use we might make of this old barn, but if the roof collapses, we have nothing."

When they returned to the house, their company had left. Scott spoke to Sandra quietly then Sandra clapped her hands. "Papa Scott said we're having a family meeting at the kitchen table. Let's go."

The children followed Sandra and Scott into the house.

"Does that mean us too?" Judge asked.

"Yes," Rosalie said as she hurried to join the children. Aimee Louise and Stuart rushed to follow Rosalie. Peyton shrugged and followed the judge.

After everyone settled down, Sandra passed around crackers.

Scott cleared his throat as he looked around the table. "We need to be more careful about security. The family at the farm in Florida follows some safety measures that might work for us too. Deputy Stuart will tell us what they are and how they work."

Stuart nodded. "Sometimes it's important for everyone to act right away for the safety of the family. Because of the immediate danger, there's no time for questions. The Florida family has a code word. It is *Inside*. When an adult shouts *Inside*, everyone drops whatever they are doing and runs to the house."

"Even the adults?" Sandra asked as she glanced around the table.

"Yes," Rosalie said. "If the adults don't run to the house, they won't know what the problem is, but worse than that, they are showing the children it isn't important to be safe."

"Ouch," Peyton mumbled.

"*Inside* hasn't been called very often," Aimee Louise said.

"But when it was," Stuart added, "It was critical to get everyone together as fast as possible."

"Let's do a practice run," Scott said.

"I'll go to the garden," the judge said.

"I can go with Gramps," Dolly said. "Just in case he doesn't hear the inside call."

Peyton snorted, and the judge glared as he and Dolly left the kitchen.

"I was showing Mom the chickens," Brandon said. "We can go to the chicken coop."

"Excellent idea," Peyton said as Brandon took her hand.

"Henry, let's go to the equipment shed," Aimee Louise said. "We can check to make sure everything is in its place."

"What do you think, Sandra? Will this work?" Scott asked.

"I think it might. The adults are the key, and Rosalie nailed their cooperation with her comment about safety. Let's give them a little time to be bored. Care for a cup of hot tea?"

"Best offer I've had all day," Scott smiled.

""Rosalie, come with me," Stuart said. "I'd like to repeat our test."

When they reached the front of the house, Rosalie said, "I'll run out to the field."

Stuart gave Rosalie time to get to the field then said in a clear voice, "I wonder how many puppies will end up here."

"You can talk now," Rosalie shouted.

"If there is only one puppy, I wonder who will name it? Will we get a—"

"Go ahead," Rosalie shouted. "You can talk now."

Stuart snickered then shouted back. "Come to the front of the house."

Rosalie ran to join him. "I didn't hear you at all until you yelled. How did you fix it?"

Stuart pointed to the tree stumps on both sides of the house. "We had a natural amphitheater. Removing the trees took away the curvature that directed the sound. Let's sit on the porch while we wait."

After they sat on the steps, Rosalie said, "Brilliant. Your idea, right?"

"Kind of. Aimee Louise knew exactly what would happen when we took down the trees."

"Does it bother you that she's so smart?"

"Not at all. Almost forgot to tell you that the front door stays locked. We'll have to run to the kitchen door when Dad calls *inside*."

Stuart rose and paced. "I'm worried about the family here. I'm not sure they're ready to defend themselves. What do you think?"

"The adults need to know what they can expect from each other as far as defense is concerned. We know Peyton can shoot a pistol, but is there a rifle for her? After we leave, there are four adults, and they all need to be able to protect the children. Five if Charo is well enough."

"I'll talk to Dad."

"Inside!" Sandra shouted.

Stuart and Rosalie raced to the kitchen door and were the first two inside the house.

Peyton and Brandon were next, followed by the judge, Dolly, Henry, and Aimee Louise.

"Aimee Louise told me to run as fast as I could, and I did," Henry said.

"Well done, everyone." Scott said. "When we hear *Inside*, what do we do?"

Brandon raised his hand. "Run fast to the house."

"Faster," Dolly said. "That's what I told Gramps, and we ran faster."

"Good answers," Sandra said. "Everyone did great and can have a cracker before you go back to what you were doing."

After Brandon picked up his cracker, he said, "Want to go with Mom and me to the chicken coop, Henry? I was about ready to gather eggs for Mama Sandra."

"Is that okay with you, Angel? Brandon and I always get the eggs together."

"Yes. It's good to do things with friends, and I have something to show Rosalie."

"Can I come too?" Stuart asked as he followed Aimee Louise and Rosalie out the door.

"Let's show Rosalie the barn and the driveway to the road," Aimee Louise said.

When they reached the barn, Stuart said, "I wanted to talk to you about what we're going to do next. We have several options. We could go to South Carolina, but I'm not sure why, go back home to Florida, or go pick up Nate and bring him here."

"Or stay here for a while," Rosalie said. "That's another option."

Stuart furrowed his brow. "Stay here to help with the defense. They could definitely use the help."

"We need an antenna or a good skip, so we can talk to the Florida farm to tell them about David and check on his condition, and we need to tell them we're needed here," Aimee Louise said.

"I'll talk to Dad and ask him about the sheriff's office. The sheriffs' communication network got word to me after Dad fell, but I don't know if they are still active here."

Before they left the barn, Stuart glanced around. "This old barn's a good meeting place."

When they reached the house, Scott was cutting the trees they had felled from the front of the house and was stacking them for firewood. When the three approached him, he set down his chainsaw and listened while Stuart caught him up on the discussion.

"Our first priority is to talk to Pops, and Andy said his family had a good radio set up," Rosalie said.

"His uncle Leo Webster is a longtime ham and has the best set up around. It's on solar. Leo's more than happy to meet someone who shares his enthusiasm for radios."

"That's Aimee Louise," Stuart said. "She's our radio guru."

"Leo's farm isn't hard to find if you know where to look. I'll draw you a map then explain it to you. Who's going? Just you and Aimee Louise?"

"And Rosalie," Stuart said. "We keep our team together."

Scott nodded. "Let's go inside. I don't know anything about the sheriff's communication network. I haven't heard much of anything about the sheriff or deputies in a while. Leo would know. I'll draw your map, and your mother will want to give you something to take to Andy's aunt, Jennie."

"While we're gone, Dad, Peyton and the boys could check the house lights from the field after dark. Henry knows what to look for, and he can show Peyton."

Scott chuckled. "Isn't that something? A six-year-old boy the team leader of an FBI agent on an important security mission."

Stuart snorted. "Let's hope she can live up to his expectations."

When they entered the house, Sandra glanced up from the stove. "Peyton and the boys are picking more vegetables for our soup tonight. I've got my broth almost ready."

After Scott explained the evening's plan, Sandra said, "I made a big batch of flatbread. I'll wrap some for Jennie. You should eat before you go. Get your things pulled together then come to the table, and I'll dish up your soup. Jennie will want to feed you, but you may want to spend your time on the radio or talking to Leo. If she offers you fried pies, don't turn them down. Hers are the best I've ever eaten."

"Shall we check our go-bags?" Rosalie asked.

"Yes. They're in the truck," Aimee Louise said. As they headed out the door, she added, "We'll grab yours too, Stuart."

After they reorganized their go-bags and sat at the table for their soup, Scott joined them as he drew the map then turned it so they could see. "Go past three farms. Take the dirt road on your left that looks more like a cow path. The path eventually curves to the left then after you pass a pecan grove on your right, watch for a barbed wire fence on your right. There will be an opening and a path that leads to their house. Shout to announce yourselves before you get too near the house. When you get close to the house, the dogs will raise a fuss, but they're in pens; otherwise, they'd rush you. Wait for Leo or Andy to come out to get you. I know you'd do all this anyway, but I feel better telling you."

Sandra gave Rosalie the flatbread. "You all be safe."

After they finished eating, Stuart put the map in his pocket, and Rosalie stuck the flatbread into her bag.

"Will you need a flashlight?" Sandra asked. "Sky's clear, and it doesn't feel like rain. You'll be back tonight, right?"

"We'll be fine," Stuart said. "We plan to be back tonight, but it might be late."

Sandra hugged each one. "I won't try to wait up. See you in the morning."

Scott hugged the girls then his son. "There shouldn't be any traffic on the road after dark. If there is, duck into the woods. I know you'll take care, but I feel better saying Dad things."

As they trekked up the driveway to the road, quail flew up from their hidden nests in the brush around the trees. Aimee Louise said, "Your mom will wait up."

"I know," Stuart said.

"Do we run or walk?" Rosalie asked.

"Run until we get to the path," Stuart said.

The girls ran on the road in front, and Stuart followed. After they passed the third farm, they slowed to a jog to watch for the cow path on the left. The light wind from the west shifted to a brisker northwest wind.

"Clouds may roll in later tonight; if they do, we'll have storms tomorrow," Rosalie said.

"I'd forgotten the kids at the farm called you Weather Girl, Rosalie, before Josh came up with Dead Eye Red," Stuart said.

"I still like keeping up with the weather," she said.

"Here." Aimee Louise turned left and dashed down the cow path. Stuart caught up with her.

"Glad we're off the road," he said.

Rosalie rushed to join them. "There's a car heading our way."

They raced to the closest grove of trees. Aimee Louise disappeared into the woods, and Rosalie climbed an oak with low-hanging branches.

Stuart stepped away from the trees and closer to the road as he pulled out the binoculars from his go-bag and scanned the road in the direction of the sound. When he spotted the vehicle, he stepped behind a tree to continue his surveillance. *Pickup truck. Two in the cab and three in the bed with rifles.*

Rosalie dropped to the ground next to him. "They didn't slow down. Do you think they're just passing through?"

Aimee Louise sprinted down the path from the road. "No license plate. Danger."

Stuart rolled his eyes. *I'm getting used to her doing the unexpected.*

"That's odd," Rosalie said as they continued on the path. "It's not like there's anyone to check their license plate. Seems like that would call attention to them at a roadblock. Maybe it fell off, and they don't know."

"Danger clouds."

Stuart froze. "Rosalie, are you sure they didn't slow down? I'm worried about Dad's farm."

"They didn't, as far as I could see."

"We need to go back and check," he said.

"Yes," Aimee Louise said. "You and Rosalie go check. I need to get on the radio."

"No. We don't split up." Stuart scowled and crossed his arms.

Aimee Louise turned and strolled away on the cow path toward the farm.

Stuart's face reddened. "Come back, Aimee Louise. We need to talk first."

CHAPTER EIGHT

"Stuart, wait; we can do this," Rosalie said. "I can run faster than you can. If you have my back, I can get close enough to your Dad's farm to be sure everything is okay then we can return to join Aimee Louise. Or we can spend another fifteen minutes arguing with Aimee Louise, who has already disappeared on the path."

"What if everything's not okay?"

"Then we've got a fight on our hands, and Aimee Louise is safe."

Stuart glared. "You're good. Let's go."

* * *

After Aimee Louise trotted down the driveway, she stopped when she neared the house. "Hello! It's Aimee Louise. Hello!" She relaxed and listened.

"Who is with you?" A voice called out.

"By myself. Stuart and Rosalie will be here soon."

Andy carried a rifle as he trotted up the driveway to her. "By yourself? Are you okay?"

"I'm fine. Stuart and Rosalie needed to check on a pickup truck that went by on the road on our way here. I need to contact Pops in Florida on the ham radio."

As they strolled to the house, the dogs whimpered. "Mr. Scott said the dogs would bark."

"They bark at strangers. Evidently you're not a stranger. You don't carry a rifle or pistol?" he asked.

"Pops tried to teach me to shoot, but the noise hurt my ears even with ear protection."

"Rosalie said you were a ham operator. Uncle Leo will be excited to meet you."

When they entered the house, Jennie rushed to hug Aimee Louse.

"Aunt Jennie, everything's okay," Andy said. "Aimee Louise needs to use Uncle Leo's ham radio to contact her Florida folks, and Stuart and Rosalie are investigating a pickup truck. They'll be along shortly."

"Good. I was afraid something was wrong," Jennie said.

Leo stood in the doorway of a room off the kitchen. He was short and wiry, and his gray hair had thinned to the point of a halo of fuzz. "Welcome, Aimee Louise. Come on in, and I'll show you my radio set up. It's been giving me a few problems lately. Maybe you'll have some ideas. Rosalie told Andy you're an expert."

When she joined him in his radio room, Aimee Louise stared at his equipment with awe. "This is nice, Mr. Leo. What do you think is wrong?"

"After lightning hit a tree near the house a week or so ago, the radio cuts in and out. I'm guessing the strike blew a fuse, but I've checked them all and didn't find a problem. I don't think it's the antenna, but I've run out of ideas."

When they sat in front of the transceiver, he fumbled with the dial with his gnarled hand. "My arthritis makes some things more difficult these days, and fine motor skills are not my strong suit." He chuckled. "Do you have the frequencies of the repeaters we might use?"

Aimee Louise pulled her list out of her pocket, and Leo read it.

"I've hit these two before. Let's see what I can get. It might be a little early, but I think we've got some weather heading this way, so we might pick up weather chatter."

After Leo turned on his radio, he tuned to his nearest repeater. "Nothing. Now I wonder if it's the repeater, not me."

"Want me to check your equipment?" Aimee Louise asked.

"Go ahead. Tools are in the top right desk drawer. I have a few things to do outside."

After Leo left, Andy came into the radio room while Aimee Louise checked the fuses and handed her a glass of water. She took a long drink then gave him the glass. He pulled the second chair away from the desk to give her room to work.

After a half hour, she rose. "Where's Leo?"

"I'll get him," Andy left.

When Leo came in, he asked, "You find something?"

"I think this fuse is bad. Do you have a replacement?"

"Getting dark in here." Leo lit the kerosene lamp that was on top of his file cabinet then opened the top drawer that served as a parts cabinet and sorted through fuses. "This one should be good."

Aimee Louise seated it then turned on the transceiver and clicked the microphone. "That's it."

Leo picked up the bad fuse. "Looks fine to me."

"It didn't feel right." She put the transceiver back together and replaced the tools into the desk drawer.

Andy remained in the doorway while Leo scooted the second chair next to her. "See if you can raise your folks."

When Aimee Louise reached Mr. Young, she said, "Need to talk to Major too."

When Major came on the radio, he asked, "Is everyone okay?"

"Yes. Brandon's dad is David Griffin. That's who is at your farm."

"Good to know. He was bitten by a snake in his travel here. We think a cottonmouth. Dr. Jody checked him. He's bedridden, and we're treating him for infection, but we'll have to wait it out as far as the venom is concerned. He's not out of the woods yet."

"We may have to stay here a while. There were signs of home invasions to the south of us; they are getting closer and maybe more frequent. A farm nearby was attacked with fatalities and possible kidnapping. We left Nate where he was. Peyton and Charo are with us. I'm using a neighbor's radio."

"Understood."

"Can you get a message to Phil? We need to know what Nate's condition is and whether he's ready to travel. Charo wants him here."

Mr. Young said, "I'll take care of it. How do we get back with you?"

Leo scooted closer to the radio and gave his call sign. "I can get messages to your family. They are within walking distance. I'm on the radio every morning and evening."

After Aimee Louise signed off, Andy asked, "Are you all really going to stay a while?"

"It's an option."

"Stuart just hollered from the driveway, Andy. Would you run out there?" Jennie asked.

Aimee Louise stepped into the kitchen as Jennie lit a candle on the dining table. "Is there anything I can get you, Aimee Louise? I'm glad Leo will have someone close to talk to about radios."

When Andy came inside with Stuart and Rosalie, he said, "You were right, Rosalie. Aimee Louise really is a whiz with the radio." He strode to Aimee Louise. "I couldn't see what was wrong with that bad fuse. I can't believe you found it because it didn't feel right. Sometime I'd like to spend some time with you to pick your brain about radios." Andy beamed as he gazed at Aimee Louise.

She glanced at Rosalie and Stuart, who still stood in the doorway, and tilted her head. *Strange clouds. Exactly alike. Angry and sad. Not very pretty.*

"Everything okay at the farm?" Aimee Louise asked.

"Yes." Rosalie crossed her arms.

"I talked to Pops. David was bitten by a cottonmouth snake before he arrived at the farm. Dr. Jody checked him. Pops said David's not out of the woods yet. I don't know what that means, do you? Molly moved David from the camper to the house because Dr. Jody wanted them to observe his condition closely. Sara reads to David. Pops said that was the best medicine of all. Mr. Young will get a message to Mr. Phil." Aimee Louise headed to the outside door.

"Mr. Young has my call sign," Leo said from his radio room. "We'll get you any messages from them."

"Supper will be ready soon. You all will stay, right? No reason to run off," Jennie said.

"Sounds smart to me." Andy smiled at Aimee Louise.

"Sorry, but we can't stay," Stuart said. "We need to head back before it gets much darker."

"Ms. Jennie, Stuart's mom sent you some flatbread." Rosalie pulled the flatbread out of her go-bag.

"This is just perfect to go with our supper. Tell her thank you for me," Jennie said.

"You'll have to come here earlier next time," Andy said to Aimee Louise. "I'd like to know enough about radios to help Uncle Leo."

"Let me give you fried pies for your trip back," Jennie said. "Next time, I'll have enough for you to take pies back for everyone else."

Stuart and Rosalie thanked Jennie then went outside.

Aimee Louise turned and stepped into the radio room as she put her fried pie into her go-bag. "Any weather news?"

Leo swung around in his chair. "Glad you stayed a minute. We've got storms heading our way. They're expected to be fairly strong and hit as soon as after midnight."

Aimee Louise sat and listened while Andy stood in the doorway.

"Thank you, Mr. Leo. Sounds like we have a rough night ahead." Aimee Louise rose to leave. "Thank you for the fried pie, Ms. Jennie."

"I'll walk out with you," Andy said.

Stuart and Rosalie stood in the driveway and turned to leave as Aimee Louise strolled toward them.

"See you," Andy called out.

"Good night," Aimee Louise said.

* * *

Stuart fumed as Rosalie set the pace up the driveway. *I don't like Andy and his sudden interest in learning more about radios. His uncle could teach him. What a phony.*

After they reached the road, Aimee Louise led the run, and Rosalie followed her. Stuart jogged then sprinted to get behind Rosalie. He caught up with her at the Newton farm driveway then when they neared the house, Aimee Louise waited for them at the kitchen door.

As they went inside, Sandra smiled. "Glad you weren't late. We haven't eaten yet. Everyone is washing up."

Aimee Louise pulled her fried pie out of her go-bag. "Ms. Jennie gave us fried pies, just like you said. Maybe you can cut it into pieces for us to share."

Rosalie rolled her eyes. "Here's mine."

"And mine," Stuart said. "There should be plenty for everyone. I'll put the go-bags into the truck."

"I'll help," Aimee Louise said.

"I can carry my own." Rosalie stomped out the door.

After they put their go-bags into the back of the truck, Rosalie asked, "Did you have a nice visit, Aimee Louise?"

Aimee Louise tilted her head. "Yes."

Stuart stared at the two girls. *She doesn't know Rosalie is angry. Or maybe she does and doesn't understand.*

"Can I talk to you a second, Aimee Louise?" Stuart asked.

Rosalie hurried into the house.

"What do you think is wrong with Rosalie?" he asked.

"She's angry and sad.."

"Did you see that in her cloud?"

"Yes, and yours too."

Stuart put his arm around Aimee Louise. "My angry and sad cloud was because I was jealous. I didn't like all the attention Andy was paying to you."

"That's odd." Aimee Louise stared over his head. "It's not there anymore."

Stuart exhaled. "Good."

"Yes. It was an ugly cloud."

As they walked inside, Stuart said, "After Rosalie's cloud isn't ugly anymore, she'll tell you what was wrong with her too."

"If she doesn't, it wasn't important."

Stuart snorted. *That's Aimee Louise. Straight to the point.*

When they strolled into the house together, Dolly was explaining the secret of pulling weeds. "I pull up the weeds easy, so I don't scare the fairies who live in the garden. It isn't good for them to be close to the weeds because fairies are allergic to weeds."

"I knew that," Henry said.

"No, you didn't," Dolly said.

"Actually, I did," Henry said. "You told me yesterday."

"Oh."

"Eat your soup and bread," Sandra said. "We have a special treat after supper."

Stuart blew on his spoonful of hot soup before he ate it. "Mmm. This is great. Love the extra vegetables. It was a good idea to go to Leo's. He has a great setup. I think his radio room was originally the dining room."

"I got through to Pops," Aimee Louise said. "We can talk after supper."

"Charo wants to come to the table tomorrow for breakfast," Sandra said.

"Glad we have your old wheelchair, Scott, or Charo said I'd be pulling her in the wagon. She's determined to sit with us." Judge chuckled.

"I'm glad Charo is back to her feisty self." Peyton smiled.

"Is feisty like a fairy?" Dolly asked.

Peyton furrowed her brow as she gazed at the ceiling. "The garden fairies are feisty, but feisty means fearless."

"My mama is feisty," Dolly said.

"She sure is, darling," Judge said.

After everyone had eaten, Sandra cut each fried pie into quarters. "I've got this all figured out. If my math's wrong, we're in trouble. Everyone gets one piece. That's ten. We have two pieces left over; if I cut each one in half, Dolly, Brandon, and Henry can have an extra half piece, and Charo can have a half piece too. I'll smash the apples for her."

Brandon and Henry applauded then everyone joined in. Sandra rose and bowed.

Peyton smiled. "Did you grow up in a big family, Sandra?"

"Nope. Just had lots of greedy cousins."

While everyone ate dessert, Stuart said, "The wind changed direction, and Rosalie said we can expect storms tonight."

"The ham operators said the same thing," Aimee Louise said. "Mr. Leo said it will be a rough night."

Scott said, "I think we may need extra hot water for clean up tonight, Sandra. I'll fill two big pots."

"Brandon and I will help," Peyton said.

"And Henry. Henry likes to help too," Brandon added.

"Dolly and I will help with the dishes, Sandra. We might not be the fastest, but we're the most entertaining," Judge said. "In fact, I can clear the table if you and Dolly would like to help Charo with her fried pie."

"We'll check outside for any equipment that needs to be put away." Stuart headed to the door, and Aimee Louise and Rosalie followed him.

"Let's check around the house before we go to the barn," Stuart said.

Aimee Louise found the wagon in the back and pulled it to the front. Rosalie carried a shovel, and Stuart added empty seedling pots to the wagon.

As they headed to the barn, Rosalie said, "I think we should empty the truck; at least pull out our go-bags, rifles, and ammunition."

"We can use the wagon to haul our things to the house. We're staying, right?" Stuart asked.

"Yes, we're staying," Aimee Louise said.

They emptied the wagon at the barn then filled it at the truck. After they emptied the wagon into the kitchen, they headed to the barn with the wagon.

Crack, crack.

Gunfire shattered the quiet night.

"Inside!" Rosalie shouted with her command voice, and everyone raced to the house.

"Sandra, can you look after the children and Charo?" Scott asked. "Peyton and Judge, we're the inside defense."

"We'll investigate," Stuart said as he and Rosalie grabbed their rifles and extra ammo. Aimee Louise joined them before they rushed outside.

"Shots sounded like they're beyond the Smith farm to me," Stuart said.

"Yes," Aimee Louise said.

Stuart led the way until Aimee Louise and Rosalie passed him on the wide path. As they ran past the barn, the sound of rapid-fire shots then more deliberate gunfire came from the direction of Leo's farm.

"To the road?" Rosalie asked.

"It's the fastest," Stuart said.

They dashed to the road and sprinted to the cow path. The closer they were to the Websters', the louder the gunfire. When they reached the curve, Aimee Louise stopped abruptly and pointed. "Pickup," she whispered. "One man. Danger."

"Aimee Louise, be our eyes. Barred owl. Rosalie, take the left, and I'll be on the right. When we're closer, I'll toss a rock or pecan into the truck bed. Our usual shots. After he's down, grab the keys, and I'll grab any weapons. Ready?"

"Always," Rosalie said.

"Keep me in sight. Stay together. Go."

The two of them crept along on opposite sides of the path. Stuart raised his left hand, and Rosalie stopped.

Stuart glanced down then picked up a pecan and lobbed it into the truck bed. The driver opened his door and hesitated before he climbed out with his pistol drawn. He walked around the truck while he scanned the area. He shrugged and aimed his pistol into the woods. He didn't flinch at the sound of the rapid fire coming from the Webster homestead behind him.

Crack. Crack. He dropped.

Rosalie ran to the man and stuck his pistol into her waistband then reached into the open driver's door and grabbed the keys and an ammo box. Stuart dragged the man into the brush, hopped into the back of the truck, and jumped out with two rifles. Rosalie and Stuart joined Aimee Louise.

"Where do we stash these?" Stuart asked.

"I'll take care of them." Aimee Louise removed her sweatshirt and tied it into a sling to carry the rifles then picked up the ammo can. "Won't be long." She trotted toward the road.

When she returned, Stuart said. "Rosalie, take left again and use the trees for cover. Aimee Louise, stay a little farther from the cow path. Barred owl, and we freeze. Let's go."

As they eased down the path to the driveway the wind picked up, and a man shouted, "Need more ammo."

Rosalie wheeled and bolted toward the road. Aimee Louise yanked on Stuart's shirt and hissed, "Run."

Stuart raced after Aimee Louise. When they reached the end of the cow path, Aimee Louise led the dash across the road and into the stand of oak trees.

"What?" Stuart bent over as he labored to catch his breath. "Why did we run?"

"They were headed back to the truck," Rosalie said. "I'll bet there was more ammunition that I missed."

The three of them crouched in the brush when the shouts neared the road then a loose group of men scrambled in panic as they reached the road.

"Which way?" a man shouted as he stood in the middle of the cow path and looked wildly around.

Another man pushed him out of the way to run in the direction away from the Newton farm.

"Six," Rosalie counted as the rest of the group followed the fleeing man. Stuart kept his rifle aimed on the group until he couldn't see the last man.

"Be right back." Aimee Louise darted across the road then returned with the rifles and ammunition can. "Ready."

"We need to hurry if we're going to make it to the Newton farm before the storm hits. The stars are obliterated in the west, and the gusts are getting stronger," Rosalie said.

"You okay carrying the rifles?" Stuart asked.

"Yes. Let's go." Aimee Louise set the pace. When they reached the Smith farm, she turned at the gate, and Stuart reached over the barbed wire and opened it.

As they neared the barn, Aimee Louise asked, "Is there a good place in the barn we can leave the rifles for now? They need to be checked out before anyone uses them."

"The door's gone to the tack room but it's dry, and we can toss some wood scraps over them. They should be fine until the storm blows over. I can't imagine anyone would find the barn tonight."

They left the rifles and raced to the house as the gusts pushed them.

"We need to get to the house as fast as we can," Stuart shouted over the roar of the wind.

Before they reached the house, pea-sized hail pelted them then grew to penny-sized as Stuart jerked open the kitchen door and slammed it when they were inside. Aimee Louise and Rosalie leaned against him as he held them and exhaled in relief. A single candle on the kitchen table gave a soft, welcoming glow to the room. Sandra peered out of the bathroom then raised her eyebrows. "Is that hail? The boys are finishing up their baths. There's hot water on the stove if you want tea."

Scott strode into the kitchen as Stuart released the girls. "Glad you're back. Okay if we stand down?"

"Yes," Stuart said as he poured hot water into a smaller pot then dropped the tea ball into the pot. Rosalie shivered and stayed close to Stuart. After Aimee Louise set three cups next to the steeping tea, she clapped her hands over her ears as the hail pounded the side of the house.

When the racket subsided, Aimee Louise said, "I think the hail stopped." She moved to the window and peeked outside. "It's just raining now."

"That was awful," Rosalie said. "I don't like hail."

Scott returned to the kitchen. "Bring your tea to the living room. Peyton and the judge will meet us there. I have an idea that your evening was more interesting than ours."

While everyone found a seat, Scott lit the two candles on the fireplace mantel, and the three children galloped to the kitchen for their snacks.

"Bath, snack, bed," Judge said. "Never realized how comforting a familiar routine could be."

Peyton nodded. "I love how safe the children feel here."

"That's Sandra's goal," Scott said. "What did you find, Stuart?"

"The gunfire was from the Websters' farm," Stuart said. "Thugs attempted a home invasion. The Websters turned them back, but we'd immobilized the gang's truck and driver and took their extra rifles and a can of ammunition. They fled on foot and went in the other direction. We were almost here when the hail hit. I'm glad we were as close as we were; I'd forgotten how much hail stings."

"I'll bet Jennie was in one of the upstairs bedrooms," Scott said. "She was in the Army; in fact, that's where she and Leo met. She hunts every fall, and Leo processes the meat. I'll bet the home invaders didn't expect a skilled shooter."

"They aren't from around here. I would think most households in rural Georgia rely on game to feed the family, which would mean at least one seasoned hunter in the home," Judge said. "Either somebody's importing talent, or the thugs are branching out, and the pickings are sparse in the cities now."

"I think you're right," Peyton said. "When the locals don't stop by their usual gathering places, a stranger could easily move around the community without anyone noticing; but why would a criminal move his operation from central Florida to a rural area in Georgia?"

"There is something or someone that drew them—a connection," Aimee Louise said.

"And back to Peyton's point, as long as they didn't draw attention to themselves, they're under the radar," Rosalie said.

Stuart rose. "Before I do the perimeter check, I'd like to tell Henry good night."

"I'll go with you," Aimee Louise said. "You coming, Rosalie?"

"I think I'll spend a little time with Charo. I'd rather stay inside, at least tonight."

When they went into the kitchen, Stuart said, "We're going to do our perimeter check for the night, Henry, but we wanted to say good night first. Did you have a good day?"

"It was a great day, Deputy Stuart. We put hay in the chicken boxes, got real dirty, and Brandon's mama said we did real good helping to fill the water pots."

"Sounds practically perfect, Henry. Good night."

"Good night, Henry." Aimee Louise hugged Henry, and he wrapped his arms around her neck then grinned at Stuart over her shoulder.

"You got my girl, Henry?" Stuart asked.

"Yes, Deputy."

"Good man. See you in the morning."

After they checked the barn, Aimee Louise asked, "Why did you ask Henry if he had your girl?"

Stuart chuckled. "When you hugged him, he gave me a look and grinned. I couldn't pass that up. He was really proud that you hugged him."

"That's sweet, right?" she asked.

"Yes," he said. "I think I know why Rosalie didn't come with us."

"You might. Tell me what you think."

"She thinks Charo may know what Peyton's not saying. Charo's not FBI and enjoys talking."

"You're right," Aimee Louise said.

"Was it okay with you that I said you were my girl?" he asked.

Aimee Louise furrowed her brow then headed up the driveway. When Stuart caught up, she said, "I don't know what that means."

Stuart nodded. "Think about it. We can talk another time."

When they reached the end of the driveway, they examined the ground around the downed tree.

"No signs of intruders," Stuart said.

"Man in the field." Aimee Louise stepped behind a tree, and Stuart did the same.

He peered at the field then spotted the figure that appeared as a silhouette against the red horizon. A lone man with a walking stick staggered toward them from the field across the road. His head was down as he dragged his right leg when he crossed the ditch to the road.

"Hurt, not dangerous." She stepped to the middle of the driveway and waved her arms. Stuart removed his sidearm from its holster and stepped in front of the tree where he'd have a better view of the young man.

"Hello," she called out. "Do you need help?"

"What?" He leaned on his stick. "Who are you?"

"I'm Angel. How'd you get hurt? What's your name?"

He took three steps forward then lost his balance and fell into the high weeds. He rose to his feet with the help of his sturdy stick. "I'm Wynn. I stepped in a hole and twisted my ankle yesterday."

"Do you have any ID?" she asked.

His chuckle was weak as he reached into his back pocket and pulled out his wallet. "Yeah, I got ID. What are you? A cop?"

"No, but I am," Stuart said.

The young man's eyes widened. "I was mesmerized by the angel voice. I didn't see you, sir."

CHAPTER NINE

"Get Dad," Stuart whispered.

As Aimee Louise raced away, Wynn winced as he shifted his weight to watch her. "She flies like an angel too."

"I'd like to see that ID," Stuart said in a flat voice.

"Yes sir." Wynn limped across the road to hand his license to Stuart.

After Stuart read the license, he narrowed his eyes at Wynn; according to his license, Wynn was twenty-two. *Older than he looks.*

The young man's jeans were muddy, his shirt had a tear near the seam on the right shoulder, and he wore a Georgia Bulldogs ballcap.

"What's your birthdate and address?"

Wynn cleared his throat before he replied.

Agrees with his license. Stuart slipped his pistol back into its holster then examined Wynn's face and hands as he returned the driver's license. "How long have you been on the road?"

Wynn leaned against his stick. "I'm starting to lose track of time. Four or five days, I think."

"You live in Athens long?" Stuart asked.

"Almost five years. I was a biology major at the University of Georgia and worked at an animal hospital. I wanted to be a vet, but things changed. After the grid collapsed, we worked in a tent for a while where our customers would bring their animals for us to examine. We ran out of medicine ages ago, but we cleaned and bandaged wounds—simple stuff. After the vet closed the practice and left town, I worked odd jobs, mostly manual labor, for food and a place to stay until even those jobs dried up. I knew if I could get to Grandpa's farm, he'd put me to work and feed me. His farm's close to here, if I'm remembering right. He's Wynn Smith too. I'm the third, like my license says. You know where his farm is?"

"Did your grandpa ever mention Mr. Newton?"

Wynn slumped against a nearby tree. "His neighbor? Sure. Grandpa thought a lot of Mr. Newton."

"This is the Newton farm. Mr. Smith moved to Alabama."

"Grandpa went to Alabama?" Wynn sighed. "My aunt and uncle have a farm there. He must have gone to stay with them."

Scott and Aimee Louise joined them while Wynn spoke.

Scott peered at the young man. "Last time I saw you, Wynn, you were eight years old, but I'd know you anywhere. You look just like your dad."

Wynn squinted as the evening moved to twilight. "Mr. Newton? I thought you'd be an old man by now, but you look the same."

Scott chuckled. "Can you make it to the house if we help?"

"Sure," Wynn grinned. "If Angel helps me."

"Yeah, I'll be helping you," Stuart growled.

Scott strolled alongside the young man while Stuart supported Wynn's weak side, and Aimee Louise remained near the road.

Stuart glanced back at Aimee Louise. *Why is she staying behind?*

When the three men reached the house, Rosalie opened the door.

"Red, Angel is finishing up our perimeter check," Stuart said.

"Gotcha." She grabbed her rifle and raced up the driveway.

As they went inside the house, Wynn asked, "Do all the girls here fly?"

"Who's this?" Sandra asked.

"Mr. Smith's grandson, Wynn," Stuart said. "He walked here to stay with his grandfather."

"Scott, help Wynn to the sink to wash in the soapy water, and I'll pull together something for him to eat." She poured water from a pitcher into a glass and set it on the table. After Wynn washed his hands and face, Scott helped him to the table while Sandra heated soup. When the judge came into the kitchen, she said, "Judge, this is

Mr. Smith's grandson, Wynn. Would you give him a bite to munch on while I stir the soup?"

Judge handed Wynn the last two rolls left over from their supper and joined him at the table.

"So, how long have you been walking?" the judge asked.

"Wynn's in capable hands," Scott said. "Shall we check on Angel and Red?"

When Stuart grabbed his rifle, Scott frowned then picked up his rifle too. As they strode up the driveway, Scott asked, "What are your thoughts about Wynn?"

"Mom will fix a pallet for him to sleep on tonight, but we're pretty much at capacity. We were planning to go to the Websters tomorrow; we'll see if they can take him in."

"Why did Aimee Louise stay near the road?"

"I don't know. I didn't want to leave her, but for some reason, she wanted me to go with you to the house. Rosalie knew I wanted her to go back up Aimee Louise. I can't explain, but somehow, the three of us operate on the same frequency."

"I've seen that. The judge said you three are spooky sometimes."

Stuart snorted. "I feel the same way."

"How does Rosalie feel about you and Aimee Louise?"

"Rosalie will always be in our lives, and she knows it."

The men slowed their pace to approach the road silently. Stuart hooted the call of the barred owl and was answered by the same call. They continued on their way in silence.

Rosalie hooted a soft call from the trees. Scott slipped to the side of the driveway behind a tree as Stuart made his way to Rosalie.

She spoke softly. "A large truck like the ones we've seen before stopped in front of the Smith property. Two men searched along the ditches on both sides of the road from the far edge of the Smith farm to ours. They stopped near our driveway to talk. They're looking for Wynn. They decided he couldn't have made it this far and left. We're waiting a few minutes to see if they return."

Stuart frowned. "There's more, isn't there?"

Rosalie disappeared into the trees, and Stuart listened to the buzz of the cicadas that announced the coming nightfall.

"We can go inside now," Aimee Louise said.

Stuart met Rosalie in the middle of the driveway, and they waited for Aimee Louise. Aimee Louise carried two rifles and had a holster with a pistol slung over her shoulder.

"Where did those come from?"

"Wynn dropped them."

Stuart narrowed his eyes. "When he fell. He left them in the grass."

Aimee Louise handed him one of the rifles. "Right."

Stuart examined the rifle. "Nice scope. Pretty expensive rifle for a starving vet tech to carry. Why would he have two rapid fire rifles?"

He held it to his shoulder and sighted to a point across the road then whistled. "Night vision."

Rosalie took the other rifle. "This one's the same."

"Dad, we're ready to go inside," Stuart said.

When they met up with Scott, Rosalie repeated what she and Aimee Louise heard.

"Aimee Louise saw Wynn drop the rifles and pistol in the field across the road," Stuart said. "We'll lock them in the truck for now."

"I'll grab the truck keys." Rosalie handed the rifle she carried back to Aimee Louise before she sprinted down the driveway.

"Fancy rifles. Wonder if Wynn defected from their gang?" Scott asked as they headed to the house.

"Ask him," Aimee Louise said.

"What?" Scott asked.

"It's a good idea, Dad. You can talk to Wynn while we're at the Websters."

Aimee Louise slipped her hand into Stuart's, and he smiled.

"You going to tell the Websters about the men looking for Wynn?" Scott asked.

"Sure will. If you decide it isn't safe to have Wynn around after you talk to him tomorrow, I'm not interested in sending him to the Websters."

"Agreed," Scott said. "I'll fill in Peyton in the morning; she'll be another set of eyes. Wynn's already on the judge's radar."

"What about Mom?" Stuart asked.

"She knows."

Rosalie waited for them at the truck. Stuart placed the rifles and pistol on the back seat. Aimee Louise tossed a blanket from the pickup bed over the weapons.

When they went into the house, the judge waited for them at the table. "Sandra and I moved the boxes out of the storage room under the stairs. I suspect if Brandon and Henry learn we turned it into a temporary bedroom, they're going to want it for themselves. Wynn practically collapsed on the sleeping pallet Sandra made for him. Hot water on the stove, if you want tea."

When Scott pointed to the hot water, Stuart, Aimee Louise, and Rosalie declined; he fixed a cup for himself before the four of them joined the judge at the table.

"I don't know exactly what's going on with Wynn; he's likeable enough, but my experience with troubled youth tells me he got himself in a bad situation and is in trouble. I think he's looking for a refuge where he can hide," Judge said. "Unless he's more forthcoming, I'd hand him a week's worth of supplies and wish him Godspeed."

* * *

It was still dark when Stuart woke. Brandon mumbled and flopped in his bed, and Henry giggled in his sleep. Stuart dressed in the dark and slipped out of the bedroom. The third stair from the bottom creaked, and his mother said, "Good morning, Stuart."

"How did you know it was me?" Stuart asked when he reached the kitchen.

"Because the girls are already outside. You want coffee to take with you?" The glow from the candle on the table gave her graying hair the illusion of a halo.

Mom's an angel too. He smiled as he hugged her. "Thank you, yes."

Stuart threw on his jacket and carried his cup outside to find Aimee Louise and Rosalie. When he neared the barn, Rosalie waved, and he joined them to relax and sip his coffee while they waited on their bench for the sun to rise. Stuart smiled when Rosalie stretched her legs and twitched her feet. *Rosalie is always restless right before the sun appears on the horizon.*

"Good morning, sun," Aimee Louise said.

Rosalie jumped up from the bench that Scott and the boys made for her and Aimee Louise. "Breakfast then Websters?" she asked.

Stuart raced to the house, but the girls caught up then passed him.

As they burst through the door, Stuart chuckled. "I thought I could beat you if I cheated."

Rosalie laughed. "Aimee Louise knew that, but we waited for you to go first. Didn't you notice that she shifted her feet for the race before you took off?"

"I spent too much time planning it, didn't I?"

"Yes," Aimee Louise said.

Sandra frowned at Stuart. "I can't believe you tried to cheat those two sweet girls."

"Sweet?" Stuart snorted. "More like devious."

Peyton came into the kitchen, "I don't know what's going on, but seems to me you'd know by now nothing gets past Aimee Louise. I need coffee, please."

Sandra laughed and poured a cup. "I'll have breakfast ready in two shakes."

When Aimee Louise tilted her head, Stuart leaned close to her and whispered, "Figure of speech. It means really soon."

"Thanks." She smiled, and Stuart hugged her. *I'll lose a race anytime if my reward is an Aimee Louise smile.*

Scott came into the kitchen. "Sounds like a party in here. What's the plan?"

"After breakfast, we've got a trail to clear," Stuart said.

"Looking forward to that being done," Scott poured himself a cup of coffee while Sandra cooked eggs and grits.

As Sandra dished up breakfast, Rosalie whisked the plates to the table and served everyone, beginning with Scott.

"What's the weather supposed to be like today, Rosalie?" Stuart asked as he finished off his eggs and grits.

"I expect it to be cool most of the day, but I don't think we'll see any rain until later in the week."

"How do you know that?" Scott asked.

Rosalie shrugged "I pay attention to the cicadas, birds, wind, and sky. Sometimes I can smell the rain coming. Weather interests me."

"Let's go." Aimee Louise finished off her breakfast.

Stuart and Rosalie picked up their rifles on the way out, and Sandra handed Aimee Louise a small jar of honey.

"Which way?" Rosalie asked.

"Smith farm," Stuart said. "The less time we're on the road, the better."

As they jogged along the path to the Smith barn, Aimee Louise asked, "Could there be a path through the woods from the Smith farm to the Websters'?"

"Good thought. Leo would know," Stuart said. "If there was a path, seems like it would be close to the homestead, but I assume it would be overgrown like the path between Dad's house and the Smith barn."

"It would make traveling back and forth to the Websters' easier," Rosalie said.

When they reached the lone chimney, Aimee Louise paced along the edge of the clearing along the woods. Rosalie jogged to the back of the house while Stuart stood where he could see both girls and scan the area.

Aimee Louise froze. "Truck on the road."

Stuart concentrated on listening before he heard the faint rumble. "They're either still looking for Wynn or making one last pass. The Smith farm is hard to find from the road; even Wynn wasn't sure where it was.

"I might have found a path," Rosalie said.

Stuart examined where she pointed. "Maybe. It would still take a lot of work to clear it even with a tractor. I have another thought. Let's head to the Websters'."

When Stuart set a slow, deliberate pace with Aimee Louise alongside him, Rosalie followed. After a few turns in the driveway,

Stuart stopped. "This is the closest the driveway comes to the Webster farm."

Aimee Louise crept along the driveway as she stared at the overgrown grass and trees. *Reminds me of a dowser searching for water.* Stuart smiled.

"Here." Aimee Louise pushed through the weeds and into the woods. Stuart raised his eyebrows as Rosalie tied a string on a branch and dashed after her before he followed. He noticed pieces of string tied onto branches at his chest-height along the way and snickered. *Rosalie's eye level.*

After thirty yards, he caught up with them, and Aimee Louise maintained her fast pace with Rosalie at her side. Stuart turned to glance back at the pathway behind him. *Not sure I could find this without Rosalie's strings. Seems to open up as we go along.* He shook his head and snorted. *My imagination is in high gear.*

When the trees thinned, Aimee Louise pointed. "The Webster driveway is there."

"I used the last of my string," Rosalie mumbled. "Need more."

After Stuart shouted to announce their arrival, Andy came out of the barn. "That you, Red?"

Rosalie snickered as Stuart replied, "It's Stuart and friends."

Andy loped to them and grinned at Rosalie's smile. "Thought you'd like that. We had some excitement last night, but I think you already know that. I found the red truck last night and cleaned up after you. Come inside for a warm-up."

"How did you know Rosalie's nickname was Red?" Stuart asked.

"It is? Makes sense to me," Andy said. "What's Aimee Louise's?"

"Aimee Louise's nickname is Angel," Rosalie said. "We haven't thought of one for Stuart yet."

"Thank goodness," Stuart mumbled. As they sauntered to the house, he asked, "What did you do before the grid collapsed?"

"I went to college in Macon and have a master's degree in teaching. After I graduated, I taught physics at a boys' prep school. Almost got fired when I turned the lab into a woodworking shop," Andy chuckled. "My education and degrees were impressive on paper, but I'll always be a country boy. I figured those sheltered, book-educated boys would get a kick out of working with their hands, and I was right. Took some fancy talking to explain to the director of the school that structural integrity, dovetails, end grain versus side grain, traditional versus modern joinery methods, and planning angles were valid topics for physics; when I threw in chisels and the Offerman Theory of Craftsmanship, the Director nodded as he took notes and commended me for teaching advanced topics."

Stuart laughed. "He had no idea of what you were talking about, but I'd be surprised if you hadn't been in line for a raise, after that."

"What about you?" Andy asked.

"Deputy sheriff and farmer. Best of two worlds for me."

"And Angel." Andy's eyes twinkled.

Stuart's eyebrows rose, and Andy grinned. "Teachers see everything."

Andy stepped alongside Rosalie. "What about you, Red? What's your passion?"

"Weather. I love being outdoors and discovered there was a lot to learn from birds, insects, and paying attention to sudden shifts in the wind or the air temperature."

"That's amazing. You're a valuable person to have around," he said. "Not many of us pay attention to the weather until we're wet, cold, overheated, or blown across the yard."

Rosalie giggled, and Stuart rolled his eyes.

When they went into the house, Andy said, "We've got company, Aunt Jennie."

Jennie came to the kitchen from the back of the house. "I'll heat up the coffee. It's nippy out there."

"Hello, Ms. Jennie," Rosalie said as she and Aimee Louise hurried to the radio room.

When the coffee was hot, Jennie poured three cups. "Thank you for your help last night, Stuart. I've never seen a knee and headshot like that before. Yours?"

"Rosalie and me. The knee shot is hers, and the headshot is mine. I couldn't duplicate that knee shot."

Jennie raised her eyebrows. "Not sure I could either. Where'd she learn that? She's only what? Sixteen?"

"Eighteen. Major Dave Elliott taught her. Aimee Louise is his granddaughter, and he adopted Rosalie as his granddaughter two years ago after her mother died."

"She's older than she looks. One of the advantages of having the right genes. Right, Andy?" Jennie chuckled. "I know Major by reputation. He's a remarkable marksman and instructor. Should have known she was Elliott-trained. What about Aimee Louise?"

"Not a shooter. She's sensitive to sounds."

"Many brilliant people are. Autistic too, right?"

Stuart shrugged. "I don't know. Never thought about it before. I guess so."

"She's herself." Jennie smiled. "The rest of us could learn from her."

"Dad said you were a crack shot yourself."

"I was surprised to learn I was a natural after I joined the Army, and I love to hunt. I keep us and a couple of neighbors in venison. We do lots of trading around here."

"Got a cup for me?" Leo came into the kitchen. "Aimee Louise is amazing with the radio. The Florida folks found a booster for their system, and Aimee Louise is talking to Major and Mr. Young. Rosalie will give a full report when they're finished. Those two are quite a team, aren't they?"

Jennie poured him a cup as he joined the young men at the table.

"What's going on in here?" Leo asked.

"We're waiting to hear Rosalie's report then I'm sure Stuart would be interested in hearing about our visitors."

Leo nodded. "If the dogs hadn't given us warning, they might have been successful."

"How are the puppies doing?" Stuart asked.

"Cute as ever. Want to go look at them?" Jennie asked.

Stuart drained his cup. "Are you kidding? Without Aimee Louise and Rosalie? I think I'll wait."

When Aimee Louise and Rosalie joined them in the kitchen, Rosalie said, "We've got a lot to talk about. I made a list." She handed the list to Stuart. "Can we start with last night's attack?"

"A large group of men came down the driveway, which was their downfall because they set off the dogs," Leo said. "If they'd had sense enough to spread out in the brush to approach the house from different directions, they might have had more success."

Jennie laughed. "Honey, I'm so glad you weren't at the driveway to direct them in the proper ways to invade our home."

Leo smiled. "Jennie and I were in the house, and Andy was in the barn. Andy challenged them, and they fired on him. Andy shot back and hit one man then Jennie took her shots from the upstairs window. When the third man dropped, a fourth one took cover behind my tractor while he shot at Andy in the barn, but I had a clear shot and took it. That's when the rest of them retreated in a panic up the driveway."

"Of course, it didn't happen quite as quickly as it sounds," Jennie said. "The attackers had rapid fire rifles, and they did reload several times. I wasn't sure where Andy was, and it was a while before I had a clean shot, but Leo gave a good summary."

"We were headed back when the remaining group fled," Stuart said. "We gave them room to escape. They stopped at their truck for more ammunition, but Rosalie had grabbed it and the truck keys, and I took their spare rifles. They ran in the opposite direction of Dad's farm."

"I didn't realize you all were there during most of the firefight," Jennie said. "Why didn't you come to the house afterwards?"

"We needed to get back to Dad's before the storm," Stuart said. "We made it before the worst of the hail hit."

"Radio next?" Rosalie held up her notes.

"Go ahead," Stuart said.

"David's still ill. Dr. Jody didn't expect him to show any improvement for a few more days. The attacks around Pops' farm are increasing. Pops said the purpose of the attacks seemed to be for food, guns, and ammunition, not kidnapping like they were for a while. The cities have been stripped and looted, and most of the people fled or died, so the gangs expanded their turf. Pops said we may see gang wars now too. Pastor John might take in a family with small children that doesn't have any nearby neighbors. The ham near Phil said our friend is well enough to travel. There's another storm brewing in the Gulf. Mr. Young said with it being this late in the season, it will be unpredictable. That's it, except we talked to the sheriff after Mr. Leo left then we signed off."

"Smith," Aimee Louise said as she read from Rosalie's agenda.

"Wynn Smith showed up yesterday near our farm. He said he walked from Athens to come to his grandfather's, and I believed he'd been traveling on foot for several days because he was exhausted," Stuart said. "He didn't know the house had burned or that Mr. Smith had left for Alabama. After we'd helped him to Dad's house, two men in a transport truck stopped near our gate and were looking for him. Aimee Louise overheard them talking. She also found the two expensive rifles and a pistol Wynn left in the field across from our farm. Mom made a bed for him for the night, but we've got a houseful. I'm not sure how truthful he's been. Dad planned to talk to Wynn after he wakes up."

"I wasn't around him much when we were kids because Mom and I visited here mostly in the summer. He's a year older than I am and was always bulkier. He was a bully until I called his bluff then he left me alone," Andy said.

"What did you do?" Rosalie asked.

"He got himself grounded," Jennie said.

"I punched him in the nose when I was twelve," Andy said. "I still remember the satisfaction of the crunch, the blood running down his shirt, and his surprised look. Mom grounded me for two weeks, but it was worth it because he stayed away from me after that. He told all the other kids I was a crazed farm boy. I kind of liked having a fierce farm nickname."

Stuart snorted. "He sure had a limited vocabulary."

"Right?" Andy chuckled. "My city slicker students could have helped him out with something far more scathing."

"We've got room here, but seems like he needs to be a little more forthcoming, or else we give him enough supplies for him to travel to Alabama. It's actually a shorter trip than coming here from Athens," Jennie said.

"We're going to head out. We'll get back to you with the consensus about Wynn," Stuart said. "Leo, did you know about a footpath between here and the Smith farm?"

"I'd forgotten all about it. Did you all find it?"

"We might have. We made our way here through the brush and trees, but it was overgrown. Rosalie marked trees with string as we pushed through so we could find our way back."

"I've got some green plastic tape. Would you be interested in marking the trail with that?" Jennie asked.

"I'd like to give it a try," Rosalie said. "Stuart wants us to be on the road as little as possible."

"Smart," Jennie said.

After they said their goodbyes, Rosalie placed the green tape at their entrance to the path from the Websters' farm. "I'll leave the string because we know it's there and can see it," she said.

"Makes sense to avoid making the path too easy to find."

When they reached the Smith farm, Aimee Louise said, "We have more information, but Sheriff asked us to keep it quiet."

"Let's go into the barn to talk," Stuart said.

Aimee Louise and Rosalie sat on the dirt floor while Stuart stayed near the doorway.

Rosalie said, "After Mr. Leo left the room, the sheriff told us he went to town yesterday to check his office. When he arrived, a man said he'd been in town for two days trying to find someone who could tell him about Peyton. Sheriff said she came through a while ago, but he hadn't seen her lately. Then the man, who claimed to be her husband, Troy, asked about her partner, and Sheriff said he never met her partner. Troy said he heard Peyton was near the Georgia border with her partner and another woman. Sheriff said she was alone and on her way to South Carolina, but the last he knew, she diverted to the east and was near Savannah."

"What a complication," Stuart said. "What did Troy say? Did the sheriff think it was the real Troy? Peyton said he'd never bother to look for her. I wonder what's going on."

"Sheriff told us the man might be the real Troy or an imposter, but either way, he had the feeling the man was a danger to Peyton. Sheriff admitted he could have used Aimee Louise by his side," Rosalie said. "We snickered because the sheriff has always been a skeptic when it came to clouds."

Stuart paced. "I need to talk to Peyton."

"Yes." Aimee Louise rose and headed to the wide path toward the Newton farm, and Rosalie followed while Stuart examined where they had placed the rifles earlier. *We need a place more secure for our growing collection of rifles. I'll talk to Dad.*

Stuart caught up with his companions before they reached the house. When they went into the house, the three children, the judge, and Charo sat at the kitchen table.

"Mommy's having breakfast with us," Dolly said with her best squeal.

"Hey there," Charo said in a soft voice.

Rosalie grinned. "I knew you'd do it. You're amazing."

"She is, isn't she?" Sandra smiled.

Stuart frowned. "Wynn still asleep?"

"He's changing in my bedroom," Judge said. "He'll be out soon."

While Rosalie and Aimee Louise helped Sandra serve breakfast, Stuart said, "Dad, I need your opinion."

"Let's take a walk," Scott said.

The two men strolled up the driveway. "The road bothers me. I'm not sure one tree across the driveway is enough," Scott said. "We can pile the downed trees close to the entrance, unless it would look like we're trying too hard."

When they neared the road, Stuart said. "If we drag the trees and branches near to the tree line and across the driveway like you said, it will look like storms had knocked the trees down."

As they headed down the driveway, Stuart asked, "Dad, where would be a good place to store our growing collection of rifles? We need a secure place where they'll be safe from inquisitive kids and bad guys."

"I'd like to check them first. If there are any we'd like to use, they could go into the gun safe. We could store the rest in the attic. Normally, I wouldn't suggest the attic because of the humidity and extreme temperatures, but it's more secure than any locked closet in the house or my shop."

"Rosalie is our gun expert. She'll want to help clean and inspect them. She's fast and meticulous," Stuart said.

Scott chuckled. "Barn might be the best place to clean them. I'll clear off the workbench and put out my cleaning supplies then find Rosalie."

"Thanks, Dad. Did you have a chance to talk to Wynn this morning?"

"Not yet. He wasn't awake when I left the house."

"If we go inside and he's up, I'll stick around and ask a few questions to keep him occupied while you and Rosalie clean firearms," Stuart said.

On their way back to the house, Scott said, "After we finish with the project, I'll move some tree trunks and boughs to the front of the driveway. When I rev up the tractor, Henry will appear. I'll most likely have expert help with that too."

When they went inside the house, Wynn sat at the table with eggs and a biscuit on the plate in front of him while Sandra washed dishes.

"Hello, Deputy," Wynn said. "Thanks for giving me a place to sleep last night, Mr. Newton."

Scott nodded. "I'll find Rosalie, and we'll get started on our project, Stuart."

"Thanks, Dad. Aimee Louise and Rosalie know where everything is."

"We'll take care of it."

Stuart poured a cup of coffee then joined Wynn at the table.

"The girls are at the garden, and Charo is napping," Sandra said. "I'll be out in just a minute. The boys and I will plant lettuce in flats while the judge builds a small cold frame to protect our seedlings."

Scott left in search of Rosalie and Aimee Louise. Sandra rinsed the last dish and followed him outside. After Wynn finished eating, Stuart cleared the plate and silverware and washed them.

"More coffee?" Stuart poured himself a refill, and Wynn nodded.

"I'm glad you got a good night's sleep," Stuart said as he pulled out his chair to join Wynn. "Nothing like feeling safe to be able to relax."

"That's the truth. I can't remember the last time I slept as well as I did last night." Wynn frowned. "Deputy, your folks are great, but there's really not room for an extra person here. I know I need to move on, but while I build up my strength, I'm strong enough to stay in the barn."

Stuart narrowed his eyes. "I know about the men looking for you. I need some straight answers."

"Oh." Wynn sipped his coffee as Aimee Louise came into the house.

"Rosalie and your dad are working on their project. I came inside to help you," she said.

Stuart smiled and pulled out her chair. "Glad you're here; please join us. Wynn was about to explain why the men were looking for him."

After Aimee Louise sat at the table, Stuart said, "Wynn, you've got one chance. You could bamboozle me if you're slick enough, but you can't fool both of us. Your choice. We're listening."

CHAPTER TEN

Wynn stared at Stuart and Aimee Louise. Stuart sipped his coffee and waited while Aimee Louise watched Wynn.

Wynn shifted his gaze to the table. "I got this job driving a truck," he mumbled then spoke louder. "Dad died a few years ago, and I didn't know where Mom was. I didn't have anywhere to turn, and I was desperate for work. I was hungry and living on the street. You were right about needing to feel safe to sleep. I dozed but never really slept and moved at the slightest sound from one spot to another every night."

He placed his hands on the table and stared at them. "I'm not making excuses. It's just how it was. Another guy who lived on the street told me about an outfit looking for transport truck drivers, and I went to see if it was true. They told me the pay was two meals a day, and I could sleep in the truck cab with the understanding that I had to do as I was told, or I'd be gone. It was clear that gone didn't mean fired."

He exhaled and scooted his chair back as he stared at the empty chair across from him. "It was an easy job. I just drove from one place to another—usually from Florida to South or North Carolina with a load then back to Florida or Georgia. I never knew what the cargo was—"

Stuart cleared his throat, and Wynn bit his lip before he continued. "I knew the cargo was people, so I was careful with turns. A supervisor always rode up front with me. The truck was full on the trips north, and the trips south included two or three men who rode in the back. On this last trip south, there was only one man in the back. The supervisor told me to stop a couple of hours after we crossed the state line into Florida, and he took his handheld radio into a field. It wasn't unusual for a supervisor to check in regularly on the trip south. When he climbed back into the truck, he told me to turn around and complained about the bosses changing the plan. He got madder with each mile, and when he slammed his fist on the dash and cursed at me, I knew I was in trouble."

Wynn rose and carried his cup to the sink then stared out the window. "When we were just south of Albany, he screamed at me to pull over, and I slammed on the brakes. He and the guy in the back went into the field together, and the supervisor waved his hands as he talked and pointed to the truck. His face was red, and I could tell he was yelling. I snatched up my backpack and the pistol in the glove compartment then slipped to the back and found two rifles. I grabbed them then ran into the trees and kept running until I collapsed. I wasn't sure where I was, but I knew I took off to the west before I made a sharp turn to the south. I found a rickety, old hunting stand and climbed up into it for the night. I knew I was too far into the woods for them to find and bet they wouldn't think to look up even if they did venture that far from the road. When I woke at dawn, I realized I had headed in the direction of Grandpa's farm, so I continued south. I was relieved when I started recognizing the names of towns I passed. When Angel called out to me, I dropped the rifles and pistol in the field. I planned to pick them up when I left. You know the rest."

Wynn sat in his chair and stared at the table.

"Do you have any questions, Angel?" Stuart asked.

"Do you miss the animals?" she gazed in the direction of the wall above him.

Wynn jerked up his head and stared at her. "Yes, I do. They were my friends."

Stuart rose. "Let's go outside, Aimee Louise."

As they strolled to the barn, Stuart asked, "What did you see?"

"He's angry. He knew what the cargo going north was and lied about that. It was hard to tell what was true and what wasn't because he mixes the truth and lies so well. He left a part out, but I don't know what it was."

Stuart nodded. "Is it okay if he stays around?"

"I wouldn't trust him in the house because what he left out is important. He cared about the dogs and cats—that was true. He's never had anyone else to care about."

"Interesting."

When they reached the barn, Scott grinned. "Rosalie cleaned four rifles, and I'm still working on mine, but it's not a competition. How did it go inside?"

Stuart explained what Wynn had said.

"Do you believe him?" Scott asked.

"With a grain of salt; Aimee Louise said he mixed truth and lies and he left something out," Stuart said.

"So what do we do with him?"

"He offered to stay in the barn. I think we take him up on it for a few days. Aimee Louise said we need to know what he left out because it's important."

Scott nodded. "That's what we'll do. Do you want to tell him?"

"I can, but because this is your farm, maybe you should. That will also let him know we talked with you."

Scott finished the final touches on the rifle he cleaned then pointed to the scoped rifles. "Rosalie and I decided we want these two in the gun case. Would you put the rest in the attic? I'll take Wynn for a short stroll, so you all won't be parading guns past him."

They waited until Scott came outside with Wynn and headed toward the front of the house before they left the barn.

"Rosalie, take the two scoped rifles to Mom and Dad's bedroom. He'll put the rifles in his gun safe. I'll pull down the attic ladder then we can store the rest of the rifles."

They carried all the rifles into the house. After Stuart pulled down the ladder, he climbed into the attic. Aimee Louise stood midway on the ladder, and Rosalie handed her one rifle at a time until they were all put away. Aimee Louise hopped down as Stuart descended the ladder.

After Stuart closed up the access to the attic, Rosalie said, "We want to check in with Pops in the morning. You don't have to go if you don't want to because now we have the off-road trail to get there."

"I'll go," Stuart said. "Aimee Louise, I need to talk to Peyton. Would you be there with me when I do?"

"Yes."

Stuart and Aimee Louise strolled to the garden as Rosalie skipped ahead to help the judge with the cold frame.

When they reached the garden, the boys were dumping dirt into the flat, and Dolly held the seed packet. Sandra held the bag of soil for the boys, and Peyton put the final touches on the cold frame she had built while the judge applied the plastic onto the top.

"Peyton, you have a little time for a discussion?" Stuart asked.

"Sure, Rosalie can install the lid for the frame. Judge can tell her what we had planned."

She brushed off her hands, and Stuart said, "How about the front porch? The breeze will feel good."

When they reached the porch, Peyton flopped onto a rocker. "What's up?"

Before he sat, Stuart slid a chair to an angle that was more conducive to conversation, and Peyton scooted her chair to see Stuart. Aimee Louise sat on the porch steps and faced the house, so she could see both of them.

"We have a lot of news and a lot of questions. Can we start with the questions first?"

Peyton narrowed her eyes, and her face tightened. "Sure."

"Why don't you trust me?" Stuart gazed at her.

She glared. "This isn't fair. I know Aimee Louise can tell—"

She crossed her arms and pursed her lips, and Stuart shrugged.

"I can leave if you want me to," Aimee Louise said.

Peyton's eyes widened. "No, not at all." She rocked and stared at the sky.

"Okay, Stuart. I don't trust easily because I've been betrayed too often in the past. I actually think I do trust you even though it scares me."

"I'm going to trust you, Peyton. We have to start somewhere, right?"

Peyton sighed. "Yes, go ahead."

"News," Aimee Louise said.

Stuart nodded. "Sheriff, Aimee Louise, and Rosalie found David Griffin at Pete's Diner on Monday. He was looking for you, but he said he was Troy. I think he said he was Troy because he thought we'd never believe him if he said he was David, Brandon's father. What's interesting is that Aimee Louise kept saying that he was Brandon's father, but I didn't believe he was Troy. The sheriff and I weren't hearing what she said."

Peyton smiled. "I trust Aimee Louise."

Stuart returned her smile. "Having someone to trust feels good, doesn't it? On his travels to the farm from Orlando, David was bitten by a snake. Major thinks it was a cottonmouth, and he's been very sick. One of the reasons Aimee Louise has been so adamant about the radio contact with Major's farm is to keep in touch with David's condition."

"We're going to the Websters' in the morning," Aimee Louise said.

Peyton rose and paced the porch. When she returned to her chair, she said, "If I could run as fast as Aimee Louise and Rosalie, I'd be tempted to hit the road right now to see David, except I wouldn't leave without Brandon."

"There's more," Stuart said. "A man who said he was Troy showed up at the sheriff's office and said he was trying to find you."

Peyton's face paled.

"What is it about Troy that scares you?" Stuart asked.

"Nothing," she said.

She gazed at Stuart. "That's not true. The last time I saw Troy he told me I knew something important, and I needed to tell him for my own safety. When I told him I didn't know what he was talking about, he told me I'd regret not telling him. When I asked him if he was threatening me, he laughed and said it was a friendly warning for old times' sake."

Peyton shuddered. "I think he ordered the attack on me. One of the men asked, *Which one is Peyton?* before they came into the room where they held us. I know Charo heard it too and knew what their intentions were."

Peyton choked back tears. "Charo must have thought she could survive the attack or felt like it was important for me to survive. I can't tell you how heavy the burden of Charo's and Nate's conditions are on me. They trusted me, and see what happened?"

Peyton rose. "Give me a minute. I'll be back." She paced to the driveway and back several times before she returned to her seat.

"Remember the list that FBI agent Rex Wilson gave me of turncoat agents and Nate was on the list? Even after Major proved to me that the list was phony, I didn't trust Nate. Nate must have known Troy thought I knew something because he told me that someone close to me intended to do harm, but I thought he meant David and wouldn't listen."

"One of the reasons we're sharing everything we know is that we have some decisions to make and want you to participate in the discussion. We learned that Nate wants to come here to be with his family."

"Nate's well enough to want to travel to be with his family? That's wonderful." Peyton frowned. "But how would he get here? That's the problem, isn't it?"

"Our additional problem is that the attacks on farms that were reported south of us are moving closer. We let Major know that we need to stay here for a while to help keep the farm safe. The Websters' farm was attacked last night."

"I'm in," Peyton said. "I'm done with feeling sorry for myself. You can count on me."

"Thank you," Aimee Louise said.

Peyton's eyes welled up as she gazed at Aimee Louise. "You are amazing." She hugged Aimee Louise then rushed to the garden.

"Did we miss anything?" Stuart asked.

"All the rifles."

"I'd forgotten about them. Peyton might want one of the new scope rifles," Stuart said.

"And Charo."

Stuart frowned as he held out his hand to help Aimee Louise up. "Charo's too injured to shoot."

"Time to talk to Charo." Aimee Louise strolled to the house.

Stuart raised his eyebrows then hurried to catch up with her. When he rounded the corner of the house, he met Wynn who was returning from the barn.

"Mr. Newton said I could stay a few days in the barn." Wynn beamed. "We talked about the potential attacks on the farm, and we agreed I'd help the family by being on duty where I can hear any threats. After all the time I spent sleeping on the streets, the barn is a luxury, and I sleep light. Mrs. Newton said she'd make up a bed for me, but I asked for the bedding so I can make my own. She said I have to eat meals at the table with the family because that's her rule."

When they reached the house, Stuart said, "I'm glad you'll be guarding the family at night. The attacks are getting closer."

Sandra handed Wynn a stack of blankets and sheets. "Come back for your pillow. Is there anything else you'll need? There's a wool blanket in there if it gets cold. Stuart, don't we have a cot in the attic?"

"I'll check," Stuart said as Wynn carried out his blankets.

Stuart found the cot in the attic and set it by the kitchen door then continued to Charo's room. Charo sat in the wheelchair next to the window and smiled when Stuart entered her room.

"Hello, Stuart. Aimee Louise said I can have a rifle as soon as my bones heal in my arms. We thought a regular dose of sunlight might help."

"I'm sure you're right," Stuart returned her smile. "Where's Aimee Louise?"

"I'm not sure. She said something was bothering her. I think she went out the front door."

Nobody goes out the front door.

Stuart hurried to the living room and opened the front door. Aimee Louise was rocking on the porch.

Stuart sat in the chair next to her. "What's bothering you?"

"Wynn may still have a bond with the attackers. I talked to Charo because I don't understand, and I was hoping with her past experience as a domestic violence counselor, she could help me."

"What is it you don't understand?" Stuart rocked in rhythm with Aimee Louise's rocker.

"How someone can break away from a gang. If a gang is like family to a lonely person, it would be like breaking away from your family. Charo said it's possible, but the ties are still there even if the person turns their back on them."

"Is that the part you think Wynn was hiding?"

"Maybe. I'm not sure."

"Do we send him away? What do we do?"

"Charo said we use it. I think we go talk to Andy. He'd know how."

Stuart rose from his chair. "I'll get Rosalie."

"Tell her to cover for us. If all three of us disappear, that's noticeable. As long as Rosalie is around, everyone will assume we're nearby."

"She'll be mad about being left out."

"Yes. She likes Andy."

Stuart sauntered to the garden and spoke quietly to Rosalie.

She growled, "Your idea?"

"Are you mad?" he asked.

She rolled her eyes. "No, I know it was Aimee Louise's idea. She's right. I've got your back."

Stuart strolled to the kitchen door, picked up his rifle, and went out the front door. "Ready."

When they came out near the trees at the Websters' farm, Stuart called out. "Hello! Neighbors are here."

"That you, Elmer?" Andy called back.

"Not this time," Stuart answered. "Just me with my angel."

Andy strode to them and grinned.

"We have the best passwords," Stuart said. "They're so secret, we don't even know what they mean."

As the three of them strolled toward the house, Andy said, "I know this isn't a social visit. What's up?"

Stuart explained the dilemma with Wynn. "How do we use his bond with the attacking thugs, assuming it exists?"

"I've seen other Wynns at the school where I teach. Very lonely kids, and the group, good or bad, became their family. My method was to put pressure on the group leaders for the behavior I wanted; for example, studying for exams or turning in homework on time. In this case, we could transfer the bond. From what you said, that's what your parents are doing. You'll need a way to reinforce the new bond."

"Explain," Aimee Louise said.

"If you adopt a puppy that was mistreated, the puppy still wants to go back to its original home, even though it was a terrible place, because it takes time to adjust and bond to the new life. Foster kids have the same behavior."

"We need a puppy," Aimee Louise said.

Stuart and Andy stared at her then Andy tilted his head. "I think I get it. His old gang didn't have a puppy. The new family does. What's our plan?"

"Bring the puppies to the farm. The kids and the puppy will choose," Aimee Louise bounded to the trail back to the farm.

Andy shook his head. "You're a lucky man, Stuart, but how do you deal with keeping up with a brilliant woman?"

"Badly." Stuart raced to catch up with Aimee Louise.

When they arrived at the farm, they went into the house through the front door then locked it behind them.

"Secret door." Aimee Louise headed to the kitchen then went outside.

Love how she sees things. Stuart smiled as he watched her leave before he strolled to Charo's room and tapped on the door frame.

Charo leaned against the windowsill for a better view of the garden; she turned her head at his tap. Wild flowers floated in the small bowl next to her neatly made bed, and her hair was pulled back with a bright green ribbon. The sunlight brightened the room, and her face glowed.

"Feel like talking?" Stuart asked. "I've got some in-depth questions that can wait until you have more energy."

"I'm bored because I feel great, at least inside my head. It's my body that can't quite keep up. Pull up a chair. I'd love some in-depth questions, but I warn you, I might have only shallow answers." Her eyes crinkled as she smiled.

"Tell me if you get tired or if I'm out of line," Stuart said. "Do you know who Brandon's father is?"

Charo narrowed her eyes. "I do. Do you?"

"David," Stuart said.

Charo sighed in relief. "Good. Now we can talk, right?"

"Yes. It's a convoluted story." Stuart explained that David, who claimed to be Troy, showed up at Pete's in his search to find Peyton and Brandon.

"Aimee Louise told us he was Brandon's father, but the sheriff and I didn't hear what she said."

Charo chuckled. "We let our preconceptions cloud our judgement sometimes, and yes, I doubled up my cloud word on purpose. Did I do as good as Josh?"

Stuart snorted. "I'm glad you're feeling better. There's more about David." He told her about the snake bite and the slow healing.

"I know he's pushing himself to get better. He'll be fine. I don't know David very well, but I've met him a few times. He's a great guy."

"I'm going to get into a touchy subject, but first, I have news for you. Nate is much better. Aimee Louise and Rosalie have been checking on him through the ham radio network."

Charo's eyes welled up before she sobbed. "I've been so worried about him. When no one mentioned him, I assumed the worst. I've been too afraid to ask."

Stuart grabbed a cloth from her bedside table and handed it to her.

When her tears slowed, she said, "I'm so grateful for the good news. Those two girls are amazing."

"Yes, they are. Nate is probably well enough to travel, but the roads are dangerous and for now, we're all staying here."

"I can't tell you how relieved I am that he's better."

"Peyton feels guilty about the attack, just to let you know."

"Understandable, and a normal reaction under the circumstances. Does she know who ordered the attack?"

"She's not sure or not saying. Do you?"

"Of course. Troy did. Nate tried to warn her, but she'd been listening to the wrong people and thought Nate was one of the bad guys for a while."

Stuart nodded. "There's more news about Troy too."

"Wow, I'm excited to be brought back into the team. I was starting to feel like an invalid outcast back here all by myself. That sounded dramatic, didn't it?" Charo giggled. "I haven't been as lonely as that sounded because of the constant flow of visitors. Do outcasts have visitors? Oops, I interrupted. What's the news about Troy?"

Stuart told her about the man who claimed to be Troy asking about Peyton at the sheriff's office.

"Oh, no, what did the sheriff say?"

"Hadn't seen Peyton in a long time, but he'd heard she was headed to Savannah."

"I always knew the sheriff had good instincts, but you have more, don't you?"

"Do you know why Troy is so determined to find Peyton?" Stuart asked.

"Yes. Troy thinks Peyton has his list of agents who are sympathetic to his human trafficking organization."

Stuart frowned. "She had a list that Rex Wilson gave her. Is this a second list? Does she have Troy's list? Is Troy part of McNeill's scheme to disrupt the government and the economy? I thought that whole operation was dead."

"Yes, McNeill's operation is dead, but this is a completely different list than the phony one from Rex Wilson. Peyton doesn't have Troy's physical list—someone in Troy's organization has it and plans to depose Troy. Peyton remembers everything she sees. She saw Troy's list and memorized it ages ago but didn't know about his criminal operation. When she realized Nate had been trying to warn her about Troy, she put the pieces together. She and Nate planned to go to the Georgia Bureau of Investigation in Macon, Georgia, so she could recite the list to them before we continued to South Carolina. Troy was never an agent or a part of McNeill's organization, but he had contacts in the agency because of Peyton and seized the opportunity to recruit crooked agents to increase his trafficking business after McNeill's organization folded."

Stuart frowned then rose to pace. "Sounds like the usurper could be just as interested in silencing Peyton as Troy is."

Charo stared out the window. "A real possibility."

Stuart stopped pacing. "Nate's in danger too, isn't he?" Stuart winced at the pain he saw on her face when she turned then stared at the floor.

"He needs me."

We have to team up with Nate.

"How soon before you can shoot?" Stuart asked.

Charo met his gaze. "Two days. What are you thinking?"

"I don't know yet." Stuart rose and left to search for Aimee Louise and his dad.

Sandra and Peyton were in the kitchen when Stuart strode past them to the door. After he stepped outside, Henry ran to him and tugged on his hand. "I was coming to get you, Deputy Stuart. We have a surprise in the barn."

Henry led Stuart to the barn. When they reached the wide doorway, Aimee Louise waited for them. Henry rushed inside and slid to sit next to Brandon and four puppies. "We got puppies, Deputy Stuart."

The puppies climbed on Henry and Brandon and explored the barn. While Wynn corralled wandering puppies and returned them to the boys, Andy and Rosalie stood apart from the group as they chatted.

The judge stood close to Dolly who sat crisscross on the ground and cooed to the puppy that climbed over her legs to her lap.

"Mommy loves puppies. Can we take all the puppies to go see Mommy? I can carry two, and Brandon can carry one, and Henry can carry one."

Dolly picked up her puppy, but it wiggled and scrambled to its feet after it fell onto her legs.

"Stay right there, Dolly. I'll bring your mommy to the barn. I think she'd like to come outside," Stuart said.

"I'll help," Aimee Louise said.

On their way to the house, Stuart asked, "Do you know where Dad is? Mom may come out to see the puppies."

Aimee Louise said, "Your dad asked Ms. Jennie if she'd like to see the driveway. I think I saw your Mom head that way just now."

When they reached Charo's room, Stuart said, "The kids and some puppies are in the barn. Want to see puppies?"

"Let's go," Charo tried to scoot her wheelchair with her uninjured foot.

"Is it okay if I push your wheelchair?" Aimee Louise asked.

"Bless you, sweet girl, for asking. Of course it is." Charo brushed away a tear that slipped down her cheek. "Sorry. I'm a little emotional today. I'll probably weep over the puppies too."

When Charo entered the barn, Dolly jumped up with the puppy in her arms. "Look, Mommy. He likes me." Dolly plopped the puppy in Charo's lap. "Ms. Jennie told me he's a girl."

Charo stroked the puppy's head with one finger as her eyes welled up. "What a pretty girl."

When Stuart hurried toward the driveway, Aimee Louise trotted alongside him.

"What are we going to do?" she asked.

"We need to bring Nate here, and Rosalie has to go with us. I need to know if Mom or Charo can help back up Dad and Peyton."

"The judge," Aimee Louise said.

Stuart slowed. "I was thinking the judge would supervise the children, but Dad assigned him to help with defense when we left because the Websters were under fire. We just need to know whether Dad thinks three of them could cover the farm or if we need to wait until Charo can shoot too." They resumed their pace up the driveway.

"Wynn stays at the Websters and take care of the puppies until we get back," Aimee Louise said.

Stuart frowned. "I'll ask Jennie. Why don't you want him here if we aren't here?"

"His cloud has even more anger since he's moved from the house to the barn; doesn't match his words. Andy needs to watch him while we're gone."

"We need Rosalie and Andy in on our discussion," Stuart said.

"Yes." Aimee Louise raced back toward the barn while Stuart waited until Aimee Louise and Rosalie returned ahead of Andy.

When Andy joined them, he asked, "Stuart, can you keep up with those two? They left me in the dust."

Stuart snorted. "Welcome to the club. We need you and Rosalie in on the discussion. The three of us need to go to Florida near the state line to pick up Charo's husband. Aimee Louise thinks it would be best if Wynn stays at your place while we're gone, so you can keep an eye on him. We don't trust him quite yet."

"I don't either. I think it would work. Aunt Jennie already told the kids the puppies are too little to leave Holly quite yet. It would make sense for Wynn to help us out with the puppies because he is good with them. Okay with me, but we'll see what she says. How long do you expect to be gone?"

"Expect and actual don't always match, but if we leave tomorrow morning, we'd expect to return no later than the next day."

"I take it you wouldn't want Wynn to know you'd left," Andy said.

"True."

Scott, Sandra, and Jennie strolled down the driveway. Scott saw the four waiting for them. "Is this a meeting?"

"Yes, Dad. We need to go get Charo's husband and bring him here. Aimee Louise, Rosalie, and I plan to leave in the morning, and we expect to return on the next day. Because of everything that's gone on lately, we're worried our farm will be attacked. We know you and Peyton can defend the house, but I think you'll need a third shooter."

Scott nodded. "Judge can handle a rifle or a shotgun, and your mom's a good shot, but we'll need her to look after the children."

"That's what we thought," Stuart said. "Charo is a crack shot too, and her hand will soon be strong enough to hold and fire a pistol; she could fire a shot right now in an emergency."

"We'll make sure she has a pistol she's comfortable with," Scott said.

"Aunt Jennie, we'd rather not leave Wynn here with Stuart and the girls gone because we don't want him to know they aren't around," Andy said.

"I'll ask him to come to our farm to take care of the puppies until they're old enough to be separated from Holly because they've become too much for me with all the work. I always wear my pistol, but do we need to be on high alert too?" Jennie asked.

"Always," Andy said.

"Andy's right," Stuart said.

"Aunt Jennie, Wynn doesn't have any firearms, and Stuart and I don't want him to have access to any," Andy said.

She narrowed her eyes. "We're getting him away from the children. Scott, let's go chat with Wynn. The rest of you make yourself scarce."

"One more thing," Stuart said, "we don't want Wynn to know about the shortcut. When you take him back to the farm with you, go along the road. I'll trail behind you in case you need me."

"And me," Rosalie added.

Andy smiled. "We get Dead Eye Red?"

"In the flesh." Rosalie giggled.

Scott raised his eyebrows at Stuart, who shrugged.

"It's time for the kids' snack," Sandra said, "I'll have it ready."

"Thanks. You're always thinking." Scott smiled.

When they reached the end of the driveway, Rosalie and Andy strolled to the front of the house, and Aimee Louise and Stuart went inside with Sandra while Scott and Jennie continued to the barn.

Stuart and Aimee Louise helped Sandra set the table with the children's snacks and drinks when Henry, Dolly, Brandon, and Peyton came into the house.

"Gramps is pushing Mommy's wheelchair. We're here for our snack. We don't have to wash our hands first, do we? The puppies were clean." Dolly sat in her seat.

"Come wash your hands," Sandra said.

Dolly jumped up as Peyton and the boys finished washing. She peered at the water then plunged her hands into the washbowl. "See the water's not even dirty." She rubbed her hands then dried them.

Before the children and Peyton began eating their snacks, the judge rolled Charo's wheelchair into the house.

"Mommy, come have a snack with me," Dolly said.

"Are you tired, Charo?" the judge asked.

"Not at all. I need my snack." Charo smiled as the judge pushed the wheelchair next to Dolly. Sandra handed Charo a wet cloth to clean her hands.

"You have to wash your hands—" Dolly clapped a hand over her full mouth when Charo raised one eyebrow in a mom look.

Aimee Louise tapped the judge on the arm and pointed to Stuart who waved for him to follow. When the judge rose and held out his arm, Aimee Louise linked hers through his, and the three of them strolled out the front door.

"We need to talk to you, Judge." Stuart explained the plan for the next few days.

After Stuart finished, the judge said, "I agree with your concerns. I've been worried about Mr. Wynn myself. A little too perfect. Does your Aunt Jennie know to be careful, Andy?"

"She does," Andy said. "Ready to go to the barn?"

"You first," Stuart said as the judge slipped back into the house and locked the front door.

Rosalie and Andy strolled around the house toward the barn.

"Are we missing anything, Aimee Louise?" Stuart asked as they headed to the barn.

"We need to tell Ms. Jennie and Andy about the trees across the driveway so they aren't surprised."

"You're right."

Aimee Louise sprinted up the driveway while Stuart waited. When she returned, she said, "I moved a few branches for a narrow path from the driveway to the road."

Andy waved as they approached the barn. Rosalie rushed to Aimee Louise, and the two girls ambled to the barn together with their arms linked and heads together.

"Wynn's going to take care of the puppies until they're old enough to leave their mother," Andy said. "It'll be what, Wynn? Maybe a week?"

Wynn rose from folding his few clothes into his backpack. "Sounds about right. I'm happy to help Ms. Jennie."

"Did you have trouble getting through the trees that the storm blew down?" Stuart asked Andy.

Rosalie smiled. "I'll bet you found that path Stuart made."

Andy returned her smile and nodded.

"We'll try to get the driveway cleared before the next time you come," Stuart said. "It hasn't been high on our storm clean up priority."

"I meant to ask about the garden. Did you have much damage?" Jennie asked.

"Some, but not as much as Mama Sandra was afraid there'd be," Rosalie said.

"Is it time for me to gather up the pups?" Andy asked.

"I'll do it." Wynn gently scooped up each puppy and placed it in the box that Jennie used as a carrier. "We're ready."

When Andy and Rosalie headed to the driveway, Stuart said, "Guess we're going with you as far as the road."

Jennie chuckled as she and Wynn followed Andy and Rosalie.

"See you later." Aimee Louise waved as she headed to the house.

Stuart frowned then quickened his pace. *She'll bring us our rifles.*

CHAPTER ELEVEN

Stuart and Rosalie stood on the road to watch while Jennie and Wynn left for the Websters' farm; Andy dropped back five yards with his rifle in the crook of his arm.

"She's here," Rosalie said as Aimee Louise popped through the brush with their rifles.

Stuart and Rosalie jogged along the road then slowed when Stuart saw Andy. After their neighbors turned at their farm's driveway, Rosalie said, "You set the pace back."

Stuart ran at his comfortable speed, and Rosalie stayed alongside him. When they returned to the Newton farm, Stuart moved the branches back into place across the driveway before they returned to the house. Scott and Aimee Louise waited outside for them.

"Everything go okay?" Scott asked.

"So far, so good," Stuart said. "I've been thinking—"

"We're ready when you are," Rosalie said.

Stuart rolled his eyes. "Was I thinking before or after lunch?"

"After lunch," Aimee Louise said.

Scott laughed. "Face it, Son; these womenfolk are always a step ahead."

"Get our list together, and I'll pack," Stuart said.

Rosalie dashed into the house.

"She'll work off her inventory list. I'll talk to Mama Sandra," Aimee Louise said.

The sound of squealing came from the garden.

"I'd like to call all the adults together," Scott said.

"I'm sure Peyton's at the garden, I'll send her to the house. I'll need to talk to Henry anyway; I might as well talk to all the kids at once," Stuart said.

When Stuart reached the garden, Peyton and the boys knelt next to the broccoli seedlings while Dolly weeded around the lettuce.

"Hi, Deputy Stuart," Henry said. "We're squashing bad bugs."

Peyton leaned back on her heels and grinned. "It's as much fun as it sounds too. Mama Sandra taught us which bugs are bad and which bugs are good."

Brandon glanced up with a serious face. "Not even the chickens will eat the bad bugs. We tried. Squashing works."

"Peyton, Dad's calling a meeting for adults in the house. I'm calling a meeting for the kids right here in the garden."

"I guess I'm an adult, right?" Peyton rose and brushed her pants.

"Yes, Ms. Peyton. We're the kids. Me, Brandon, and Henry," Dolly said.

"Good to know," Peyton chuckled as she hurried toward the house.

Stuart crouched alongside Henry. "Before we have our meeting, show me a bad bug and how to squash it."

Henry examined a plant. "Here, Deputy Stuart. Look. Mama Sandra said it's a cabbage worm." Henry picked it up and squashed the bug then rubbed dirt on his hands. "Ms. Peyton told us not to rub our hands on our pants, so we clean our hands with dirt."

"That was Henry's idea," Brandon said. "He's a smart little kid."

"He sure is," Stuart said.

"I don't like to squash bugs," Dolly said. "Mama Sandra said she'd make me a jar of soapy water to drown them."

Stuart stifled a snicker. *Mom's raising real gardeners here.*

"Meeting called to order," Stuart said.

"That means we're supposed to listen," Brandon said.

"Angel, Red, and I are going on a short trip after lunch. We'll be back in two or three days. We wanted you to know."

While Stuart talked, Aimee Louise joined them.

"This is a kids' meeting," Dolly said, "but you can be a kid, Angel."

"Thank you."

"Does anybody have any questions?" Stuart asked.

"Are you going far?" Henry furrowed his brow and scooted close to Aimee Louise.

"Too far to come back for supper tonight, but not so far that we can't find our way back in two days," Stuart said.

"That's good," Henry said. "That's not too far."

"What do we do while you're gone?" Brandon asked.

"Your biggest assignments are to gather eggs and keep bugs out of the garden," Stuart said.

"Aren't there any other assignments for us?" Brandon frowned.

"I have an assignment for you," Aimee Louise said. "If you're outside and there is no farm adult with you, call *Inside* for yourselves in a quiet voice."

"And run inside?" Henry asked.

"Yes, and run inside," Stuart said.

"What if we're inside, and there's no adult with us?" Brandon frowned.

"I would say go to Ms. Charo's room, but maybe we should ask Papa Scott," Aimee Louise said.

"Yes," Brandon said, "we'll ask Papa Scott."

"Meeting is over," Stuart said. "Let's squash more bugs."

"I'm going inside, and I'll ask Papa Scott to come outside for questions when he's not busy," Aimee Louise said.

Not long after Aimee Louise left, Scott and the judge strolled to the garden.

The judge sat on his garden bench. "I'm here to supervise the garden work so you can go pack whenever you're ready, Stuart."

Scott leaned against the fence. "I understand you have some questions for me."

"We were talking about what the kids should do if there is no farm adult with them when they are outside. They'll call a quiet *Inside* for themselves then run to the house. If they are inside the house, and there is no farm adult with them, what do they do?" Stuart asked.

"The quiet *Inside* idea is excellent and takes a worry off my mind. What did Angel say to do if you're inside?"

"Angel told us to go to Mommy's room," Dolly said.

"I like that, and if your mommy isn't there then wait for her."

"Angel is smart," Henry squashed a bug then rubbed dirt between his hands.

"Yes, she is," Scott said.

As Scott and Stuart strolled to the house, Scott asked, "Why did Henry rub dirt on his hands?"

"Because Peyton told them they couldn't brush their hands on their pants after they squashed a bug."

Scott snorted. "So he's scrubbing his hands with dirt. Got it."

As they continued to the house, Scott said, "I'll unlock the gun safe if you're ready to load your truck."

"Sounds good. Rosalie and I need our second rifles."

Aimee Louise passed them on her way to the barn. "Getting the wagon."

When they walked into the kitchen, Sandra stirred soup on the stove. Without turning, she said, "You two walk just alike. I'd know your footsteps anywhere. The girls have everything pulled together for the trip except for the rifles. Charo wants to talk to you, Stuart."

Charo stood one-legged next to her bed. "I've been testing my ankle. It's not quite at the weightbearing stage." She grimaced as she dropped into her wheelchair. "I could hop, but I'm not that coordinated. Stuart, my hands are strong. If you'd help me rig up a support on my wheelchair, I could easily shoot a rifle."

"Be right back." Stuart went to the kitchen. "Mom, I need to set up a table for Charo so she could shoot a rifle. Do you have any lightweight, tall tables?"

"Look in the attic. I might have just what you need. It's an old table I got at an auction, but it was too tall after all for everyday use."

Stuart climbed the ladder to the attic and found the table. It was sturdy but lightweight when he picked it up. *This is perfect.*

After he closed up the attic, he carried the table to Charo's room.

"It's the right height," she said, "but it looks too heavy for me to move around."

"Give it a try," Stuart said.

Charo used her good foot to move her wheelchair, and the wheel pushed the table. "Lighter than it looks. I could decide where I want it and set it up in advance myself. Thanks, Stuart. Now I need a rifle."

She flipped open a latch on the bottom of her closet door with her foot, and the door swung open. "Scott fixed this for me. It's not perfect, but it's relatively secure because if you try to open the door, it seems locked."

"Good. I'll get your rifle. Do you want a pistol you can keep with you?"

"I'd love it."

Stuart went to his dad's bedroom. "I'll need a pistol and a rifle for Charo."

Scott opened the gun safe. "Here is Rosalie's rifle, and here's yours. I have a rifle for Charo. I'm not sure what kind of pistol she prefers, but for now, take her this one. Did you want extra ammunition?"

"Some, but not a lot. We can't run with a lot of extra ammo, and I don't want to give the bad guys a supply if we have to abandon the truck."

Scott froze. "Is that a possibility?"

"One thing I've learned from Aimee Louise is to consider all possibilities."

"I don't like that one," Scott grumbled as he locked the safe.

Neither do I, Dad.

"That was fast." Charo unlocked her closet and pointed. "Lean it against the side wall. I can grab it from there."

After she locked her closet, Stuart said, "Here's your pistol and two extra magazines."

"Thanks. I feel better knowing I can defend my side of the house."

"Soup's ready," Sandra called from the kitchen.

As Stuart passed through the kitchen, Sandra dished up soup while Peyton placed the bowls on the table. The judge brought the children into the house.

"Red told us lunch was ready." Judge led the children to the sink to wash.

Stuart carried the rifles and ammunition to the truck. Aimee Louise unloaded the wagon, and Rosalie organized the boxes and items in the back.

"I've set it up almost like you did, Stuart," Rosalie said. "Ms. Sandra suggested we take extra blankets in case we have to spend the night in the back of the truck. I think our weather may turn cold tonight, so we've included warm coats. We have your go-bag but not your backpack. We thought you might want to check it before it goes on the truck. Your dad came by a few minutes ago and gave me a chainsaw and can of gas for the chainsaw. He said it was a contingency."

Stuart smiled. *Thanks, Dad.*

"All ready except for me?".

"You and lunch," Rosalie said.

While they ate lunch, Scott asked Henry to explain their quiet *Inside* plan.

"That's a great idea. You'll be the most important part of our defense team if we have any problems," Peyton said.

After lunch, Stuart said, "We're ready to go. Be safe, everybody. Thank you, Henry, Brandon, and Dolly for your service on the defense team."

Henry hugged Stuart then approached Aimee Louise with his head down. "You won't forget me, will you, Angel? I wrote you a note."

Aimee Louise stooped to hug Henry and kissed him on his forehead. "I could never forget you, Henry. Never, ever."

She read her note then asked, "Thank you, Henry. This is a nice note. Can I show it to Deputy Stuart and Red?"

"Yes." Henry flung his arms around her neck in a hug that almost knocked her down, but she regained her balance as he stepped back and held out his fist. They bumped fists then Aimee Louise rose and hurried to start the truck.

When Stuart was in the passenger's seat, and Rosalie was in the back seat, Aimee Louise drove through to the shortcut path then past the Smith barn before she handed the note to Stuart. *To My Angel From Your Boy Henry M.*

"He's going back with us to Major's farm, isn't he?" Stuart smiled as he handed the note to Rosalie.

"I never had any doubt," Rosalie said. "He's your boy too, Stuart." She read the note. "This is awesome. Your first love letter, Aimee Louise."

She snickered when Stuart jerked his head to glare at her then he sighed. "I think you're right, Red."

After Aimee Louise turned onto the road in the direction away from the Smith farm, she asked, "Any change to our route?"

Stuart opened the glove compartment, removed the county map, and studied it. "There's a county road coming up that angles to meet the state road thirty or so miles south of here. It could save us time, assuming we don't run across any problems, but the transport trucks use the state road, and we know they're a problem. Turn right onto County Line Road in two or three miles. It should be paved."

Aimee Louise turned on the mobile ham radio receiver. "Needs to be on simplex."

Stuart pulled out the list of repeaters and tuned the receiver to the closest repeater in addition to scanning simplex.

Rosalie opened the window between the cab and the pickup bed. "I'm going to keep an eye on what might be coming up behind us." She pulled out her binoculars from her backpack and climbed into the back.

The squelch broke on the radio. "…eastbound…"

Stuart turned up the volume. "…white…"

"We're going eastbound in a white truck." Aimee Louise accelerated.

"They're breaking up. Not quite close enough to make out what they're saying." Stuart glanced back. "That's a good set up, Rosalie. You can see out both side windows and you've got a clear view of the road behind us. I like the idea of watching all sides."

"Everything except the sky above us. I won't see a drone," she said.

"Seems kind of far-fetched this far out, but now you've got me worried," Stuart said.

Rosalie snickered then scooted closer to the tailgate. "Oops. Vehicle coming up behind us. Can't see it well enough yet to know what it is."

Stuart peered into the passenger's side mirror. "I don't see anything yet."

"Right turn coming up," Aimee Louise said. "Hang on. I'm taking it fast."

"Get situated, Rosalie," Stuart called out. "Fast, hard turn to the right coming up."

Rosalie slid close to the cab and held on in preparation for the turn. Aimee Louise slammed on the brakes and spun into her turn then accelerated down the county road. "Do I pull over in a few miles?"

Squelch. "...south..."

"They know we turned south," Aimee Louise pushed the accelerator to the floor. "Need a grove of trees."

"Rosalie, are you watching the road behind us?"

"Nothing yet." Rosalie had returned with her binoculars to the edge of the pickup bed near the tailgate.

"Got it. Right side." Aimee Louise sped to the grove then slowed as she inspected the ditch for a way to cross.

"They made the turn and are behind us again." Rosalie scooted to her spot close to the cab.

"Looking for a place to jump the trench? There, ahead." Stuart pointed before he grabbed onto the dash and the console and called to the back. "Hang on, Rosalie, ditch then trees."

"Braced for the Angel maneuver," Rosalie shouted.

Aimee Louise accelerated into then out of the gulley before she plowed through the brush and into the trees as far away from the road as she could get. After Aimee Louise turned off the engine, she and Stuart jumped out. Aimee Louise bent down behind the truck then raced to the roadway before she threw herself down into the tall grass.

Stuart scowled as he crouched when the truck approached then slowed to a crawl as it drove past them. *Dang it. Wish she wouldn't do that.*

After the truck was gone, Stuart started their truck and eased it out of the trees where Aimee Louise had wedged it.

Squelch. "…close…faulty…"

"Hey," Rosalie said from the back. "Did someone on the radio just say close and faulty?"

"I haven't been paying attention—" Stuart turned off the engine and jumped out of the truck. He ran his hand along the back bumper then behind the rear wheel well and pulled out a black plastic disk the diameter and height of three stacked quarters stuck in the well. He stared at it. *A GPS tracker.*

"Rosalie, I found something."

Rosalie climbed through the window and into the cab then hopped out of the truck. "What did you find?"

"I think it might be a GPS tracker. I found it on the underside of the rear wheel well, but it has a significant crack—maybe from road debris. See if you can find any more."

Rosalie hurried to the front bumper. Stuart checked the back bumper again then the rear wheel well on the passenger's side. Rosalie checked the front wheel wells.

"Nothing else," Rosalie said. "How could this work? I thought all of the cell towers were down."

"GPS works by satellite, not cell towers."

"So what do we do?"

"Smash it," Aimee Louise said.

Stuart's eyes widened. *She's quiet. Didn't hear her coming up behind me.*

He opened the tailgate and grabbed the toolbox then slammed the GPS with the hammer, and it shattered. "Done. So, why smash it?"

"There were two. I grabbed the first one then tossed it into the back of their truck when they passed us. They're going to always be close to their tracker."

"You did what? That's phenomenal," Stuart said.

"Everything Aimee Louise does is phenomenal, Stuart." Rosalie snorted. "So, that's why the guy on the radio said close and faulty. Now their faulty one has lost its signal."

"The only way two GPS devices could have been put on our truck at Dad's farm was if Jennie, Andy, Peyton, or Wynn put it there," Stuart said.

"Actually, the discs could have been put into place any time after we left Pops' farm," Aimee Louise said. "They just never needed to stop us before."

Rosalie shuddered. "Someone does not want us to team up with Nate."

"No. Someone does not want Peyton and Nate together," Aimee Louise said.

"I think you're on to something there. The first time Nate came to Major's farm, Peyton had been told he was a bad guy," Stuart said.

"We need to go back to the state road," Aimee Louise said.

Stuart nodded. "Load up."

After Aimee Louise made the turn for their original route to the state road, Rosalie said, "I checked everything back here and didn't find any trackers on our gear."

"Thanks." Stuart squinted at the map. "I've found another alternative to the state road. I didn't consider it earlier because it's not a county road and probably wasn't well-maintained even before the grid went down. It's four or five miles past the state road but shouldn't cost us more than fifteen minutes in time, depending on the road condition."

"I have your ballcap, Aimee Louise. You look too much like a girl," Rosalie said.

"Catch, Stuart." She leaned through the window and tossed the cap to Stuart who plucked it mid-air then handed it to Aimee Louise. He held the steering wheel steady while Aimee Louise swept up her hair with one hand then crammed on her ballcap.

"Thank you," Aimee Louise said.

Aimee Louise approached the intersection to the state road at a moderate, steady speed. When she neared the intersection, she flipped on her left turn signal and slowed at first then accelerated to continue past the state road.

"A couple of men jumped out of the ravine at the turn to the north. One's waving a pistol. Guess we ruined their ambush plans. Good call, Stuart," Rosalie said from the back.

After she moved closer to the cab, Rosalie asked, "Why did you put on your turn signal, Aimee Louise?"

"Just to check," Aimee Louise said.

"I like it. Definitely worth remembering." Stuart squinted at the map and the road ahead. "The road will be coming up soon."

"Car behind us," Rosalie said.

"Here's our road on the right." Stuart scanned the empty fields.

Aimee Louise slowed before she turned.

"Paved. I hoped it would be," Stuart said.

"How far until we turn back toward the state road?" Aimee Louise asked.

"The road curves back to the state road in seventy miles. We'll be close to the state line and have the option to continue north on the state road or cross it and take the backroads to Keith and Leslie's farm."

Stuart scanned the fields as they continued their travels.

When the countryside changed from farmland to planted pines and rows of pecan trees then overgrown forests, Rosalie asked, "Do people live out here?"

"There may be a few hunting cabins back in the woods but not much else," Stuart said.

"That's good, right? There aren't any homes to invade, so maybe this is the best route for us to return."

"Might be," Stuart said.

"Unless one of the hunting cabins is a hideout," Rosalie said.

"Shh," Stuart said. "Don't give the bad guys any ideas."

Rosalie giggled. "We'd be a pretty good team of bad guys."

Stuart scanned the roadside that had become more overrun with brush and fallen tree trunks and limbs before he examined the map. "We'll come to a side road that heads toward the state road in about five miles. After that, we'll have a stretch of about ten miles where the only way for us to bypass any road barriers is to turn around or try to continue through them. What do you think?"

"Stay on this road." Aimee Louise dropped her speed.

Stuart leaned to peer at the speedometer. "Why did you slow down?"

"Deer trails."

Stuart squinted at the roadside. "Now, I see them."

Rosalie moved to the backseat of the cab. "I think I saw a bobcat."

The potholes became more frequent.

"Road hasn't had any maintenance in a while," Rosalie said after Aimee Louise steered to avoid a deep hole.

"Might be hard on the truck to travel this at night for the first time, but might not be so bad coming back if we take it slow." Stuart glanced at Aimee Louise. "In case we decide we want to take a short break then head back this evening."

"If we don't have any cloud cover, the moon should be bright enough for us to drive without headlights," Rosalie said.

"What! Are you serious?" Stuart glowered at Rosalie.

"Need them to see deer," Aimee Louise said.

Rosalie sighed. "Guess Deputy Stuart won't have to write you a ticket, after all."

"The road that goes to the state road is coming up," Stuart said. When they reached the side road, Stuart frowned. "Never mind. It looks like sugar sand."

"What's that?" Rosalie asked.

Stuart chuckled. "It's a sand that is extra soft and real easy to get stuck in and takes forever to get out of. It's easy to spot because it's a lighter color than the other sand. I never heard of it until I moved to Florida. I got stuck one time in sugar sand, and it took me hours to get out. I finally pulled out my floor mats for traction."

"Pops always kept a couple of boards and a shovel in the back of his truck, but I never knew why," Rosalie said. "They're back there now if we ever need them."

Aimee Louise slowed as she pointed ahead. "Doe in the middle of the road."

The doe stared at them then bounded into the woods. A smaller doe dashed across the road after her.

The squelch broke on the radio. "…Gulf…weather…"

"That doesn't sound good," Rosalie said. "Anytime someone mentions Gulf and weather in the same sentence, I think storm."

Stuart grabbed the sheet with the list of repeaters. "Here's one closer to us," he mumbled as he changed the frequency.

The voice on the receiver was much clearer. "Yep. Heard about it. When do you think we'll see it?"

"One or two days, according to a guy in Tampa I talked to this morning."

"I got things to do then."

The two ham operators signed off.

"We go back tonight," Stuart said.

"I'm really glad we didn't wait until tomorrow morning. Tomorrow night might be iffy coming this way with all the trees so near the road," Rosalie said.

When Aimee Louise slowed down, Stuart frowned at the road ahead. "Pull over, Aimee Louise. Would you hand me the binoculars, Rosalie?"

After Aimee Louise stopped the truck, Stuart jumped out and hurried to the front of the truck. Rosalie stepped out of the truck on the driver's side with her rifle and joined Stuart. The two of them climbed back into the truck.

"There's a large oak across the road. Looks like it uprooted recently because its branches have green leaves. Unless somebody's taking advantage of it being down, I think we're okay. Dad threw in a chainsaw and extra gas. Let's get closer and see what we can do."

Stuart handed the binoculars back to Rosalie who placed the strap around her neck.

"Go slow, Aimee Louise." Rosalie lowered the window on the driver's side. "I'm going to sit in the window with my rifle."

Aimee Louise stopped fifteen yards from the tree, and Rosalie opened her door then examined the tree and surrounding area with the binoculars before she assumed her shooting position and continued her surveillance of the tree. Stuart strode to the back of the truck and removed the chainsaw and its accompanying bag of equipment. He started the chainsaw while he stood behind the truck; after he revved it, he turned it off.

"See anything, Red?" he asked.

"Nothing."

Stuart stayed close to the shoulder as he approached the treetop then shifted to the opposite side of the roadway to the root ball. He brushed away the debris and leaves then walked the length of the tree across the road and studied the branches. He returned to the massive root ball and started the chainsaw to cut the oak's trunk as near as he could to the base of the tree and the roots that were covered with dirt. After he made his cuts, he stood back as the severed root ball flipped back into its hole. He exhaled. *Went well. Next, cut the trunk.*

Stuart cut the trunk across the roadway into three sections. With the use of the hook from the equipment bag, he rolled the first trunk section to the shoulder near the stump then rolled the farther section to the opposite shoulder. After he cut the middle section into two, Rosalie joined him, and they rolled the two remaining sections out of the roadway.

"That was awesome, Stuart," Rosalie said as she helped put the chainsaw and equipment back into the truck. "I've never seen a tree flip like that."

Stuart smiled. "It's what they do. People don't realize how heavy all that dirt is. If they know what they're doing and they're careful, it's easy; if they don't, it's deadly."

"Is that why you walked to the other end of the tree?"

"Yep, otherwise, I'd focus on the root ball and miss something else that might hurt me." Stuart raised the tailgate and closed up the back of the topper before they climbed into the truck.

"I couldn't have done that in the dark," Stuart said. "If there's a lot of wind when we leave Keith's tonight, it might be too dangerous to come this way."

"Another reason to leave as soon as we can." Aimee Louise checked her rearview mirror to be sure Rosalie was ready to move before she drove past the tree then accelerated. "More talk on the radio about the storm in the Gulf except the latest is it's moving faster. Might be here by morning."

"Won't be long until we'll either cross over the state road or continue the back road on the west side. So far, the back roads seem to be our best bet," Stuart said.

"When we were putting away the chainsaw and equipment, there was a light breeze, but it didn't seem tropical," Rosalie said. "This storm might catch a lot of people by surprise."

"I never had a real appreciation for the ham radio network until the grid went down," Stuart said.

"What?" Aimee Louise asked.

"Just to let you know, Stuart, we're horrified." Rosalie chuckled.

Stuart turned to look out his window and rolled his eyes. "I guess I am too."

"You are not," Aimee Louise said.

"Busted," he mumbled.

As they neared the state road, Aimee Louise slowed then pulled onto the shoulder. "Shots fired." She lowered her window.

"I hear them." Stuart grabbed his rifle, jumped out of the truck, and raced to the intersection; Rosalie caught up with him.

"What are we going to do?" Rosalie asked.

"I have no idea." Stuart glanced back at Major's truck that crept along two yards behind them.

CHAPTER TWELVE

Stuart and Rosalie took cover in the trees before they reached the intersection. "It's Phil," Rosalie said. "They're being attacked by a transport truck."

Rosalie stepped out of the trees and shot the two transport assailants in their knees as Stuart followed with head shots. The third assailant shifted to aim at Rosalie, and Phil stood up and shot him in the shoulder. When the attacker turned his weapon toward Phil, Stuart fired, and he dropped.

Stuart raced to the back of the transport truck and pulled back the flap. Three young boys with wide eyes held up their hands. "We give up, Mister," the smallest one said.

Stuart's smile was weak. *Just broke my heart hearing that.* "I'm Deputy Stuart. I'm a good guy. Who are you?"

The smallest one put down his hands. "I'm Corey."

The oldest one left his hands up. "I'm John, and this is my brother, Travis."

Travis put his hands in his lap. "I'm six. John is nine."

"I'm six," Corey said.

"Come with me," Stuart said. "I know someone named Red who has snacks."

"Snacks?" Corey rushed to the back of the truck, and Stuart helped him out. John climbed out then helped his brother.

"Hey, Red. Got three boys who wouldn't mind having a snack."

Rosalie raced to the back of the truck. "Hey there. Come with me."

"Wow," John said. "You run fast."

"We'll walk. You don't have to run," Rosalie said.

While Rosalie led the boys to the truck, Stuart joined Phil and his team behind their barrier.

"What happened?"

"When the truck drove up, we told them to turn around, and they started firing. We were outclassed in terms of weapons, but we're all hunters. They didn't seem to be familiar with their rifles and were slow. Anyway, we dived behind our barrier but they had the upper hand until you arrived. What are you doing here, anyway? Where's my Angel?"

"Angel's with the truck. She's our driver."

Aimee Louise had driven the truck close to the barrier. When she stepped out to open the back door for Rosalie and the boys, Phil shouted, "There she is. My Angel."

Phil rushed to Aimee Louise and hugged her. "Thank you for bringing Stuart and Red to our rescue."

"There were three little boys in the back of the truck," Stuart said. "Can they stay with you?"

"Are you kidding? Deana would love to have them. Do we know where their parents are?"

"We don't know anything about them except their names and ages," Stuart said.

"No matter. We'll take care of them as long as they need us."

"Thank you," Stuart said. "We'll take them to your house while they eat their snacks. Red always has snacks for kids."

"Let's go then. Follow me, Angel."

As they parked at Phil's house, Phil met Deana as she came outside. Stuart helped the boys out of the truck. When Red climbed out, the two younger boys clung to her, and John held his brother's hand.

"See, Deana? I told you I brought special company home."

"Good guys," Rosalie said. "Just like we talked about in the truck."

Corey hung back and peered at Stuart.

"Red's right," Stuart said. "You'll be safe here with the good guys."

"Are you hungry?" Deana asked as they went inside.

The two younger boys stared at the floor.

"Red gave us a snack, but we're still hungry," John said.

"Follow me to the kitchen, and I'll give you a late lunch then we'll have supper later. I'm Gramma Deana. Who are you?"

After Red and the boys followed Deana, Aimee Louise tapped on the front door, and Phil opened it.

"Come on in, Angel," he said. "Did we leave you?"

"No, I was listening to the radio. There's more news about the Gulf storm. We can't stay long."

Phil frowned. "Heard about that. Are they still saying tomorrow?"

"Yes, but early in the morning."

"We're on our way to pick up Nate at Keith's then we'll head back to my folks' farm right away," Stuart said. "I'll see how quickly Red can leave."

Stuart strode to the kitchen. The boys ate bread while Deana warmed soup.

"We're going to have to leave because there's a big storm coming," Stuart said. "Red has to go with us. Is that okay?"

"Yes. Red told us she has to leave because there's a big storm," Corey said.

"But we're safe here, right, Red?" Travis asked.

"Absolutely. This is the best place to be," Rosalie said.

John rose and saluted Stuart. "Thank you for your service, Deputy Stuart."

Stuart returned his salute.

Deana wiped her eyes with her apron. "That was very nice, John."

Stuart joined the boys at the table. "John, what can you tell me about the men and the truck? Where are you boys from?"

"We're from Orlando. We didn't know Corey until the men threw us into the truck. I was afraid they'd hurt Travis. They kept waving their guns around. Travis and I were in our front yard. Corey said he was at his friend's house, but his friend was inside when the man grabbed him. We don't know anything about the men except they're bad guys. They didn't talk much. Just waved their guns."

"Are your folks in law enforcement?" Stuart asked.

"No, Dad is a chef. Mom is an engineer. She designs things."

"My dad is a pastor, and my mom is a nurse," Corey said.

"After the storm, Phil will try to find a way to let your parents know you're okay. We have to go now."

"Goodbye, boys." Rosalie hugged each boy then Stuart and Rosalie hurried to the living room.

"Sorry we're in a rush, Phil. Thank you for taking in the boys," Stuart said.

Phil walked with them to the truck. "Wait just a second, Angel. I want to give you some diesel for your trip."

"Thank you, but we have some spare if we need it," she said.

Phil had left a can next to the truck and was filling the tank from his can before she could get out all her words.

"There you go. The road's clear between here and Keith's. Be safe. Thanks again, Angel, for always showing up when I need you but didn't know it." Phil hugged Aimee Louise and Rosalie and shook hands with Stuart.

On their way to Keith's, Stuart said, "I expected the back of the truck to be empty."

"I was surprised none of their folks were in law enforcement," Rosalie said.

"It does look more like human trafficking, which is different than McNeill's motive of blackmail," Stuart said.

"Here's the driveway." Aimee Louise tapped the horn twice as they neared the house then stopped.

When Keith peered out from the house, Stuart called out, "Hello, Keith. It's Stuart, Angel, and Red."

Keith and Nate stepped out while Aimee Louise drove closer and parked. Stuart climbed out of the truck while Aimee Louise and Rosalie waited.

"How's Charo?" Nate asked.

"She's doing very well," Stuart said.

"Are you here to pick me up?" Nate asked. "I hope so because I've been packed for two days."

"We sure are. Have you heard about the storm, Keith?" Stuart asked as Nate hurried into the house.

Keith nodded. "It'll hit us in one or two days is the last I heard."

"The latest is it'll be here early in the morning. We'll have to run."

Keith raised his eyebrows. "I'll have to rearrange my plans; I thought I'd do storm prep tomorrow. I'll let Leslie know you're here. She'll want to at least say hello."

When Keith opened the door, Leslie dashed out. "Nate told me you were here. He'll be out in just a minute."

"Storm's going to be here in the morning," Keith said. "We need to spend the rest of the day getting ready, and Stuart and his band will need to head north right away."

"Well, I hate that you'll have to leave hungry, Stuart. I'll be right back."

Nate carried his duffle bag to the truck and tossed it into the back. "I have a pistol that Keith gave me, but I don't have a rifle. Do you have a spare?"

"Sure do." Stuart climbed into the back of the pickup and pulled out a rifle and ammunition and handed the rifle to Nate.

Leslie came out of the house with a tote bag. "Here's a pound cake and some apples for your trip home." She hugged Nate. "Be safe, and tell Charo and Peyton hello for us."

Nate carried the tote to the truck; after he and Stuart jumped in, Aimee Louise pulled away.

"Tell me more about Charo, Dolly, and my dad. How are they doing?" Nate asked.

Rosalie told him how well Charo was doing and how his dad helped at the farm then followed up with stories about Dolly. Stuart added his version of the adult and kid meetings when Dolly said Angel could be a kid and attend their meeting.

"Back way or state road?" Aimee Louise asked.

"Back way," Stuart said. "You could have talked me into the state road if we hadn't come across another transport truck."

"What truck?" Nate asked.

Rosalie explained their recent encounter with the transport truck and finding the boys.

Nate slammed his fist into the seat.

"You know who's behind this, don't you?" Stuart asked.

"Yeah, but I'm not the one with evidence," Nate said.

"That's what Charo said. Peyton has the evidence, and Troy wants to stop her before his organization crumbles."

"Right, and someone inside Troy's organization plans to push out Troy, but Peyton's in his way. What does Peyton say?" Nate asked.

"Not much."

Nate shook his head. "Peyton and her old partner were together since the day she was hired. She never trusted anyone but him, and for a long time, it made sense. Unfortunately, I don't think she ever really trusted me, and I'm one of the good guys."

Stuart snorted. "You'd have to be, or Charo and Dolly would straighten you out."

"You're right about that." Nate furrowed his brow. "Those two mean the world to me. So, what's the plan?"

"Our first priority is to return to my folks' farm. You may not have heard about the rash of home invasions, robberies, and murders in the rural areas. I'm not positive, but I think the main goal is the stolen items – firearms, ammunition, jewelry, alcohol, drugs, silver, gold, and whatever else they can find that has trading value."

"Kids?" Nate asked.

"We think so," Stuart said.

"That's why Charo pretended to be Peyton, and it still kills me to think about it. She wanted Peyton to be able to get the evidence on Troy to the Georgia Bureau of Investigation. Peyton told me they were the only organization she could trust."

Stuart narrowed his eyes. "It's time for Peyton to trust us, so we can help her."

"You've got my full support," Nate said.

After they passed the state road, Stuart said, "We came this way earlier today and didn't see anyone, but that doesn't mean it's clear now."

Rosalie slid the window open to the pickup bed and climbed to the back.

Nate chuckled. "Dead Eye Red is the perfect lookout, and I can't think of a better crow's nest than a pickup bed.."

"I'd forgotten you knew about Dead Eye Red," Stuart said. "Do you know David Griffin?"

"Brandon's father? Peyton introduced me to him not long after we became partners. I had the feeling that if David didn't like me,

I'd be looking for a new partner. Brandon dotes on his father, and the feeling's mutual. I never understood why Peyton married Troy."

"David's at Major's farm. He was bitten by a snake and is fighting to recover." Stuart told Nate about David walking to the farm from Orlando and impersonating Troy in his effort to find Peyton and Brandon.

"You had people scattered all over the place, didn't you? Are you going back to Major's farm after you reunite me with my family?"

"Eventually. Peyton and Brandon will want to reunite with David, but she won't be able to until Troy and his rival are stopped. It would be really convenient if they'd annihilate each other."

"We should think about that, in all seriousness," Nate said. "There ought to be a way to step out of their way to each other. What if Peyton gets the list to GBI? Would that help?"

"It would be logical that she would no longer be a threat, but either she knows something else that we don't know about, or Troy has taken this to a personal level."

Nate narrowed his eyes. "Back to Peyton again. Maybe instead of being focused on convincing Peyton to trust us as a group, we need to look at Peyton trusting one of us. Who is Peyton closest to?"

"Annie," Aimee Louise said.

"She and Annie certainly hit it off at the farm, didn't they?" Stuart furrowed his brow in thought. "When I told her about David, she said she trusted you, Aimee Louise. What do you think?"

"I'm the logical choice." Aimee Louise slowed the truck then pulled over to the shoulder. "Check our downed tree."

"Binoculars, Rosalie," he called.

Rosalie handed them to Nate who passed them to Stuart. Stuart peered at the road ahead. "One of our logs has been rolled back to the roadway."

Nate lowered his window and aimed his rifle. Stuart hopped out of the truck and examined the road ahead.

When he resumed his passenger's seat, he said, "The larger of the three logs has been rolled to the middle of the road. There's no way to get around it. Ambushers have the perfect cover with the downed branches."

"Could they be in the woods across the road from the branches?"

"They could, but the downed branches are perfect to hide in."

"Can we get within a hundred yards of the branches? Maybe we can flush them out," Nate said.

"We can do that," Aimee Louise said. "There's enough room on the right shoulder to get by because the log they rolled to the middle was blocking the right side."

Stuart nodded. "Oh, I see it now, you're right. Nate and Red, after Aimee Louise gets close enough to draw their fire, shoot into the branches. When Aimee Louise accelerates and swerves to the right side to get past their blockade, cover our left side. Our other choice is to backtrack to the state road."

"I vote go forward." Rosalie climbed back to the pickup bed.

"I agree." Nate positioned himself at the lowered window.

Stuart lowered his window. "I'll cover the right side. Let's roll."

Aimee Louise accelerated toward the downed tree then slowed as she approached the tree trunk. When the truck was less than a hundred yards away, a shot came from the tree branches with a crack.

"Hold your fire," Stuart said. "That was a twenty-two rifle. Aimee Louise, drive like we're under attack."

Aimee Louise accelerated slowly, and another crack sounded.

"They're warning shots," Stuart said. "Hang on. Hit it, Aimee Louise."

Aimee Louise accelerated and veered to the right and cleared the logs on the road. On the other side of the branches was a transport truck. Aimee Louise slammed on the brakes.

"What did you do that for?" Nate remained at his window.

When no more shots were fired, Stuart shouted, "Are you in trouble?"

Nate and Rosalie maintained their positions as a young voice said, "We're lost."

"Throw out your gun, and we can help you. Are you hungry?"

A small rifle skittered onto the roadway, and two boys stepped away from the back of the transport truck.

"Yes," one of them said.

Two faces popped out of the back of the transport truck. "We're hungry too."

"Two boys and two girls," Stuart said. "Boys look fourteen and twelve; twin girls look six."

"Everybody come over here. We have snacks," Rosalie said.

"That was a lady," one of the boys said.

The girls jumped out of the back. "She has snacks."

"Whoa," Nate said. "Did they steal the truck?"

Stuart dropped the tailgate, and Rosalie sat with her backpack on the tailgate and swung her feet.

The children ran to the back of the pickup, and Rosalie hopped down to lift the girls onto the tailgate for their snacks.

"I'm Red," Rosalie said. "Who are you?"

"I'm Sam," the first girl said as she bit into the piece of pound cake Rosalie had given her.

"I am," the second one said.

"Oh, I get it. That's so funny," Rosalie chuckled.

"Thank you," the second girl grinned. "I'm Cami. I like to tell jokes."

"How do I tell you apart?" Rosalie asked.

"Sam is serious, and I have dimples." Cami smiled to show her dimples.

"I'm left-handed, and Cami is younger," Sam said.

"Only three minutes." Cami rolled her eyes.

"Anyone else at the truck?" Stuart asked the boys.

"No," the older boy said. "There were two men, but they never saw us; we watched from the woods. We're not really lost; I couldn't figure out what to say. We live near Mr. Phil. You know him? We were out hunting for squirrels."

"Except we never get one," the younger boy said.

"One of the guys said time for an ambush or something like, and they rolled that big log into the road from the shoulder," the older boy said. "We heard gunfire from the state road, and one guy walked down the road then back like twenty times. Later the other guy jumped out of the truck and yelled that vigilantes were coming. Are you the vigilantes? They cussed at each other then ran away. I don't know why they didn't move that log and drive away in the truck."

"Vigilantes," the second boy said.

"Oh, yeah. They was sure scared of the vigilantes."

"We was going to roll back the log and take the truck home, but we don't know how to drive," the younger boy said.

"I looked in the back of the truck and seen them little girls," the older boy said. "I asked them if they were waiting for their dad to come back, but they said the men stole them, and I got scared. We were afraid to leave them, but we didn't want anybody to think we stole them. We thought we might help them hide in the woods, but we were afraid they'd get lost. That's why I said we were lost."

"Then you showed up, and we were afraid you might be the vigilantes. What's vigilantes?"

"It's local folks that step in when there are no deputies around, but sometimes vigilantes go overboard. We aren't vigilantes," Stuart said.

"Can we go home now?" the younger boy asked. "We didn't want to leave the little kids by themselves, but you got snacks. You'll take care of them, right?"

"They'll be safe with us," Rosalie said. "Go straight home. There's a bad storm coming."

"We will," the older boy said. "Thanks for the cake."

The two boys raced to the woods and disappeared.

"Rosalie cut an apple in half and cored the halves before she handed a piece to each girl. "We'd like for you to go home with us so you'll be safe. Is that okay with you?"

"Yes, ma'am," Sam said.

"We were scared." Cami bit into her apple.

"And hungry," Sam said.

"Figure out seating, Red," Stuart said. "I'm going to check out the truck. Want to come along, Aimee Louise?"

"Are you okay, Red?" Nate stood near the back of the truck to scan the road and surrounding woods.

"We're fine," Rosalie said. "We'll figure out where we'll sit, and we've got snacks." Rosalie hopped into the back of the pickup to join the girls. "Put up the tailgate for us?"

Stuart slammed the tailgate closed. "We won't be long." He strode away with Aimee Louise by his side.

Aimee Louise checked the truck cab. "I have the keys. There's a rifle under the passenger seat and a pistol in the glove compartment."

"I'll grab those before we leave." Stuart hurried to the back of the truck then whistled when he pulled back the canvas flap. "Ammo, cases of food, a case of water, and two cans of diesel. Stinks back here. They must not have stopped for the girls to take a break at all. Would you back the truck so we can transfer the contents before we leave. Won't take us long."

Aimee Louise dashed to the truck and backed it into position while Stuart moved the transport truck contents close to the back.

Nate joined Stuart as Aimee Louise maneuvered the pickup into position. "Wouldn't it be easier to steal the truck?" Nate's eyes twinkled. "Never mind. The vigilantes might come after us."

Stuart snorted. "I couldn't decide whether we were the vigilantes or not, but then I remembered I'm a deputy, and we aren't locals."

After Aimee Louise backed into position with her usual efficiency and precision, Stuart and Nate loaded the supplies into the pickup bed, and Rosalie slid them into place.

While Stuart secured the fuel cans in the back of the pickup, Rosalie said, "We'll ride back here. The girls have already settled in their spot. Ready when you are."

Stuart closed the tailgate then he and Nate jumped into the truck.

After twenty minutes of travel, Rosalie leaned through the window to the cab. "The girls have fallen asleep on the bed they made. They said bad men came to their house, and their mama told them to run outside and hide in the woods, but the bad men found them. Their last name is Mitchell."

"Wow," Stuart said. "Looters invaded and murdered the Mitchells at their farm near Dad's, and the twin girls have been missing. The grandparents will be thrilled that we found them."

"They reminded me of how much I missed Dolly," Nate said. "I'm glad these girls are safe. I understand how the grandparents will feel; it's like I felt when I learned Dolly and my dad were okay."

"The girls told me they dumped out a box and used it for their potty. I wouldn't mind going all vigilante on those two guys if I had the chance," Rosalie said before she disappeared back into the pickup bed.

After an hour, Rosalie said, "The twins woke up. Can we take a stretch break?"

"Sure can," Stuart said.

Aimee Louise pulled onto the wide shoulder and stopped. Stuart opened the tailgate, and Aimee Louise accompanied Rosalie and the twins to the first row of trees. Nate hurried to the front of the truck to watch the road, and Stuart scanned the road behind them.

Aimee Louise led the girls back to the truck, and Rosalie brought up the rear. "We saw a baby deer hiding in the bushes," Sam said.

"But we were quiet and didn't scare it," Cami added.

After Rosalie loaded the girls into the back of the truck and joined them, Stuart closed up the tailgate.

Nate waited until Stuart reached the passenger's door before he spoke. "Did you come across anyone on this back road when you were going to Keith's? Seeing the transport truck off the state road worried me."

"No, we didn't. It bothered me that they were going south because the trucks we've seen with children in the back were going north. Everything about the truck was off."

Nate frowned as he climbed into the truck; Stuart scanned the road before he shook off his dread and jumped inside.

As the afternoon faded to twilight, the twins squealed, and Rosalie laughed. "We just saw a mama raccoon run across the road behind us with three babies following her."

When Aimee Louise slowed her speed, Stuart asked, "Do you expect animals to move to cover because of the upcoming storm?"

"Yes, but there's no scientific evidence that it's true," Aimee Louise said.

"I have a theory about that," Nate said. "Scientists work in an environment that is removed from nature, so they miss the finer points."

"Exactly." Aimee Louise tapped the brakes when two does bounded across the road in front of them.

As Aimee Louise slowed for the turn to head west, a band of heavy rain swept through.

"I'd say we should be home before the storm hits full force, but I don't want to jinx us," Stuart said.

As they reached the intersection, a lone car sped north. After Aimee Louise continued on their road, Nate said, "I wouldn't have known about the storm if you all hadn't told me. I wonder how many other people will be caught short by the storm."

"I'm not sure how we could have managed without our ham experts, Aimee Louise and Mr. Young," Stuart said. "The ham radio system has been critical for us."

Nate nodded. "There were a few local radio stations that broadcasted after the grid went down, but I think they must have been using generators for power because it wasn't long until they went off the air."

"Someone's on the side of the road ahead," Aimee Louise said. "I don't see a vehicle around."

As the truck approached, the figure disappeared.

"He ducked into the trees, so we wouldn't see him," Stuart said as Aimee Louise sped past him..

When the next band of heavy rain blew across the road, Aimee Louise slowed and turned the wipers on high. As they approached a slow-moving vehicle, Stuart narrowed his eyes for a better view. After Aimee Louise passed the car, he said, "Until I realized it was a car not a truck, I was afraid they'd try to force us off the road, but a car can't see as well as we can because we sit higher."

"Yes," she said.

"The rain is noisy back here," Rosalie said. "We're having a snack to drown out the noise."

"Good plan, Rosalie. Want me to make room for you all up here?" Nate asked.

Rosalie leaned through the window. "Thanks, but we're fine. Sam said she likes her window seat, and Cami said she likes hers better." Rosalie snickered.

Nate chuckled. "Are you sure you don't have Dolly back there too?"

"Won't be much longer, and we'll have the whole crowd together," Stuart said.

The rain slowed then stopped. "Our turn is coming up," Aimee Louise said.

When Aimee Louise turned at the Smith farm, Stuart said, "We're at the farm next door to my folks' farm. Dad and I blocked the driveway to his farm."

Nate peered at the driveway. "I don't see any farms."

"Great, isn't it?" Stuart grinned.

After they traveled the circuitous driveway to the barn, Nate said, "I saw the remains of a chimney, and this barn looks like it's been abandoned for years. I'm worried about you people."

"It's a perfectly good barn," Rosalie called out from the back. "Just needs a little paint."

Nate snorted.

When they came out of the brush and passed the Newton house, Aimee Louise tapped the horn before she parked. After Scott opened the kitchen door, Stuart met his father in the yard.

Scott hugged Stuart. "Everything okay?"

Stuart smiled, "All good. We have Nate, and we found the two Mitchell girls."

Scott's eyes widened. "Wow. Sure didn't expect that. Let's get everyone inside. Your mother has supper almost ready. After we eat, we can take them to their grandparents' house. It's not that far away, but too far for little girls to walk."

Stuart motioned for Nate to join them.

"I'm Scott." The two men shook hands. "Come with me, Nate. Charo, Dolly, and your dad have been waiting for you."

Scott and Nate hurried to the house while Stuart opened the back tailgate. "Go on in, Rosalie. Aimee Louise and I will be right behind you. We'll lock up the truck and unload later."

Stuart helped the twins out of the truck, and they clung to Rosalie as she herded them to the house.

After Aimee Louise locked the truck, Stuart said, "Ready to go inside? It's going to be loud."

Henry ran out of the house to Stuart and Aimee Louise. Aimee Louise knelt to hug him, and he wrapped his arms around her neck.

"Missed you, Angel and Deputy Stuart," Henry said.

Stuart hugged the two of them, and Aimee Louise smiled. "I missed you more," she said.

I love her smile. Stuart grinned. "I missed you the most."

Henry giggled. "You win, Deputy Stuart."

The three of them held hands as they headed to the house.

When they walked inside the house, Dolly squealed, "Henry, my daddy came to see me."

Henry squeezed Stuart's hand. "My deputy came home too," Henry said.

"Come on, Henry," Brandon said. "We're washing our hands for supper."

Henry glanced up at Stuart who nodded, and Henry joined Brandon.

CHAPTER THIRTEEN

"We're having carrot soup with tiny pork sausage meatballs." Sandra dished up bowls of soup while Peyton set two platters of biscuits on the table. Charo was at the table in her wheelchair, and Nate knelt beside her.

"Here's a chair, Nate," Scott said.

Nate scooted his chair close to Charo, and when Dolly dried her hands, he pulled her chair close to his other side. Rosalie sat in between the twins, and Peyton gestured for Brandon to sit next to her.

"Judge, go ahead and eat with your family. We'll eat in shifts," Sandra said. "Here's a biscuit for you, Henry, while you wait. I know you want to eat with Stuart and Angel. Scott, go ahead and take your seat."

"I'll wait for you, honey," Scott said.

Sandra put another batch of biscuits in the oven. "There's plenty of soup and more biscuits to come, so eat what you want."

No one talked during the meal. After the first shift had eaten, Peyton and Nate cleared the table, and the judge washed dishes while Rosalie and Charo led the children to the living room for a game.

After they sat at the table, Scott said, "Stuart and I will take the twins to their grandparents after we eat."

"Rosalie will need to go along, Dad. The twins have bonded with her."

"Henry and I would like to go too, but we'll stay here," Aimee Louise said.

Stuart furrowed his brow. "I need you to drive, and Henry doesn't take up a lot of room."

Scott nodded. "We'll leave right after we eat, if you don't mind being stuck with the dishes, Sandra."

"The judge will help me. We'll wait for baths until you get back, so Henry doesn't miss out on his snack."

After the last group finished eating, Stuart and Henry went to the living room. "When you're at a stopping point in your game, Red, we're ready. We'll unload the truck after we get back."

"We can leave now," Rosalie said.

"It's a very fluid game," Charo chuckled.

On the way to the truck, Scott said, "I'll sit in the backseat behind you, Stuart. I know you're Angel's navigator."

When they reached the truck, Sam said, "Can we ride in our seats in the back?"

"We like our special seats," Cami said.

"Stuart, is it okay if we ride in our seats?" Rosalie asked.

"Your call, Red," he smiled.

Rosalie helped the twins into the back. After she jumped in with them, Stuart raised the tailgate.

"You want to ride up front with Angel and me, Henry?" Stuart asked.

Henry nodded and hurried to the passenger's door.

When everyone was in, Aimee Louise headed to their shortcut to the Smith farm.

"There's another Gulf storm headed toward us. We might see it in the morning, Dad, unless it bypasses us."

"I'll check to see if there's anything we need to do after we get back, but I think we're fine."

"We'll look around," Stuart said.

"This worked out really well," Scott said as Aimee Louise drove through to the wide path. "When we get to the road, turn right. The Mitchell farm is on the left about a quarter mile before the state road."

As they neared the end of the driveway before the road, Stuart said, "I saw a light on the road to our left." Aimee Louise lowered her window and cut off the headlights and the engine.

"Lights to our left," Scott said when Rosalie leaned through the opening.

"We'll watch," she said.

"I hear it," Aimee Louise said.

"I see the light," Henry pointed.

"Medium speed," Aimee Louise said. "Accelerated after the Websters' driveway."

After the car sped past them, Aimee Louise turned on the engine then drove to the road. As she raised her window, Stuart lowered his.

"I don't hear it. Let's go," he said.

Aimee Louise turned on the headlights before she drove on the paved road and toward the state road.

"Up ahead after the group of three trees," Scott said.

Aimee Louise slowed when she reached the trees.

"Here," Scott said.

Aimee Louise turned left at an overgrown driveway. As the truck crept down the driveway, the twins squealed.

"Do all five-year-old girls sound alike?" Scott asked.

"Yes, Papa Scott," Henry said.

Scott chuckled. "Thank you, Henry. Good to know."

Aimee Louise stopped before they were close to the house and honked. Scott stepped out and stood next to the truck.

The side door of the farmhouse opened, and a gruff voice called out, "We're heavily armed. Whoever you are, get off my property."

"It's Scott Newton from down the road," Scott shouted.

"Scott? What's your kid's name?"

"Stuart is my son," Scott said.

"What are you doing here so late?" Mr. Mitchell stepped outside.

"My son and his friends found the twins. We have them with us. Can we bring them to you?"

"The girls?" He shouted into the house. "Scott Newton's boy found the twins. They're here."

Aimee Louise slowly drove closer to the house, and Scott walked alongside. After she stopped, Scott opened the tailgate, and Rosalie hopped out then helped the twins to the ground.

"Grandma! Grandpa!"

The girls ran toward the house. When Sam stopped, Cami turned, "Come on, Red. We're at Grandma's."

Rosalie followed them. "I'm coming. Run on ahead."

Stuart joined Rosalie as she walked to the house. Rosalie hugged the twins then returned to the truck when Mrs. Mitchell took the girls inside.

Stuart spoke in a quiet voice. "We found them this afternoon. They were exhausted and hungry. They were filthy and will need baths. We don't think they were mistreated in any other way. Mom fed them supper then we brought them to you. They didn't seem to know about their parents. The girls may talk about Red. She bonded with them when we found them. One more thing—we may have a storm hit tomorrow, maybe in the morning."

"Thank you, Stuart." Mr. Mitchell's eyes welled, and the two men shook hands.

Stuart and Scott returned to the truck. After they were inside, Rosalie said, "I almost climbed into the back. It's really comfortable back there."

"Can I ride in the back sometime with Red?" Henry asked.

"That would be fun," Rosalie said.

Aimee Louise turned the truck around and headed to the road. She and Stuart lowered their windows and listened.

"Okay," Stuart said; Aimee Louise turned and accelerated to the Smith driveway.

When Aimee Louise parked at the house, Scott exhaled. "Is this what it's like driving around with you three? I'll stay at the farm."

It's never dull.

"Henry and I will go inside, so he doesn't miss bath time," Aimee Louise said.

Stuart, Scott, and Rosalie carried in their bags and the first few cartons from the transport truck. When they went inside the house with the first load, Sandra slipped a pan into the oven. "Stack everything there, out of the way, and we'll sort through it tomorrow. Everyone has earned a relaxing evening. Peyton and the judge have bath time under control."

Aimee Louise joined in unloading all the cartons and supplies from the transport truck.

After their last trip, Sandra said, "Hot water on the stove if you want tea. The children will be here soon for their snack."

Rosalie elbowed Aimee Louise, and Stuart sniffed the air. "We'll wait for them right here." They sat at the kitchen table.

When Scott came into the kitchen and joined the three already at the table, Sandra chuckled. "I see how this works. Do you think you'll get away with it?"

When the children rushed into the kitchen, Dolly pursed her lips as she stared at the table. "Mommy, the rule—"

"Bath, snack, bed," Charo sang. "Our favorite farm rule. Eat up, sleepy heads; Mama's snacks are cool."

When everyone applauded, Charo waved her hand with a flourish and bowed.

"Love our new song, Charo, and it's nice to see everyone so clean and ready for snack." Peyton sat in the chair next to Brandon.

Judge and Nate came into the kitchen, and the judge took his seat at the table. Nate glanced at the expectant faces as he stood behind Charo's wheelchair and placed his hands lightly on her shoulders. "I'm not sure what's going on, but I don't want to miss out."

"Here you go." Sandra set two plates of cinnamon sugar cookies on the table. "It's a welcome home party for you or maybe a surprise party for us because we didn't expect you before tomorrow."

After the snack party was over and the kids were in bed, Charo asked, "Do we have another bed for my room for Nate? My twin bed isn't big enough for both of us even if I didn't have my leg in a splint."

"That room did have two twin beds, but I can't remember why we moved the second one out. Do you, Scott?"

"The second bed is in the attic, but I'm pleading the fifth on this one," Scott said.

"Oh, yes. My minimalist phase when I decided the second one cluttered the room. Now that we have a dozen people in the house, I'm over that," Sandra said.

"I'll get it," Stuart said.

While Stuart and Scott brought the bedframe, mattress, and box springs down from the attic, Sandra and Aimee Louise arranged Charo's bedroom for the second bed. After Sandra gave them sheets and a quilt, Aimee Louise and Rosalie made the bed.

"Ready for our night check?" Scott asked as he picked up his rifle.

Aimee Louise waited for Stuart and Rosalie while they grabbed their rifles then the three of them joined him outside.

"Let's split up to check the barn, chicken coop, and around the house," Scott said.

After their rounds, they met at the driveway.

"Should we let the Websters know about the storm?" Rosalie asked.

"Leo would have heard on the radio, but maybe we could let them know we're back," Stuart said.

"Y'all go on. I want to check the chainsaws and tractor in case we have any limbs or trees down tomorrow," Scott said.

The three of them trotted to the Smith farm then used the driveway to get to the road. Aimee Louise and Rosalie raced to the

Websters' driveway, and Stuart ran behind them. When they neared the house, Stuart called out.

Andy came out of the house, and Wynn peered out of the barn.

"You tell Andy, Rosalie," Stuart said. "We'll go occupy Wynn."

Rosalie dashed to meet Andy, and Aimee Louise and Stuart continued to the barn.

"How are the puppies?" Aimee Louise asked.

"Growing." Wynn watched Stuart as Stuart checked around the barn.

"Nice set up. Are you comfortable?" Stuart asked when he glanced in the tack room.

"Yes. The dogs at the shelter were restless at night, so I thought that's how all dogs are, and these aren't. Most likely because these dogs aren't cooped up during the day. They go to their kennels at night without prompting."

"There may be a storm tomorrow," Stuart said.

"Mr. Leo told me. Ms. Jennie wanted me to come to the house, but the barn is sturdy. I'll stay with the dogs, so they won't be afraid."

"I know you want to go to Alabama as soon as you can. How are you feeling?"

"Lot stronger. Ms. Jennie takes good care of me. I could probably go at any time, but I'd like for the puppies not to be a burden on Ms. Jennie before I leave."

"Have you named any of the puppies?" Amy Louise asked.

Wynn glanced at the puppies. "Oh, no. That's for someone else to do."

"We just came to hear the latest news about the storm from Mr. Leo, but Aimee Louise wanted to check on the puppies first." Stuart beamed. "We'll see you later."

Stuart took Aimee Louise by the elbow, and they strolled together to the house and knocked. Jennie opened the door, "Come on in."

After they stepped inside, Stuart said, "We wanted to make sure you knew about the storm and let you know we're back."

"Thanks for letting us know. Andy's been worried about Rosalie. He wanted to chase you down right after you left." Jennie shook her head. "Andy and Rosalie are in the radio room with Leo. I think the signal has been sketchy. Go on in."

Leo spun his chair around. "Storm seems to be gaining strength according to the barometers on the Florida coast. Unlike the forecasters before the grid collapsed, who missed most of the time anyway, nobody is guessing where or when it will hit landfall. Andy's already made sure we're storm-ready."

"Except for the tool shed, Uncle Leo. We need to check it." Andy and Rosalie hurried to the back door.

"Any way Rosalie could stay with us? I'm asking for me, not Andy. He'd drive me crazy worrying about her."

Stuart glanced at Aimee Louise who agreed with an imperceptible nod. "That's up to Rosalie," Stuart said.

"Good. We'll play it by ear then." Jennie stood in the doorway. "Care for a cup of coffee? Tea? Glass of water?"

"No, thank you," Aimee Louise said.

"I'm interested in what Rosalie has to say," Stuart said. "I'll take a glass of water."

When Rosalie and Andy returned, Jennie stood in the doorway as Andy said, "I'd left a fuel can out when I filled the tractor. Glad I checked. I put it in the fuel shed."

Andrew cleared his throat. "Rosalie and I wondered—"

"I'm staying here during the storm," Rosalie said.

"Sounds like a good idea," Stuart said. "We don't expect any raids during the storm, but we have adequate coverage at Dad's farm. Wouldn't hurt to have extra protection here."

Andy's eyes widened as he looked from Rosalie to Stuart.

Rosalie smiled. "Right."

"Y'all are amazing," Andy said. "Straight to the point. I need to learn that."

Jennie snickered, and Stuart nodded. *Hope you're a fast learner.*

"We'll head back. See you after the storm," Stuart said.

Stuart and Aimee Louise headed outside, and Rosalie and Andy followed them.

"I'll go part of the way up the driveway, in case Wynn is watching," Rosalie said.

"He's been the perfect dog trainer," Andy said. "The puppies are responding to his commands."

"Has he named them?" Aimee Louise asked.

"Yes. He calls them by name, but I wasn't paying attention," Andy said. "Is that important?"

"Not really," Stuart said.

The four of them headed up the driveway. Andy stopped and waved. When Rosalie was out of sight of the barn and house, she said, "You two are the best," as she turned back to Andy.

"Yes," Aimee Louise said, and Stuart grinned.

On the way back to the Newtons', Stuart asked, "What did you think about Wynn?"

"He's an accomplished liar. When I asked about naming the puppies, he said no, which was the professional answer, but his cloud was anger that I asked. Andy had no reason to lie when he said Wynn had named the puppies. Charo could better explain Wynn's motives, but I think he doesn't want to reveal what he perceives as a weakness."

* * *

Stuart woke in the middle of the night when the rain and wind intensified. When the rain slammed against the side of the house, and the intensity of the wind rattled the windows, he padded downstairs. A candle flickered in the kitchen, and the aroma of coffee told him his mother was awake too.

She poured his coffee, and he held the cup with two hands. "That wind is unnerving. How long have you been up, Mom?"

"Long enough to get the coffee on. You came back without Rosalie."

Stuart chuckled. "Sorry you weren't there. You know how direct Aimee Louise is, right? It's her autism. Rosalie is direct because she doesn't have time for niceties. Andy was asking me if Rosalie could stay—for security reasons, of course—"

"Of course." Sandra smiled.

"And because he's from Georgia, he was being nice as he started to explain the advantages of having Rosalie stay when Rosalie interrupted him and announced she was staying."

Sandra chortled. "I am so sorry I wasn't there. Rosalie is a hoot."

"She's that and more," Stuart nodded. "I think she's planning on staying to back up Andy and Jennie as long as Wynn is there."

After another wave of howling wind blasted the house with a loud roar, Aimee Louise padded into the kitchen. She wore her hearing protection earmuffs.

"The noise is terrible, isn't it? I'm surprised everyone else can sleep through it," Sandra said.

"It's the low," Aimee Louise said.

"If Rosalie were here, she'd have an in-depth explanation on the impact of the low barometric pressure on animals and humans. The kids at Major's farm call her our weather girl." Stuart put his arm around Aimee Louise and hugged her.

"Angel, do you care for coffee or hot tea?" Sandra asked.

"I'd like to try hot tea," Aimee Louise said.

"I'll add a dollop of honey," Sandra said.

Just before dawn, Nate came into the kitchen. "I could have slept through that wind, but the smell of coffee finally pulled me out of bed."

The abrupt sound of pounding on the kitchen door startled them all. Stuart jumped out of his seat and knocked over his chair as he hurried to the door. When he opened it, a powerful blast of wind pushed Jennie headlong inside but she caught herself before she fell to the floor.

"I need help," Jennie said. "Leo got up early this morning and went out to check on Wynn, Holly, and the puppies. When he didn't come back, Rosalie and I checked and found Leo beaten in the barn, and Wynn was gone. Rosalie took off to find Wynn. Andy helped me get Leo into the house then he left to find Rosalie. That's been hours ago. I was afraid to leave Leo, and I thought they'd be right back, but they're not back. I'm worried sick." She collapsed on a chair and sobbed.

"I'll find them." Stuart grabbed his rifle.

"I'll go with you," Nate said.

"Wait," Aimee Louise said. "Were the puppies in the barn, Ms. Jennie?"

"What? Of course, they—" Jennie furrowed her brow. "No, Holly was, but the puppies weren't there. They would have been all over me. I didn't realize they were gone because I was so worried about Leo."

"It's logical that if the attackers were after Wynn, he wouldn't leave the puppies," Aimee Louise said.

"You see more complexity in Wynn than the rest of us do," Stuart said.

"Yes. I know where he'd take them."

"Where?" Scott frowned.

"To our barn," Stuart said. "Like Aimee Louise said, it's logical. But what about Rosalie? If she left the Websters' before the storm worsened, she could be anywhere."

"Depends." Aimee Louise left the kitchen then returned with her rain gear.

As she headed for the door, Stuart rushed to go with her. "Where are we going?"

"For a walk."

"I'm going too," Nate said, "but I'm confused."

Scott followed them outside. When the four of them reached the Newton barn, it appeared empty. After they stepped inside, Scott frowned at the sound of whimpering puppies then opened the tack room door. Wynn huddled in a corner with the puppies he had wrapped in an dry, old quilt remnant. His clothes were soaked, and he shivered as he stared up at Scott.

Scott grabbed a box and plopped the puppies inside it. "Let's go into the house, Wynn. Those wet clothes are giving you the chills. Sandra will find you some dry clothes and fix you a warm breakfast. We'll take the puppies inside with us."

After Wynn scrambled to his feet, he picked up the box with the puppies and walked with Scott to the house.

Aimee Louise held up her arm to protect her face against the blowing rain as she headed to the front of the house.

"We're checking the Smith barn. That's why you said it depends, right?" Stuart asked as he and Nate caught up to her on the way to the shortcut.

"Yes."

The brush and trees provided protection from the wind, but when they came out at the wide path, they lowered their heads for protection against the assault of the storm. Aimee Louise grabbed onto Stuart's arm as they leaned into the wind to walk.

After they reached the barn and went inside, Nate said, "That was rough. I can't even imagine what it would have been like in the dark in the worst of the storm."

Aimee Louise pointed to the middle stall, and Stuart smiled at the flattened pile of straw that had been gathered from the other stalls. "Good sign that someone took refuge here. Let's go to the Websters' house."

When they reached the house, Stuart knocked then opened the door and called out. "Hello? Anybody here?"

The aroma of coffee greeted him as he stepped inside with Aimee Louise clinging to his jacket. Nate slammed the door against the wind.

"We're in the radio room," Rosalie said. "Come join us."

Leo, who sat at the transceiver, motioned for Aimee Louise to join him. She rushed to sit in the chair he had pulled close for her.

"Let's go to the kitchen," Andy said. "I need more coffee, and I can give you a full report while those three are on the radio."

Andy set two cups on the table and filled them before he refilled his own then the three men sat at the table.

"Aunt Jennie left Uncle Leo a note that she was going to the Newtons for help, but I'm getting ahead of myself. I'll start at the beginning. Uncle Leo knew that Wynn would take good care of Holly and the puppies, but he wanted to check on the rest of the dogs. When he got to their kennels, they had already moved into their part of the barn where they'd be safe and dry."

Stuart nodded. "Leo would go through a storm to check on his dogs."

"The dogs alerted Wynn when they raised a fuss as the men tried to open the back door of the barn that we had nailed shut ages ago. When Uncle Leo passed by the main barn to come back to the house, the three men jumped him and pushed him into the empty barn then wanted to know where Wynn was. Uncle Leo said he didn't know who they were talking about, and they pummeled him. After Uncle Leo dropped to the ground and feigned unconsciousness, they left."

"He took a chance doing that, but I'm not sure what else he could have done," Nate said.

"I know." Andy shook his head. "He stayed on the ground in case they came back. Aunt Jennie thought he was spending some time with the dogs, but she and Rosalie wanted to check on the puppies. They went out to the barn and found him. Aunt Jennie ran inside to get me, but by the time we reached the barn, Rosalie was gone. Uncle Leo told us she ran out of the barn the second he told her he was fine. He said he'd never seen anyone run as fast as Red. I was frantic that she took off by herself, but I helped Uncle Leo into the house against Aunt Jennie's protests. She was certain he was terribly injured and didn't want him moved. As soon as Uncle Leo was in the house, I left to find Rosalie. I was really scared for her."

"Aimee Louise scares me all the time," Stuart mumbled.

"How did you find her?" Nate asked.

"I didn't; she came back for me. By the time I reached the road, I decided Rosalie would have had a plan, which I didn't. I struggled against the wind, and by the time I reached the Smith farm driveway, the storm was fierce. When I was having difficulty staying on my feet, I realized lightweight Rosalie couldn't have withstood the wind and would have taken shelter, so I headed to the Smith barn. Would you believe she was almost at the Newton farm by way of the shortcut when she turned back to find me?"

"Not much you could tell me about Red that I wouldn't believe," Stuart said.

"I'm starting to catch onto that. I asked her how she knew I was looking for her. She said it was logical." Andy shook his head. "She told me she crawled on the wide path because the wind kept knocking her down. She was clinging to a tree when I got to her. She said she waited out gusts to run from one tree to the next to make her way to the barn door. I held onto her, but the wind still blew us around. After we made it inside, we gathered straw to sit on. Our raingear kept us relatively dry, so we were comfortable enough. We fell asleep, probably from the exhaustion of fighting the wind. When we woke, we came back here, found the note from Aunt Jennie, and made coffee. Uncle Leo was in the radio room and didn't notice he was alone in the house." Andy chuckled.

"Aimee Louise found Wynn with the puppies in Dad's barn, so Rosalie was right," Stuart said. "By the way, that's not the first time I've said that about her or Aimee Louise. I try not to say it in their hearing, though, if I can help it."

Nate snorted. "Do we need to head back and let Jennie know everyone's okay?"

"They're going to be on the radio for a while, I'll go," Andy said.

"I'll go with you," Nate said. "You and Jennie should be fine coming back together."

"As soon as Aimee Louise signs off, we'll head back too. I want to talk to Wynn. I think last night may have helped him decide where his loyalties lie, and I'd like to know," Stuart said.

Rosalie joined Andy when he stepped to the radio room doorway. "Stuart and Angel will return to the Newton farm after she signs off. Nate and I are going to get Aunt Jennie," he said. "I may be back before Stuart and Aimee Louise leave."

"I need to go too." Rosalie frowned. "No, that doesn't work. I need to stay with Leo."

"Yep." Andy hugged her. "Be back as quick as I can."

After Andy and Nate left, Stuart and Rosalie went into the radio room, and Rosalie picked up her pad to continue her notes.

When Aimee Louise signed off, Leo took over the radio. "I want to see if I can pick up any more tidbits," he said as Stuart and the young women left for the kitchen.

Rosalie sat at the kitchen table and flipped to the first page of the day's notes. "Mr. Young had heard the report about the Gulf storm, but they didn't get any rain or wind at all at the farm. He was surprised we were hit so hard. David's toes are warm, and the swelling is going down. Aunt Molly is complaining because he's walking more than she thinks he should. He asked Annie and Mr. Young to see when Dr. Jody is available for a consult because he wants to come see Brandon and Peyton. Mr. Young said he thinks David and Aunt Molly are related because all they do is bicker."

"If David's feeling well enough to argue with Molly, he'll be fine," Stuart said.

"That's exactly what Mr. Young said." Rosalie grinned. "Sheriff and the deputies are helping to staff a new roadblock near Plainview, and Pastor John's brother Chuck and Dr. Jody are helping with another one near Red Springs. Major said the roadblocks are making a difference. He thinks the bad guys are bypassing their counties."

"I might talk to Dad about that," Stuart said.

Aimee Louise joined Rosalie at the table and peered at her notes. "Best for last. Ham network news."

"Yes. Mr. Young said a small team of ham operators have been tracking conversations on simplex frequencies and have pieced together evidence there is more organization to the groups of invaders than anyone thought. The hams believe there is a big meeting between the heads of the two major groups this weekend in Macon. Leo joined the ham team and will listen to simplex to gather more information."

Stuart's eyes widened. "This is big. Do you think Troy heads one group?"

"Yes," Aimee Louise said. "Peyton and Wynn know who the other one is."

"Let's go. I need to talk to Wynn and Peyton." Stuart threw on his raingear and headed to the door then stopped. He turned to gaze at Aimee Louise and Rosalie, who had not moved from the kitchen table. "What else?"

"We have to wait for Andy and Ms. Jennie because I'm going with you. If Wynn stays at your dad's farm, there's no reason for me to stay here," Rosalie said.

Stuart tilted his head. "What about Andy?"

Rosalie nodded. "You're right. Maybe he should be part of the discussion too because he knows Macon."

Stuart blinked. *Not what I meant, but good point.*

"You already have a plan, don't you?" Stuart asked after he removed his raingear and joined them at the table.

CHAPTER FOURTEEN

"I don't think this is a friendly meeting for the two groups to join forces, in spite of the appearances. It's an ambush," Aimee Louise said.

"Troy's senior team is the list of agents that Peyton memorized and wants to get to the Georgia Bureau of Investigation," Rosalie said. "The other leader—I call him X—wants the list, and Troy wants to stop Peyton. The original kidnapping of children to force law enforcement to join McNeill's team inspired Troy to start his own operation of shipping the children to camps in South Carolina and other states for the highly lucrative overseas human trafficking business."

"X was close enough to Troy to copy the business model and start his own based near Orlando," Aimee Louise said. "His organization is smaller and less experienced. He'd like to entice some or all of Troy's senior team to his business and take over Troy's organization."

"There's no reason the crooked agents would have any loyalty to Troy. It's not like he's one of them. They'd be willing to go to the highest bidder," Rosalie said.

Stuart frowned. "How did you two come up with all this?"

"It's logical," Aimee Louise said.

"So, what's the plan?"

"You and Aimee Louise talk to Wynn; Aimee Louise talks to Peyton. It's time for them to help us," Rosalie said.

Andy and Jennie came into the house as Stuart asked, "After that?"

"We go to Macon," Aimee Louise said.

"When do we leave?" Andy asked.

"As far as leaving for Macon, we need to go over what we know first. We were waiting for you because we think you'll want to be in on the discussion at Dad's," Stuart said.

"Will you be okay, Aunt Jennie?"

"The bad guys were looking for Wynn." She hung up her raingear. "We'll be fine here. Let me know the plan and what you want me to do."

Stuart and Aimee Louise peeked in on Leo; he had put on his headset and was taking notes as he listened.

"He's picking up snippets of conversations on those traveling on the state road," Aimee Louise said as they returned to the kitchen. The four young people left for the Newton farm. The wind had slowed to a light breeze, and the rain became occasional sprinkles.

"After Aimee Louise and I talk to Wynn, she'll talk with Peyton before we have our discussion about Macon," Stuart said.

On the shortcut to the Smith farm, Rosalie gave Andy a quick rundown of the ham network news. Stuart and Aimee Louise led the way up the driveway to the road then the four of them jogged to the Newton driveway.

"Mr. Scott's at the equipment shed," Andy said. "Let's see if he could use our help." He and Rosalie headed to the equipment shed while Aimee Louise continued to the house.

Wynn and the judge watched the puppies and children play next to the barn. Wynn waved as Stuart sauntered to join them at the barn.

"How you doing, Wynn?" Stuart asked

"I'm fine. It was rough last night getting here, but I need for the puppies to be safe."

Stuart nodded. "Mind keeping an eye on the puppies too, Judge? I'd like to talk with Wynn."

"Go right ahead," the judge said. "We've got everything under control."

"What's on your mind?" Wynn asked as they strolled toward the garden.

"What happened last night? Why did you leave the Websters' barn?" Stuart asked.

Wynn stopped and stared at the ground. "I think I was hoping you wouldn't ask. Can we find somewhere to sit?"

"Sure. Let's sit on the bench near the garden if you don't mind getting wet. I don't."

When they reached the bench, Aimee Louise came out of the house and ran to join them.

"Everything's okay in the house," Aimee Louise said.

"Glad you're here too, Angel," Wynn said. "Stuart asked me about last night, and I'd like for you to hear too."

Wynn and Aimee Louise sat on the bench as Stuart stood next to Aimee Louise with his foot propped onto the edge of the bench.

Wynn cleared his throat. "I knew when I was driving the transport truck that our cargo was kids. I'd become callous; it was just a job. I had food and a place to sleep and thought I'd found my people. The big boss was Troy. His brother, Ben, drove an eighteen-wheeler until the whole trucking industry folded after the collapse. I guess I'm not quite answering your question yet. I wanted you to understand what it's been like."

"Take your time. We want to hear what you have to say," Stuart said.

"I wasn't quite just a cargo driver for Troy. I kind of stayed close to him because I was afraid of some of the men he hired, and he got used to me being around. He told me his wife was a cop and wanted to shut down his operation, and he needed her silenced." Wynn shuddered. "He was so business-like when he said it that he scared me worse than his goons did."

Stuart glanced at Aimee Louise, but her intent gaze was focused on Wynn.

Wynn furrowed his brow as he peered at Aimee Louise. "You see things, don't you, Angel?"

"More than you know," Stuart said.

"Troy had a list of his trusted guys and others that he planned to add to his organization. Ben told me he needed the list for safekeeping and asked me to bring it to him. Troy was out of town, which wasn't unusual, and I didn't think anything about Ben's request because he always filled in for Troy. When Troy returned and he couldn't find his list, he went on a rampage. He was convinced his wife had stolen it, and I was afraid to tell him I'd given it to Ben. I figured Ben would tell him after Troy calmed down, but Ben and Troy had a falling out instead. Ben started up another business just like Troy's, except Troy's destination for his cargo was South Carolina, and Ben's was Florida. Ben asked me if I'd help him grow his business. I went from a cargo driver to Ben's number two man. Heady stuff when six months earlier I was starving to death. Literally. I was excited to work with Ben until I realized he was even more cutthroat than Troy."

Wynn rose and paced in front of the bench. "I was nervous because I gave the list to Ben then I realized he wouldn't want anyone to know he had it. When I was driving the cargo truck and the team leader told me to pull over for a radio call, I knew Ben had issued my death sentence. It was the perfect location for me because I knew I was close to Grandpa's farm, so I stole the rifles and pistol and ran."

"Troy wants to kill his wife because of the list, and Ben wants to kill you because of the list, and probably Troy's wife too," Stuart said.

"Exactly." Wynn sat on the bench.

"Do you have any idea of what Ben or Troy plan to do next?" Stuart asked.

"Troy has allies in every law enforcement organization in the southeast except the Georgia Bureau of Investigation, which is why he doesn't have any operations in Georgia. Ben started operating in Georgia even though he's wary of the GBI because he didn't want open conflict with Troy right off." Wynn frowned. "I hadn't thought of that before. As far as what Ben plans next, he hinted at an upcoming meeting with Troy in Macon. That's weird, because there's a GBI office there. Maybe they considered it neutral ground. Supposedly the agenda is to discuss combining their organizations, but Ben is planning an ambush. I wouldn't be surprised if Troy is too."

"This is a lot to be carrying around," Stuart said. "What about last night?"

"The rain was heavy, but the winds hadn't really picked up yet. After the puppies settled down, I heard someone trying to break in at the back of the barn. I knew Ben's guys had found me. I put the puppies in the box and took off with them to the road and saw an empty truck on the side of the road. When I realized they hadn't seen or followed me, I ran to your dad's barn. I was glad I'd taken the puppies there because it was dry and safe, and the storm intensified after that."

"What an ordeal," Stuart said.

"I suppose," Wynn said. "I've had a lot of time to think, and I've brought the problems on myself. I fell into a way of life that I'm not proud of at all. I need to be in Alabama with my grandpa and family. I may never have the opportunity for veterinary school, but I can find a veterinarian to work with and provide a service to the small community. That's where I want to be."

When Aimee Louise rose to leave, Wynn said, "Thanks for listening. And not throwing me out."

Stuart smiled. "You'll do well."

As Wynn hurried to the barn, and Stuart and Aimee Louise strolled toward the house, Stuart asked, "So?"

"He's healing. He considers you a true friend."

"I have a feeling that's something he hasn't had in a long time. Do you believe him? Can we trust him?"

"I do."

"Good enough for me. Next, Peyton."

"She trusts me but needs to talk to you," Aimee Louise said.

"Really? I hadn't looked at it like that."

"She and Sandra were planning on picking up the fallen branches in the front yard."

When they reached the front yard, Peyton dropped a branch and hurried to them. "Any news about David?"

Stuart nodded. "According to Mr. Young, his toes are warm and the swelling in his leg is going down. The best news is that he and Molly are arguing. Mr. Young sounded like he was enjoying his latest entertainment."

Peyton chuckled. "You're right. That is the best news of all. David has sisters—I'll bet he's needling Molly."

"We have more," Stuart said. "Can we sit on the porch?"

"Is that okay with you, Sandra?" Peyton asked.

"Sure is. I need to check on the judge. He may be ready for a break too."

"What's up?" Peyton asked after Sandra left.

"We're planning a trip to Macon." Stuart asked.

"I need to go too," Peyton said.

"Why?" Stuart asked.

Peyton stared at him. "Why not?"

Stuart met her stare.

"Fine," she scowled at Stuart. "I have information for the Georgia Bureau of Investigation. Don't ask me what."

Stuart raised his eyebrows, and Aimee Louise gazed at Peyton then tilted her head.

"What information?" Aimee Louise asked.

Peyton's face softened as she turned her gaze to Aimee Louise. "It's a list. It's Troy's list of his henchmen and other sympathetic FBI agents. I memorized it."

"You can't leave Brandon." Stuart matched Peyton's soft tone.

"Dammit, Stuart," Peyton growled. "That's a low blow."

"I could deliver it for you," Aimee Louise said.

"You could, couldn't you? If I recited the list, you would memorize it. No one would know." Peyton bit her lip. "That has possibilities."

"Now," Aimee Louise said.

Peyton raised her eyebrows. "You're right." She recited her list.

"Twenty-five," Aimee Louise said before she repeated the list.

"You've got it. Very impressive, Angel." Peyton smiled.

"Do you have a contact at GBI?" Stuart asked.

"I planned to go to the office that is south of Macon first. If no one is there, Nate suggested we go to the Georgia Public Safety Training Center north of Macon."

"We'd need to watch out for Troy. Anybody else?" Stuart asked.

Peyton's eyes widened. "Ben. Troy's brother Ben. He would have gone to work with Troy, but they never really got along. Ben would try to take over Troy's business, and the best way to do that would be to have the list that Troy liked to brag about."

"We need to have a family meeting," Stuart rose.

"I'll find Sandra, She's probably in the kitchen." Peyton paused at the bottom of the steps. "What about Wynn?"

"We'll include him. We can meet at the barn," Stuart said as he and Aimee Louise hurried to find Scott, Rosalie, and Andy.

"What about the kids?" Peyton asked. "I could occupy them."

"True, but you have a unique perspective that we need. They can listen or play where we can see them," he said.

Scott strolled with Stuart and Aimee Louise to the barn while Rosalie and Andy hurried to the house to help Nate with Charo's wheelchair.

After the adults had gathered in the barn, Wynn moved to the doorway to keep an eye on the puppies and kids, and Sandra joined him.

"I'll start," Stuart said. "Rosalie and Aimee Louise will add details, but feel free to jump in with any questions."

Stuart began the discussion with a summary of Troy's business.

"Isn't that your husband, Peyton?" Sandra asked.

"Yes, but we've been estranged for a while. Brandon's father is at Major's farm in Florida recovering from a snake bite. He has been trying to find me and Brandon."

Stuart continued with a summary of the rivalry between Troy and Ben and the big meeting in Macon.

"They need to be stopped. Both of them," Judge said. "I have a question, though. If the two are put out of business, what would stop someone else from picking up one or both organizations where they left off?"

"I think we're seeing Troy's business seriously eroding from the raids on the camps in South Carolina, North Carolina, and Tennessee," Nate said.

Charo nodded. "And if Ben is trying to build up his own organization in the Orlando area, he doesn't have enough experienced people who are willing to work with him."

"I think we saw the disorganization on our last trip with the truck going south with the Mitchell twins and the other truck at Phil's roadblock with the three boys," Stuart said.

"So, who is going to Macon?" Judge asked.

"If you are asking this crowd," Scott said, "the whole lot of them are going. We need to look at making sure we're covered here and at the Websters' because even if Ben's and Troy's businesses are falling apart, we've still got the free-lancing home invaders robbing and burning homes."

"Let me take a first stab," Sandra said. "Jennie, Leo, Scott, me, Charo, Judge, Wynn, the kids, and the puppies stay here."

"Add me to your list, Sandra. I want to go, but I need to stay with Brandon," Peyton said.

"I'm another one," Nate said. "I'm not ready to be away from Charo, Dolly, and my dad quite yet."

"We're short on defense at the Webster farm," Scott said.

"The puppies and I can go back to the Webster farm," Wynn said. "With Ms. Jennie's permission, I'm a good shot with a rifle."

Stuart stared at Wynn. *Didn't see that coming.*

Aimee Louise said, "That's a good idea. We will have to talk to Ms. Jennie."

Rosalie tugged on Andy's sleeve; when he bent to listen, she whispered, "Angel said okay. It will work."

Andy straightened up and cleared his throat. "Thank you, Wynn. I'm sure Aunt Jennie will welcome your help. I'll go with you to talk to her."

"Next question: when is the team going?" Scott asked.

"Fairly soon, but we don't know when. It certainly won't be today, but it might be tomorrow. Leo is gathering information to help us with our planning," Stuart said.

"Nate, Peyton, and I are available for planning or as sounding boards, if you like," Charo said.

"Individually, or as a group," Nate said.

"If you give us an idea of how long you expect to be gone, Peyton and I can take care of planning and packing the food for you, Stuart," Sandra said.

"Thanks, Mom. I'm guessing three days, if all goes well."

"We'll plan on six."

"If there's nothing else, Wynn and I are going to the Websters' farm. You coming, Andy?" Stuart asked.

"Let's go."

"We have a shortcut, Wynn. We'll show you." Stuart pointed to the front yard.

On the way, Wynn said, "I like this much better than traveling on the road. I felt like a target every time my feet hit the pavement."

"I know exactly what you're talking about. It must have been even worse with the puppies."

As they reached the Webster farm, Andy told Wynn about the attack on Leo, and Wynn's eyes widened. "That's terrible. I never expected anyone to come out of the house in the storm. I never saw him. Is he okay?"

"He has swelling and bruises, but he's okay," Andy said. "I thought you should know."

When they went into the house, Jennie inspected each one of them. "You three look like a delegation. Do I need to sit?"

"I don't think so, Aunt Jennie." Andy said. "Let's go into the radio room, so Uncle Leo can listen if he's not too busy."

When the four of them went into the radio room, Leo removed his headset and peered at them expectantly.

"If you're in the middle of something, Uncle Leo, we don't want to interfere. We have some news to share," Andy said.

"Find a seat, if you can, and go ahead. I'll break away if I hear something."

Andy insisted that Jennie take the chair next to Leo's then explained the activities of Troy and Ben and told them that he, Stuart, and the young women were going to Macon. When he added that Wynn offered to stay with them to defend the farm, Jennie asked, "What do Angel and Red say?"

"Angel approves," Stuart said.

"Red agrees," Andy added.

"Double seal of approval. Can't get any better than that," Jennie said. "What do you prefer, Wynn? A rifle or a shotgun."

"I prefer a rifle," he said.

"I've got one you can try out. We'll go out to the practice range and you can get a feel for it. I don't know what you have in mind, but I'd feel safer with you in the house with us rather than in the barn. It will be easier to communicate, and I won't worry about you."

Wynn's eyes widened. "I didn't even think of—I'm fine with staying in the barn."

"In the house is better," Leo said. "It's not good to split up."

Wynn stared at Jennie and Leo. "Okay, if you'll let me cover Andy's chores while he's gone.".

"Let's take a walk outside, and I'll show you what I do every day and all the projects I haven't gotten around to yet," Andy said.

After they left, Jennie asked, "Who's going to Macon?"

"Andy, Aimee Louise, Rosalie, and me," Stuart said.

"That's good. Andy will be a good addition to your team, and the Newton farm will be adequately covered too. When will you leave, and how long do you expect to be gone?"

"Leo's gathering data for Aimee Louise to analyze, so we can determine the best time for us to leave, but it's hard to guess how long we'll be away because of the unexpected. We haven't made any final plans yet, but at a minimum, I'd guess three days. Mom's packing food for six days."

Jennie chuckled. "You all do seem to have a knack for the unpredictable."

Stuart shook his head. "Sometimes I wonder why we bother to plan. Of course, it does give Rosalie a chance to make a list, and we always use something she packed that I hadn't expected to need. In fact, I've finally learned the importance of her snacks."

"Do you need gas, or is your truck diesel?" Jennie asked.

"It's diesel. Aimee Louise could tell us how much we need because she keeps a close eye on our fuel, but I'll bet we're getting low."

"We've always kept gas on hand for our vehicles and diesel on hand for the farm truck and the tractors, but after we backed off going anywhere or farming crops, we've developed a backlog in the fuel shed that needs to be used in the next few months. Might as well use it now because we won't have any use for it before it goes bad."

"We'll bring a wagon over," Stuart said.

"I've got a wagon; you can return it when you bring back empty cans."

As Jennie moved the gas and diesel cans with the older dates to the front of the shed, she said, "Should have done this a long time ago, but I never had a need to rotate my fuel stock like this."

Stuart lifted the diesel cans into the wagon. "Are you sure you're comfortable with Wynn?" he asked.

Jennie stepped to the doorway. "When I was in the Army, I trained a lot of young people. When a person has a lifechanging breakthrough like Wynn did, it sticks. He always had a decided streak of loyalty to family when he was a kid. Nice to see he's accepted us as his extended family and discovered where his true loyalties lie. So, yes. I'm comfortable with Wynn."

As Stuart pulled the wagon toward the driveway he said, "I have a strong skeptical side that probably comes from my law enforcement experience, but I trust Aimee Louise's insights."

"She sees people in a way that the rest of us don't. Rare talent, there." Jennie smiled.

They reached the house at the same time as Andy and Wynn.

"I think Andy made up some extra projects for me," Wynn said.

"Who, me?" Andy raised his eyebrows in feigned surprise. "Consider it bonus homework."

Wynn smirked. "I'll make a list after they leave, Ms. Jennie, and you can prioritize the projects for me."

"You might be sorry, Wynn. She'll add some of her own," Andy said. "How do you think I got so many?"

The two of them chuckled as they headed into the house.

"Andy was skeptical at first too," Jennie said. "Good to see he agrees with you all."

When they went inside, Stuart said, "Andy, I can tell you what we usually pack in our go-bags. You can pull yours together."

"Y'all sit. I'll put on some coffee. I know Leo would like some," Jennie said.

As they sat, Wynn asked, "What's a go-bag?"

"It's a large backpack, like a hiker's pack, with essentials in case we have to walk home from somewhere. We always have our go-bags with us when we travel in the truck. Things like a change of socks, compass, space blanket, insect repellent, and other things; Rosalie has a list."

"I'll gather what I can think of then ask Rosalie for her list. I'm sure I'll forget something vital," Andy said.

"There's a hiker's pack in the attic, Andy." Jennie poured coffee then carried two cups to the radio room.

As Stuart held his cup to warm his hands, he said, "Pack a regular backpack with two changes of clothes and whatever else you want to have handy like an extra knife or a boonie hat."

Wynn furrowed his brow. "I feel like such a city-slicker. What's a boonie hat?"

Stuart smiled. "It's like a gardener's hat except its stiff brim isn't as wide, and the boonie hat can be rolled up; it's usually tan or camo. A boonie keeps the back of your neck from sunburning, and if you spray it with insect repellent, it keeps gnats away from your face."

"I need a boonie hat," Wynn said.

Jennie rushed into the kitchen. "Leo said Angel needs to hear what's going on."

Stuart rose. "I'll run get her."

"I'm with you." Andy slammed the door as they rushed out.

Stuart outran Andy on the path to the Smith farm, but Andy caught up as they neared the Newtons'.

When they reached the side of the house, Andy said, "Man, you can run fast."

"No, I can't. You'll see."

When they rushed into the house, Rosalie asked, "What's up?"

"Leo said Angel needs to hear what's going on," Stuart said.

"Go ahead," Sandra said. "We'll be fine here."

Aimee Louise waited while Rosalie grabbed her rifle then they raced out of the house.

"Wow. No way could I catch them," Andy said as he and Stuart headed toward the shortcut.

As they ran past the Smith barn, Stuart said, "I have a feeling we'll be leaving sooner than we thought. Ask Rosalie to help you finish up your packing, and I'll take the fuel to my dad's farm while Aimee Louise is on the radio."

"You're assuming she'll still be on the radio when we get there," Andy said.

Stuart snorted. "There is that."

After they went inside the farmhouse, Rosalie came out of the radio room. "We might leave early in the morning. Are you packed, Andy?"

"I need help with my go-bag," he said.

"I can look over what you have to see what else you need. Where is it?" Rosalie asked.

"In the attic. I haven't packed anything yet."

Rosalie blinked. "Get it. I'll give you a list of what you need."

Andy hurried to pull down the attic ladder and climb up for his bag.

Stuart headed to the door. "I've got a wagon full of fuel to haul to Dad's farm, and I have a few things to pack too."

"Wait for Aimee Louise. I don't think she'll be much longer. We'll see you there," Rosalie said.

When Aimee Louise came into the kitchen, Stuart said, "Ms. Jennie gave us some diesel, and we loaded it into a wagon to take to Dad's farm."

"Let's go," she said.

On the way to the Newton farm, Aimee Louise said, "From what everyone has pieced together, the meeting between the two leaders—the hams are calling the groups Old South and Beaches—is planned for Sunday morning in Macon across the river from the city park."

Stuart stopped to drag away large branches on the path that blocked the wagon's progress. "I'd like to hand this off to the Georgia Bureau of Investigation. If we have lunch on the road, we can be at the GBI office before the end of the day. If no one is there, we can push to go to the training center. What do you think?"

"Because the two groups are not familiar with each other, it will be easy for any GBI officers to infiltrate the meeting on Sunday." Aimee Louise steadied the fuel cans as the wagon rolled over uneven ground.

"If we don't make it to the training center in time today, do you think anyone will be there tomorrow?"

"Doubtful, but Leo gave me the address of a ham if we can't find anyone today. He'll find a contact for us."

Stuart frowned. "The guy gave out his address over the air? That's not good."

"True, except after the grid went down but before the other systems failed, Leo exported the names and addresses of all the hams in Georgia and printed it. It's in call sign order. He isn't the only ham who did that. Mr. Young has a list of the Florida hams."

"I'll ask Mom to pack our lunch," Stuart said. "I need to replace my dull chainsaw chains and finish packing."

"Rosalie and I are packed. I'll take care of the fuel."

"We may be ready when Rosalie and Andy get here."

"Yes."

While Stuart hurried to the equipment shed to swap his chains, Aimee Louise filled the truck's tank then strapped one of the cans to the back of the truck. Stuart and Scott walked to the truck in deep discussion.

"Dad, these are the fuel cans I was telling you about."

"I'll put them into our fuel shed and will return the Websters' cans after you all leave. Anything else I can do to help?" Scott asked.

"We may need to camp out tonight and tomorrow night," Aimee Louise said. "Do you have any camping equipment we could use?"

"On it," Scott said as the three of them hurried to the house.

"Mom, we'll leave as soon as we load up. Would you mind packing lunches for the road?"

"Already done," Sandra smiled as she pointed to the table. "There's the food for your trip, and this bag is Rosalie's snacks."

Nate came into the kitchen. "Stuart, I know I said I couldn't go, but Charo and I have been talking. I know some of the agents on

Troy's list, and I also have some GBI contacts. I need to go along. I'm packed and ready."

Stuart stared at him. "Nate, you'd be an unbelievable addition to the team. Are you sure?"

Charo rolled into the kitchen. "Yes. We both are. I'll go too if you need an undercover woman in a wheelchair with a mouthy kid in tow and a hovering father-in-law."

Sandra snickered. "Now I want to go, just to see that."

"What do you think, Angel?" Nate asked.

"Good. We need you," she said. "Let's load your bags and rifle."

Stuart kissed his mom, and she hugged Aimee Louise. "Be safe," Sandra whispered.

When they reached the truck, Stuart hopped into the pickup bed, and Nate handed him the gear.

"Rosalie will want to ride in the back. It's her favorite observation point. I'll bet she'll want Andy to ride with her. You'll probably have the backseat to yourself, Nate," Stuart said.

As they loaded the gear, Rosalie and Andy rounded the house and headed to the truck.

"You're going, right, Nate?" Rosalie asked as she peered into the back of the truck. "Perfect. Extra blankets for seats. Andy will ride in the back with me."

"Toss me your bags then load up, and we can go," Stuart said. "Your snacks are in the food box that Mom packed, Red, and you're in charge of handing out the lunches when we get on the road."

Scott and Henry sauntered to the truck as Stuart headed toward the passenger's seat. Scott hugged his son. "Be safe. I know you will, but I feel better saying it."

Henry ran to Aimee Louise and hugged her. "Don't forget me, Angel. I won't forget you."

Aimee Louise returned his hug. "I could never forget my Henry."

CHAPTER FIFTEEN

Scott and Henry stood together and waved as Aimee Louise drove past the front of the house to the shortcut. She navigated the winding Smith driveway to the road while Stuart studied the map.

"We'll stay on the state highway until we get about twenty-five miles from Macon," Stuart said. "The map doesn't show any alternatives to the interstate, but I'm sure Andy can point us to a side road that won't cost us too much time."

"Lunch," Rosalie handed Nate a small sack. "Biscuit and tomato sandwiches. We've got water to drink. Hang onto your bottles for refills." Nate took the three bottles from her.

"Did everybody get a sandwich?" Nate asked.

"Sure did," Rosalie said.

Nate frowned. "Sandra had the lunches packed before Charo and I came into the kitchen. How did that happen?"

"Mom-magic," Rosalie said. "Also, exceptional hearing."

"I can believe it," Nate chuckled. "Charo is always two steps ahead of me. Dad told me once I think too loud. So, what's the plan?"

"Rosalie, make sure Andy is where he can hear too," Stuart said.

Rosalie shifted to make room for Andy at the window. "We're set, Stuart," she said.

"Peyton's husband, Troy, is involved in human trafficking. His thugs have been kidnapping children in Florida, transporting them to camps in South Carolina and other states then the children are sold from there. North and South Carolina and Tennessee cracked down on the camps, so he's struggling. His brother, Ben, has started up a similar operation of kidnapping children in Georgia and South Carolina and transporting them to Florida. We have reliable reports that Troy and Ben are meeting in Macon on Sunday. It's supposed to be a consolidation discussion, but it will more likely be a takeover by one of the brothers."

"You said Troy is Peyton's husband?" Andy asked.

"I should have said estranged. Peyton was in the process of divorcing him," Stuart said. "Peyton memorized a list of law enforcement officers who work with Troy or who are sympathetic to Troy's criminal business. Troy believes that Peyton has his list, but his brother Ben has it. Ben may believe that Peyton has a copy. If Ben takes over Troy's organization, that list is key to helping him rapidly expand his business."

"So, are we taking on the two organizations?" Rosalie asked. "Shouldn't we have packed more ammo?"

Stuart furrowed his brow to keep from smirking. *No matter how bad the odds might be, Rosalie's ready to step up to a fight.*

"No, we're going to tell the Georgia Bureau of Investigation about the meeting and give them Peyton's list. It's significant that no one from GBI is on the list."

"Did she give you her copy or write it down for you?" Rosalie asked.

"Neither one," Stuart said. "She recited it to Aimee Louise, and Aimee Louise will recite it to the GBI. We're hoping to get to the office before they close today. If we don't, we've got the address of a ham operator who has a GBI contact."

"Are we going to the meeting on Sunday if we get the information to GBI?" Andy asked.

"There doesn't seem to be any reason to go," Stuart said.

"Might be," Nate said. "I know Troy and Ben."

"But what about the people who know you?" Rosalie asked.

"For all they know, I work for the other brother," Nate said.

"That's not very reassuring," Andy said.

"Car coming up fast behind us," Rosalie said.

Stuart peered out his side mirror then scanned the road ahead. "There's a driveway up ahead. Turn like we've arrived at our destination, Aimee Louise."

After she slowed the truck and turned at the driveway, Aimee Louise continued down the winding, overgrown path. She cleared a curve then drove the truck into the brush before the car sped by.

"I don't think they saw us at all," Rosalie said as Aimee Louise backed out of the brush and resumed travel on the state road.

As Aimee Louise sped up, Rosalie said, "I forgot. We have cookies." She handed out the sugar-cinnamon sprinkled cookies that Sandra had packed.

Stuart snickered. *Dad's always said that Mom's cookies calm the savage beasts.*

When she finished munching on her cookie, Rosalie asked, "Do you have the radio on? I just realized I haven't heard anything since we left."

"You're right. I would have thought there would be more chatter too, especially with how close we are to the interstate." Stuart checked the list of repeater frequencies and the radio's setting then adjusted the radio. "I changed to a repeater that is closer to Macon."

After a quiet, uneventful hour, Aimee Louise slowed.

"Andy, we're getting close to the exit for the interstate. Is there another way we can go?" Stuart asked.

Andy leaned through the opening to the cab and peered at the roadway ahead. "In about a mile, our road curves to the left; if we went to the right, we'd come to the ramp for the interstate. After five miles, we'll come to a stop sign. Turn right."

Andy remained at the opening to monitor their route of travel. "That was our curve even though it wasn't as much of a curve as I remembered."

"More signs of habitation around here than we usually see." Stuart pointed to a house with a dog on the porch near the road.

After Aimee Louise stopped then turned right, Andy said, "We're about twenty minutes from the office. It will be on our right."

"When we get to the building, I'll see if there's anyone there, Stuart," Nate said. "Then I'll come get you and Aimee Louise."

Aimee Louise slowed when she approached the building and turned to park in their lot. When Nate stepped out of the truck, Rosalie slipped through the opening to the cab.

"No fair," Andy said. "I can't fit through that tiny window."

"Too bad." Rosalie snickered. "I need to be up here in case we need a quick getaway while you're back there to watch."

After Nate went inside the building, Stuart, Rosalie, and Andy peered at the building while Aimee Louise scanned their surroundings.

A half hour later, Nate came out of the building with another man who was younger and slimmer than Nate, but not as tall. Stuart stepped out and waited by the side of the truck.

"Stuart, this an old friend of mine, Bob."

Bob smiled and extended his hand. "Nice to meet you, Stuart."

Stuart shook Bob's hand, and Nate said, "Let's get Aimee Louise and go inside."

Stuart motioned for Aimee Louise, and she joined the men.

Nate introduced Aimee Louise to Bob. Stuart was surprised when Bob nodded, and Aimee Louise returned his nod.

Nate prepared Bob for Aimee Louise.

After the four of them were inside, Bob said, "I know Major. He taught my first advanced shooting class. We have a large conference room with windows, and we all use it. Our radios were solar-powered before the grid went down because we had a newbie that swore it would work. We've moved our operations into the one room because of the windows."

When they walked into the conference room, a woman in a wheelchair was on the radio with a headset. Bob led them to a table on the other side of the room.

After they sat, Bob said, "Nate gave me a quick rundown on why you all are here, and I've contacted the leader of the task force investigating the trafficking, and she is sending a team here."

"Stuart, would you go over the background information?" Nate asked.

Stuart described Troy's organization then Ben's. Bob took notes and occasionally interrupted for questions. After Stuart explained the details about Troy's list of traitorous agents, Bob added, "I'm very well acquainted with Troy Romero and his brother, Ben. It's too bad they've made Peyton a target, but I'm grateful she managed to see the list and that she gave it to you. She's greatly respected here at GBI. I'm not a bit surprised that she could memorize a list of twenty-five names with a quick glance."

Stuart glanced at Nate then the two of them chuckled.

"She didn't exactly give us the note," Nate said. "We don't have anything in writing."

Bob frowned. "Then what do you have? A recording?"

"Peyton told me the list," Aimee Louise said. "I can repeat it when you're ready to write it down."

The woman at the radio set her headset down on her table then turned toward the conference table. "I'll transcribe. I'm fast."

"True," Bob said. "I'll take over the radio."

Bob hurried to the radio table while the woman wheeled toward Aimee Louise with her notepad in her lap. Her brown eyes twinkled when she rolled to the table. "I'm Delilah. I was the upstart newbie that set up the solar-powered radio system."

"I love radios. I'm a ham radio operator," Aimee Louise said.

"You're Angel, aren't you? It's a pleasure to meet you." Delilah beamed.

Stuart's eyes widened as Aimee Louise extended her hand, and the two women shook.

"I'm ready when you are, Angel." Delilah poised her pen over her notebook.

Aimee Louise recited the names in the same tone that Peyton used.

"I'll read them back to you." Delilah read her list, and Aimee Louise nodded.

"I have a radio question for you, if you have a little time," Delilah said.

While Aimee Louise and Delilah were deep in conversation, Stuart and Nate stepped into the hallway.

"When those two shook hands, I could have sworn I saw sparks," Nate said. "Have you ever seen Angel in such a deep conversation?"

"Never with anyone she just met, and I've never seen her shake hands with anyone," Stuart said. "Can we head back today in good conscience?"

"Yes. The GBI team will step in, and the information that Peyton shared through Aimee Louise will crush Troy and Ben," Nate said. "I don't know what the plans are for Sunday's meeting, of course, but I wouldn't be surprised if the task force leader has a few men embedded in Troy's organization. One of them may have jumped ship to infiltrate Ben's new venture. The list is more than likely the big break the team was waiting for. I'm guessing the highlight of Sunday's meeting will be a complete collapse of the two organizations. In a way, I'm almost sad we won't be here to see it, but I want to get back too."

"Let's see if we can break up the electronic wizards, so we can hit the road," Stuart said.

When they returned to the conference room, Delilah glanced up. "Your men are getting restless. I guess it's time for you to go." She took Aimee Louise's hands in hers. "It was a pleasure to talk electronic bits and bytes with a kindred Elmer." Delilah chuckled, and Aimee Louise smiled.

"What's an Elmer?" Nate whispered.

"It's a ham radio term for an old, knowledgeable radio operator," Stuart replied in a soft voice.

Aimee Louise rose to join Stuart and Nate, and Delilah relieved Bob at the radio.

"Wheels are in motion," Bob said when he reached the three who waited near the door. "The task force leader asked for the list on CW—that's morse code; I only know because Delilah told me once that it used to be required for an amateur radio license."

When the three of them climbed into the truck, Andy said, "I sure am glad to see you. Red was about to storm the building."

Rosalie snorted. "Only because Andy told me to."

"I know that's not true. No way would Andy have lost his mind and tried to tell you to do anything." Nate laughed, and Andy chuckled.

Rosalie stuck her tongue out at Nate then landed with a thump in her haste to slide through the window into the pickup bed, and Nate and Andy laughed harder.

"Do we go back the way we came?" Aimee Louise asked when she started the engine.

"Andy, what do you think?" Stuart asked.

"I still think it's safer than the interstate," Andy said.

Aimee Louise turned out of the parking lot and headed toward the Newton farm.

As they continued south on the state road, Nate pointed to the southwest. "That's a lot of smoke."

Stuart narrowed his eyes. "It's an active fire. See how it's billowing?"

"Try another frequency," Aimee Louise said.

Stuart consulted his list and changed the frequency on the radio.

After a few minutes, the squelch broke: "… brush fire … evacuate…"

Stuart squinted at the rising smoke. "It's hard to tell which way it's spreading. Are we likely to cross its path?"

Andy came to the window. "Rosalie's checking."

Rosalie joined Andy. "The wind from the northwest is brisk. It's driving the fire. We need to be farther east."

Andy added, "We'll have to travel on the interstate for at least twenty miles before we know we're far enough south for the fire to miss us."

"I'm not crazy about being on a highly traveled road that is a prime target for highway robbers," Stuart said.

Andy nodded. "We have the alternative when we're on the interstate to watch the fire and reassess in ten miles. That will be our last chance to divert and maintain going south. After that, we'd have to turn back north to get away from the fire if it continues its current direction."

"What do you think, Angel?" Nate asked.

"State road." Aimee Louise increased her speed.

"Okay. Rosalie, let us know if the fire or wind changes direction, and I'll check the map to see if there are any alternatives east of the interstate."

After twenty minutes, Rosalie announced, "Wind is increasing, and the smoke area is much wider. We should go farther east as soon as we can. It doesn't look good."

Nate and Stuart peered out their windows to the west. "She's right, Stuart," Nate said.

"I think I've found something," Stuart said. "Make the turn to the interstate, Aimee Louise, but continue past the interstate on the overpass then we'll come to a road that goes southeast. It's not toward the farm, but it's away from the fire. After we feel like it's safe, we can turn west. Not ideal, but it's the best I have for the circumstances."

After they were east of the interstate, Rosalie said, "We found a sack in the food box marked *Emergency Snacks*. Andy and I voted, and it was unanimous. This is an emergency. Snack, anyone?"

Nate chuckled. "I don't snack except in emergencies."

Aimee Louise nodded, and Stuart said, "We agree. This is an emergency."

"We've got crackers and a small jar of jam. I'll make cracker and jam sandwiches for us, and Andy will pass them to you."

"Sticky." Aimee Louise licked her fingers after she finished her jam crackers.

"This is good. Is this how your mom was when you were growing up?" Nate asked.

"Sure is. Dad told me she made snacks, so she could keep track of who I was hanging out with, and if any of them acted up, they didn't get snacks. She trained an entire class of boys to be polite and wash their hands." Stuart chuckled.

Aimee Louise slowed. "Roadblock ahead. Nowhere to turn."

"On alert back there. Roadblock." Stuart lowered his window, and Nate lowered both back windows.

"I've got the driver's side window, and Andy's positioned at the passenger's side," Rosalie called out.

A man with a feed store logo on his frayed ballcap and a paunch that strained across his overalls held a shotgun in the crook of his arm. Aimee Louise stopped twenty yards away and leaned out her window while she waved.

The man narrowed his eyes then scooted the flimsy wooden saw horse that was his roadblock out of the middle of the road. "You don't look like a home invader, young lady."

"Windows closed. Everybody down," Stuart hissed as he placed his rifle on the floor under his feet. Nate raised his dark-tinted windows before he scrunched down on the floor.

When Aimee Louise reached him, he raised his hand, and she stopped.

He asked, "Evacuating from the fire?"

"Trying to go south to get home, but the fire chased us away from our usual road."

He nodded. "There's some bad yahoos with a roadblock a few miles ahead. Turn right at the next road you come to. It's a dirt road, but it'll be worth it because you'll skip them."

"Thank you, sir," she said.

"Any time, young lady. Be careful." He peered at Stuart. "You aren't being kidnapped, are you?"

"No, this is my boyfriend. He worked all night, so I'm driving."

Stuart nodded and yawned.

"Smart. Got to work when you can find it. Get along, now. Y'all be safe."

Nate moaned as he rose to the seat. "I want to ride in the back if we have to hide again. I could lie down on those quilts and stay put for an hour or so at a time."

"You just caught on to why nobody's complaining about you having the back seat to yourself," Andy said.

"Looks like a driveway, but that might be our road coming up," Stuart said.

Aimee Louise slowed then turned. "The road sign was knocked down and is in the weeds."

"Road's going to be bumpy," Stuart called out then held onto his armrest as the truck bounced as it crossed a rut.. "Rough road. Glad we have four-wheel drive."

"Good news is we shouldn't run across any roadblocks or raiders," Nate said.

After a half-hour of creeping on the bone-jarring road, Rosalie asked, "How much longer are we on this road?"

Stuart checked the map and frowned. "I don't see it on the map."

"Guess it doesn't matter because we're on it, and I don't think it's taking us toward the fire, but I'll check."

A few minutes later, Rosalie said, "We are going in the right direction because, even though I can see fire in the smoke now, we're making a little progress in moving away from it."

"Oh, man," Nate said. "Look out your other window, Rosalie. I see smoke on the east side."

"That doesn't make sense," Andy said. "We're not in a dry season by any stretch."

The squelch broke on the radio: "Wild fires…shut down…interstate…"

"That doesn't sound good. What do you think, Nate?" Stuart picked up the map while Nate examined the smoke to the west then to the east.

Stuart studied the map then rubbed his eyes before he leaned back in the seat. "My eyes need a break before I try to come up with any options."

Nate leaned on the front seat and said softly, "We should keep going south. If we turn back, we'll get caught in the fire to our west. Do you want a second set of eyes, Stuart?"

"Thanks, Nate. I'd appreciate it." Stuart handed him the map.

After five minutes of staring at the map, Nate said, "I think I see something. Angel's friend knew what he was doing when he sent us this way."

Stuart turned in his seat, and Nate pointed. "See this faint blue line that looks like a creek? I think it might be a county road, and our dirt road may end there." Nate traced the light blue line with his finger. "It goes to the southwest and continues over or under the highway." Nate squinted at the map. "I can't really tell."

"It ends at our state road not too far north of Dad's farm. That's a long way for a little creek to go then suddenly end at a state road."

"Right," Nate said.

"We'll keep an eye on the fires," Andy said.

Nate handed back the map, and Stuart leaned back in his seat.

He gazed at Aimee Louise. "So, I'm your boyfriend?"

She tilted her head. "You aren't my kidnapper."

Touché.

Nate snorted and poked Stuart in the back.

"Do you need a tissue, Nate?" Rosalie giggled.

Oh, great. Rosalie and Andy heard too.

"Dolly told me you have everything, including remarkable hearing, Rosalie," Nate said. "So far, you're living up to your reputation."

When Aimee Louise came to a stop sign, she released her tight grip on the steering wheel and wiggled her fingers. "That was a hard road to travel."

As they traveled on the narrow, two-lane road, Stuart pointed to a sign. "County road—you called it, Nate. Thanks."

When they approached the overpass, Aimee Louise said, "There's more than one man hiding in the high grass on the other side of the overpass. I'm not slowing down."

Stuart and Nate lowered their windows, and Rosalie and Andy opened the topper's side windows.

As she sped across the overpass, four men appeared with pistols. Two men on opposite sides of the road aimed at the truck. Stuart shot one on the right; Nate shot the one on the left. The other two men jumped close to the road, and Stuart smirked when the man on the right side dropped with a shattered knee. Andy shot the man on the driver's side of the truck. A fifth man hefted a fifty-five-gallon drum barrel at the truck; Aimee Louise swerved to miss it as the man dropped to the ground with shattered knees.

"Both knees, Dead Eye?" Nate asked.

"Second knee was for the second barrel behind him," she said. "Just in case."

"You definitely took that idea out of his head," Nate said.

"What's our next turn?" Aimee Louise continued on the county road.

"We'll turn left at the state road." Stuart turned to the back. "How are we doing in relation to the fires?"

"East fire is less of a threat. It's not moving toward us anymore," Rosalie said. "At the angle we're headed, we should be well clear of the west fire too."

After they cleared the interstate, Stuart pointed to the cars partially hidden in the trees on both sides of the road. "It would have been hard to see the robbers at night."

"Looks like they've been doing this a while." Nate frowned as he shook his head. "If nothing else, I'm glad I came along to see them stopped."

As they continued west, Stuart said, "Look at the sunset."

"I never took the time to look at a sunset. Being out in the country definitely has its advantages," Nate said.

Andy and Rosalie leaned in the window. "That orange and red looks like the sun set the horizon on fire. Reminds me of you, Red." Andy hugged Rosalie, and she smiled.

"The fire or the color?" Nate asked.

Rosalie snickered. "I looked so much like Mom that her friends call me Mom's mini-me. One of them said I had the same fire as Mom too. Mom laughed and said our fire could warm or burn without warning."

"That's the truth," Andy mumbled.

"I'm like two inches from you, and I have exceptional hearing on top of that," Rosalie said.

"I didn't say anything. I thought something, and you eavesdropped," Andy said with a straight face, and Nate and Stuart laughed.

Rosalie growled, "Not funny."

"I have a question," Nate said. "Will we be getting back to the farm too late for supper?"

Stuart snorted. "When we walk into the house, no matter what time it is, Mom's first words will be that we're just in time for supper. No one goes hungry at the farm."

"I wonder if that's what Wynn's problem has been," Andy said. "He's needed someone to care enough to be sure he didn't go hungry for food or a sense of belonging. Wasn't it Napoleon who said, 'An army marches on its stomach.'?"

"Interesting observation, especially since an army develops a sense of camaraderie," Nate said.

"Y'all are getting too philosophical for me." Rosalie disappeared then reappeared with a sack. "Anybody interested in this sack that Mama Sandra labeled *Late Afternoon*?"

Nate laughed. "Mama Sandra knows her army so well. I'll take it."

When Nate opened the sack, he peered inside. "Thought it was heavy for crackers. We have satsumas, if I'm not mistaken, which are related to tangerines, except they are seedless. I heard they grow well in south Georgia." He handed two pieces of fruit to Stuart and took one for himself then handed the sack back to Rosalie.

"I'll peel yours for you." After Stuart peeled one of the satsumas, he handed individual sections to Aimee Louise.

"This is good," Nate said. "Charo's been saying since I'm out of a job we need to become farmers."

Aimee Louise turned on the headlights.

"We should be coming up to the state road soon," Stuart said.

Rosalie passed the sack to Nate. "Trash."

Nate collected Stuart's peels and added his then handed the sack back.

Stuart raised forward in his seat. "Someone's on the side of the road waving a light."

Aimee Louise said, "Too dark to get a good look at his cloud, but not a danger cloud. I'll slow down."

Aimee Louise slowed then eased closer as the man stepped into the roadway. Stuart lowered his window. "You need help?"

"Got a flat. I thought I'd hit a deer, but when I got out to check, two guys jumped out and started shooting. I shot back, and I think I winged one of them. They ran off, but they shot my tire, and it's flat. I've been trying to change it, but I'm worried they might try to sneak up on me when my back's turned."

"We can help," Stuart said as he jumped out. Andy hopped out of the back of the truck while Nate grabbed a flashlight before he stepped out to watch for traffic.

Stuart and Andy changed the tire as the man watched the woods. When they were finished, the man shook their hands.

"Thanks a lot, fellas. You going to the state road? I hear there's a roadblock three miles to the north, but going south should be clear."

The man hurried to his truck then drove away while Stuart, Andy, and Nate climbed into theirs.

As Aimee Louise accelerated, Stuart said, "He told us the state road is clear going south."

"If there's any trouble, we'll find it," Nate said.

When they came to the state road, Aimee Louise turned left. When she made the final turn toward the Newtons' farm, Stuart asked, "Rosalie, did Mom pack any more sacks?"

"I'm not saying. Not my job to ruin the mom mystique." Rosalie snickered.

After Aimee Louise turned at the Smith driveway, Stuart asked, "Do you want to be dropped off when we get to the barn, Andy?"

"That's a good idea. Saves me the extra few steps," Andy said.

"I'm going to the Websters too," Rosalie said. "I'll get the report from Leo, and if there's any news, I'll be back tonight. Otherwise, I'll see you in the morning when you come over for the radio call."

After they reached the charred and crumbling chimney, Rosalie and Andy climbed out of the truck with their backpacks and rifles.

"Will we see Rosalie later tonight?" Stuart asked.

"Yes," Aimee Louise said.

As Aimee Louise rounded the corner of the house, Scott strolled from the barn to meet them.

"How do you know?" Nate asked as Aimee Louise parked.

"There will be news."

Stuart snorted at Nate's puzzled look then climbed out to greet his dad.

"How was your trip?" Scott asked after he hugged his son. "We didn't expect you home so soon."

"We didn't need to stay for the meeting because GBI has a team in place, and Peyton's information was exactly what they needed. Troy's and Ben's organizations will collapse."

"Where's Rosalie?" Scott peered into the back of the truck as Stuart climbed inside to pull their gear for unloading.

"She and Andy got out at the Smith farm to walk to the Websters'. According to Aimee Louise, we'll see them later this evening."

"Did you run into any trouble?" Scott asked as Nate grabbed gear to take inside.

"Just this team's usual," Nate said.

While Nate and Aimee Louise carried the gear into the house, Stuart told his father about their trip.

"Y'all see more trouble in one day than most folks do in a lifetime. If your mother hears about all this, don't be surprised if she grounds the whole lot of you," Scott said.

"No kidding," Stuart chuckled.

When they carried the rest of the gear and the food boxes into the house, Nate met them at the door.

"Guess what? Your mom said we're just in time for supper. Good thing because I'm starved." Nate beamed, and Stuart laughed.

"Sure am glad to see you get your appetite back, Son." The judge hurried into the kitchen and hugged Nate while Dolly raced down the hallway as she pushed Charo's wheelchair.

Charo would have crashed into the table if Nate hadn't stopped her. Dolly jumped up on a chair and wrapped her arms around his neck. "You surprised us, Daddy. We missed you all day."

Nate hugged Dolly and kissed Charo.

CHAPTER SIXTEEN

Henry ran down the hallway and hugged Aimee Louise. "Welcome home, Angel. I'm glad you're back, and Deputy Stuart too."

While Aimee Louise hugged Henry, Stuart wrapped his arms around both of them. "It's good to be together," Stuart said.

"Wash your hands, travelers," Sandra said. "I'm ready to dish up your supper. Where's Rosalie?"

"She'll be here later," Nate said. "She's checking the radio news."

Sandra nodded. "Most likely with Andy."

Peyton and Brandon came into the kitchen.

"You're back early," she said. "Did everything go okay?"

"Better than we expected. Message delivered, and the wheels are in motion," Nate said. "There was no reason for us to stay any longer."

"That's a relief." Peyton dropped into a kitchen chair. "Details later?"

"Yes," Aimee Louise said.

"Where's Rosalie?" Peyton scanned the room.

"She'll be here later with Mr. Andy," Dolly said. "They want to listen to the radio news first."

"How do you know?" Brandon asked.

"My dad told us."

"Why don't we get baths out of the way?" Peyton asked.

"I'll help," Judge said as Peyton lifted the large pot of hot water off the stove to warm the bathwater.

Dolly and Brandon dashed to their respective bathrooms to undress for their baths. Henry hugged Aimee Louise then left the kitchen.

Sandra placed two platters of flatbread on the table then dished up soup into bowls. "It's hot," she said. "Root vegetable noodle soup."

Nate blew on his soup then took a bite. "Umm. Really good. Carrots, turnips, and sweet potatoes with homemade noodles and rosemary." He dropped a piece of flatbread into his bowl, then dished up the soup-soaked bread with his spoon.

Sandra laughed. "You have the palate of a gourmet."

After they ate, Stuart and Aimee Louise cleared the table while Nate washed dishes.

"The judge and I took Dolly to visit Sam and Cami today," Scott said. "The Mitchells appreciated having the company as much as the twins did. They're trying to find someone to take over their son's farm. They don't want it to be looted and trashed. On our way back, the judge told me Charo would love their greenhouse."

"Charo has always wanted a greenhouse, but it didn't make any sense in Miami," Nate said.

"Dolly wanted to go back to play with the girls tomorrow, but the judge and I convinced her that next week would be better because we wanted to wait for you all to come home," Charo said. "Maybe I'll be strong enough that I can go too."

After Nate finished the dishes, the children ran to the kitchen and sat at the table. "Bath, snack, bed," Dolly sang.

"Here you are." Sandra gave each child two crackers then inhaled. "You all smell clean."

"We scrubbed," Henry said.

"I scrubbed too," Dolly said.

When the snacks were devoured, Aimee Louise and Peyton accompanied the boys to bed, and Nate accompanied Dolly.

After the children were settled, Aimee Louise, Peyton, and Nate joined the rest of the adults in the kitchen. Scott poured hot tea while Sandra poured coffee for Charo, the judge, and Scott.

The sound of footsteps thudded on the back porch then Rosalie and Andy burst into the house. Andy was winded.

"We've got news," Rosalie said. "David is feeling much better. The swelling is going down, and he's been walking. Dr. Jody is going to check him this evening to let him know when he can travel. Aunt Vanessa is giving him her car. Don't you know Pops is relieved?"

"He's well enough to travel? Where's he going?" Peyton asked.

"Here, of course," Rosalie said. "I guess I forgot to say that. I'll bet there was all kinds of discussion about the farm rule that no one travels alone."

Peyton smiled. "I'll bet David played his visitor card and claimed the family rule didn't apply to him."

"I'll bet he did too, and Molly had fits," Stuart chuckled.

"She's certainly entitled," Sandra said. "Nobody's exempt from the house rules."

"That's all we have," Rosalie said. "It was too good to save until morning. We'll see you tomorrow."

As Rosalie rose from her chair, Andy moaned. "We're going back right away?"

"Sure." Rosalie headed to the door, and Andy pushed himself to his feet. "She runs fast."

"Tell me about it," Stuart said as they left.

"I'm excited and terrified," Peyton said. "I can't help but think of all the things that have happened to all of us on the road."

"But David walked through the woods and swamps from Orlando to Plainview and survived a cottonmouth snake bite to find you and Brandon. I don't think any puny thugs will slow him down," Nate said.

Charo giggled. "Puny thugs."

Peyton sighed. "You're right. He's not a target like we were, either. And on top of all that, he wrangled Vanessa's car." Peyton snort-laughed.

"Why is that funny?" Charo tilted her head.

"Vanessa is the absolute worst driver ever, even though she insists she's a great driver. Major won't allow her to drive since she crashed the farm's UTV. She was ejected and had a serious leg injury; Aimee Louise wore her seatbelt but still had a concussion. No one's actually told Vanessa she can't drive anymore, but it always is not quite convenient. I can't imagine what David could have said to talk her out of her car," Stuart said. "Of course, maybe Major—"

Stuart was interrupted by the sound of gunshots. Stuart, Scott, Peyton, and Nate jumped for their rifles, and Charo rolled to her room for hers as the judge and Sandra grabbed their shotguns.

"Came from the Websters'," Aimee Louise said.

Several shots hit the front of the house. "We're being invaded. To your stations," Scott said.

Sandra blew out the candle on the table and took her place at the kitchen sink where she cracked open the window for her shotgun. The judge dashed up the stairs to the boys' room, and Peyton followed him to cover the kitchen door from an upstairs window.

"Where do I go?" Nate asked.

"Upstairs. Your dad is in the boys' bedroom. Take a window to cover the front from the second floor. I'll be in the living room," Scott said.

"I'm going out the kitchen door and flank them," Stuart said as he rushed to the door. Aimee Louise slipped out with him.

When Stuart dashed to the truck, Aimee Louise stayed with him. "What are you doing here?" he whispered as the sound of gunfire from the Webster's continued.

"Follow me," she said.

Aimee Louise headed through the trees to the driveway. "There. Climb a tree." She pointed to the small grove of trees. She raced up the driveway before Stuart could say anything.

He slipped to the grove and climbed the tallest tree.

I count four men in the field.

After he dropped the first man with a shot to the head, his dad fired at the men, and Nate fired from the second story. Stuart aimed at a second man who fell from his deadly shot. A third man crawled toward the farther end of the house. When he rose to rush the house, Nate shot him.

Stuart heard his mother's shotgun at the back of the house then a single rifle shot. *Charo.*

Three men who were hidden in the trees close to the house rapid-fired at the first and second floor windows where Nate and Scott were stationed.

Can't get a clear shot.

The gunfire continued from the trees, and Stuart frowned as he realized they were providing cover for someone. He scanned the area then saw a man who crept toward the kitchen door. Stuart lifted his rifle to aim, but the man dropped from a single shot from the second floor. *Peyton.*

"He's down," one of the men in the trees shouted.

"Keep shooting," another replied. "Might be part of his plan."

The constant honking of a horn at the highway interrupted the gunfire. Stuart smiled. *They left the keys at their vehicle. Aimee Louise set off their horn.*

A man in the field shouted. "Somebody's stealing the truck." When he stood up, Stuart shot him.

The men in the trees had rushed the house but froze midway. "What do we do now?" one yelled.

Stuart shot him; Nate and Scott shot the other two.

After one more shot at the Websters', the gunfire ceased then the repeated honking stopped.

Stuart climbed down and remained still in the grove as he scanned for any motion in the field or trees near the house.

The hoot of a barred owl came from the trees near the truck, and Stuart answered the call.

Aimee Louise appeared next to him and whispered, "Clear here?"

"I think so."

"Go inside to talk," she said quietly.

After they were inside the house, she said, "We need to go to the Smith barn to meet Rosalie."

Stuart called out. "We're going to the Smith farm. We'll cross in front of the house and take the shortcut. Stay alert. We'll use the barred owl call when we return. Answer so we know it's safe to continue."

"Got it," Scott said as Charo, Nate, Peyton, and the judge acknowledged Stuart.

Sandra continued to peer out the kitchen window. "Be safe."

Stuart and Aimee Louise slipped out of the house and around to the short cut. Stuart led the way. He stopped every few feet and listened then continued.

When they reached the barn, they still hadn't heard any more shots.

"The barn?" Stuart asked.

"Yes, but outside."

They stood at the corner of the building while they waited, but they hadn't dressed for a drop in temperature, and the night air and the wind from the northwest chilled them. When Aimee Louise shivered, Stuart wrapped his arms around her.

The sound of a barred owl reached them, and Aimee Louise replied. The barred owl called a second time, and Aimee Louise answered. Stuart whistled his cardinal call, and Rosalie and Andy came out of the field to the barn.

"It's turning colder. Can we go inside the barn?" Andy asked when they joined them.

The four of them went inside the barn.

"They killed Wynn," Rosalie said. "When the gunfire started, he ran to the barn. Andy and I stepped outside to cover him, but a man was waiting next to the barn, and he shot Wynn. I took a Stuart shot, and the man dropped. We hurried to Wynn, but he was already—"

"Gone," Andy said.

"Yes. Then the raid started on the house, and Andy and I were stuck in the barn, but the attackers didn't know that. It ended up being an excellent advantage. We cleared the back of the house while Ms. Jennie cleared the front. Two men tried to break in the side window, but Mr. Leo stopped them. Then the truck horn went off, and it caused a lot of confusion. One of the bad guys shot another one then a third bad guy shot the second."

"Aunt Jennie dropped the last one. We heard the shooting at the Newton's farm. Is everyone okay?" Andy asked.

"Yes. Everyone's okay."

"We ran to the house after the horn stopped," Rosalie said. "Andy kept up with me."

"No way was she going to leave me. After we waited in the house for a while and there was no more gunfire, Rosalie said we needed to come to the Smith farm. Aunt Jennie and Uncle Leo are still on alert."

"What do you think?" Rosalie asked. "Was this a last-ditch effort by Troy to stop Wynn and Peyton or was it a coincidence of a random attack?"

"Troy," Aimee Louise said.

"I agree," Andy said. "What do we do?"

"This attack showed me that we can't leave," Stuart said.

Rosalie narrowed her eyes. "Explain."

"Charo and the judge want to move to the Mitchell house. That takes three shooters out of Dad's house. When David arrives, I'm not sure that he and Peyton will stay very long at Dad's; they may join the Cabellos. That leaves three shooters at the Websters' and two at Dad's," Stuart said. "We need to stay and help set up a roadblock to keep the bad guys away like Major and Phil did. Right now, it's wide open for an attack at any time by any roaming gangs."

"I like the part where Rosalie stays," Andy said.

"No surprise," Stuart snorted. "Let's sleep on it. We can meet in the morning after the radio call. We'll come early, and I'll help you bury Wynn, Andy."

Andy nodded. "I'll ask Aunt Jennie where she'd like for us to bury him."

"See you in the morning," Rosalie said as she and Andy headed to the Websters'.

When Aimee Louise headed to the Smiths' driveway, Stuart caught up with her.

"Where are we going?" he asked.

"I'll move the transport truck here. It has a lot of supplies that we can use."

When they reached the truck, Stuart pulled back the canvas flap that covered the back and whistled.

"You were right. This is an arsenal for an army," he said.

Aimee Louise maneuvered the transport truck down the driveway and parked it in the trees behind the chimney.

"We can go home now," she said.

Go home. I like the sound of that.

CHAPTER SEVENTEEN

The next morning, Stuart dressed then slipped down the stairs to the kitchen. The flickering candlelight and the beckoning aroma of coffee told him his mother was already up, but he was surprised to hear his father's voice.

A cup of hot coffee steamed at his seat at the table. "How did you sleep?" Sandra asked.

Stuart sipped his coffee. "Better than I expected."

She joined him at the table with her cup. "It was a long day for everyone."

"Aimee Louise, Rosalie, Andy, and I had a discussion last night at the Smith barn. We think Aimee Louise, Rosalie, and I should stay a while. Last night's attack was obviously a targeted one, but the two farms, in fact, all the farms on our road, are vulnerable for roaming gangs. We'd like to help with staffing a roadblock to protect the farms. We've seen how effective it is in Plainview and at Phil's community."

Scott nodded. "I think Nate and Charo will move to the Mitchell's farm, and it won't be long before Peyton and her family leave. They may even join the Cabellos. We'll have plenty of room for you, Aimee Louise, Rosalie, and Henry."

As Sandra stirred her biscuit dough, she asked, "Is Rosalie going to stay with the Websters?"

"That's up to Rosalie and Andy. If she does, there will be three shooters here plus Aimee Louise, and three shooters there."

"Aimee Louise's talents far exceed any mere shooter." Scott sipped his coffee. "So what's the plan for today?"

"We'll bury Wynn. I'm going to help Andy dig the grave. We'll let Jennie decide where. Then we'll need to clean up around both farms."

"I'll dig a large enough hole with the back hoe," Scott said. "I have an area of land at the back end of the property that will work, and we'll need to collect all the weapons. I don't want the kids to run across a loaded rifle."

"Aimee Louise and I are going to the Websters' first thing so she can talk to Major. I'd like to dig Wynn's grave before we leave there."

While Stuart sipped his second cup of coffee, Aimee Louise came into the kitchen.

"Eggs and biscuits before you leave?" Sandra pulled a pan of biscuits out of the oven.

Mom's timing is impeccable.

Aimee Louise sat at the table. "Yes."

"Your usual, I suppose." Sandra smiled as she scrambled Aimee Louise's eggs and fried Stuart's.

After they ate, Stuart and Aimee Louise ran to the Websters' farm. Aimee Louise followed Stuart as he tried to pick up his pace.

When they reached the Websters' farm, Stuart stopped before they headed to the door. "Just let me catch my breath. I don't want Andy to know how out of shape I am."

Aimee Louise gazed at him until he squirmed.

"Fine. That was an ego thing. Let's go inside," he said.

When they walked into the kitchen, Leo and Rosalie rose from the table.

"Let's crank up those airways," Leo said.

Rosalie and Aimee Louise accompanied Leo to his radio room.

Stuart and Andy sat at the kitchen table with their fresh cups of coffee.

"Andy told me y'all thought I'd like to decide where to bury Wynn. Thank you. I appreciate it," Jennie said. "Let's bury him at the Smith farm near the homestead site. It's where he was happy."

Stuart nodded. "Our first priority."

"I don't want to have a gathering. I just want a little private time at his gravesite after he's buried. I'll find a large rock on the Smith property sometime to use as a marker. Wynn loved those puppies. He died protecting them." Jennie sighed.

After Jennie rose from the table and refilled their coffee, Andy said, "Stuart, we talked about you three staying, and Uncle Leo was ecstatic to keep his radio partner."

"If you listen to Angel on the radio, you'd get the impressions she's a regular chatterbox, wouldn't you?" Jennie smiled.

"When I was at Major's farm after the grid went down, I used to linger outside the radio room just to listen to the sound of her voice," Stuart said.

"That's how I feel about Red's voice," Andy said. "She told me she likes to sing."

"Too bad we didn't bring our guitars," Stuart said.

"I've got three guitars and a tambourine in my closet," Jennie said. "We could use a little music around here."

"The Smith barn would be the perfect place for a party too," Stuart said.

Aimee Louise and Rosalie rushed out of the computer room.

Rosalie bounced on her toes. "We talked to Pops. He agreed it's important for us to stay. I'm going back with you because we also have David news, and Peyton will be so excited. David is on his way to Phil's. He can spend the night there if he's worn out, and Phil's expecting him. He'll be here either later today or sometime tomorrow."

"We'll collect shovels and go with you as far as the Smith farm. Aunt Jennie wants Wynn buried at the Smith homestead," Andy said.

"We'll stay with you," Aimee Louise said. "Rosalie will have her rifle."

Always thinking.

After the grave was dug, the four of them walked to the Newtons' farm. When they crossed the front yard, Peyton waved from the side yard. "I've been waiting for you. Nate and I came outside to collect rifles and move the bodies to a central location while Scott digs. Remember the guy who tried to sneak to the kitchen door? I told you about him, right? Anyway, I shot him, and he dropped. It was Troy! He is out of the picture. Completely."

Nate hurried out of the field. "Glad you're here. Peyton couldn't wait to tell you. We need to get word to Delilah and Bob. Can you do that by radio today, Angel?"

"Yes."

As Aimee Louise turned to leave, Rosalie said, "One second. Peyton, we have news for you. Good news. David left Major's farm this morning. He'll stop at Phil's, and if he's too tired to continue, he'll stay there. He'll be here today or tomorrow."

Peyton's eyes widened. "That is awesome news. I'm not going to tell Brandon quite yet. We need to clean up the yard first because he'll want to stand by the driveway until he sees David. Oh, no. David won't know how to get to the house because we've blocked the driveway. Do I need to stand by the road and watch for him."

"Not if you're talking about the same David that we know. He wouldn't let anything like a blocked driveway keep him from you and Brandon. He'll park the car and walk down," Stuart said.

"You're right. Absolutely. I'll look for more rifles."

"Now, we can go back," Rosalie said.

"I'd like to go with you," Nate said. "If you get in touch with Delilah, I'd like to hear her reaction. I was walking the field for more rifles, but Peyton can do that."

On the way back, Stuart said, "I saw Troy make his way to the side of the house, but I couldn't get a clear shot before Peyton dropped him."

"That was when those three put up their cover fire, wasn't it? I thought something was going on but couldn't tell what it was," Nate said.

When they reached the Websters' farmhouse, Rosalie and Aimee Louise ran inside.

"I need to ask Aunt Jennie if she has a quilt or something she'd like for us to use to wrap his body," Andy said.

Stuart and Nate continued to the barn to wait.

Nate eyes widened when he saw the second body near the barn. "Is this who shot Wynn?" he asked.

"Yes. He was waiting inside the barn. After the shooting started, Wynn ran out to grab the puppies to bring them inside. Andy and Rosalie hurried to the door to cover him, but this man shot him when he got to the barn. That headshot was Rosalie's," Stuart said.

"Rosalie shot Ben Romero," Nate said.

"Wow. Troy and Ben are dead." Stuart said.

"We need to go inside. This is big news," Nate said.

When the two men walked into the house, Stuart led the way to the radio room. Leo had unplugged his headset so everyone could hear the transmission.

Rosalie met them at the door and whispered, "Delilah."

Andy nodded then whispered, "Come with me to the kitchen for a second, I have news for you."

"Ready for your news, Angel."

"Just a second," Aimee Louise said as Stuart grabbed a pad and pen and wrote *Ben Romero dead here at barn.*

Leo leaned to read the note then glanced at Stuart with raised eyebrows, and Stuart nodded.

Rosalie squealed in the kitchen. "Really?"

"The brothers who were coming to see you tomorrow showed up here last night, and are going to stay," Aimee Louise said.

"The brothers?" Delilah asked. "Both of them? There? And staying, like permanently?"

"Both of them. We had a wonderful reception. Thought you'd like to know they won't be there after all."

"The brothers are there. No exit. Case closed, right?" Delilah asked.

"All but the cleanup, but you don't mind, do you?"

"Are you kidding? Cleanup is my middle name." Delilah giggled. "Catch you later, Angel. I need to share with my buddies. I'll bet they throw a big party tomorrow."

Delilah signed off then Aimee Louise signed off.

Jennie hurried downstairs to the radio room and almost collided with Andy and Rosalie.

"What on earth is going on?" Jennie asked.

"Troy and Ben Romero are dead," Andy said.

She frowned. "Aren't those the two ringleaders of the trafficking operations?"

"Yes. The most interesting part is that Peyton shot Troy, and Rosalie shot Ben."

"I knew it. Girl snipers are the best." Jennie whooped and danced a jig then flopped onto a chair.

"Clean up time here. Let's pull all the bodies to a central location. I've got a site in mind."

"After Dad digs the site at our place, he'll bring the backhoe here," Stuart said.

"Here's the blanket for Wynn. It's the one he had in the barn," she said. "Andy has a litter for you to use to carry him to his grandpa's farm. I hate that he's gone, but I'm grateful Rosalie stopped his killer."

* * *

After Stuart, Andy, Aimee Louise, Rosalie, and Nate buried Wynn at the Smith homestead, they walked to the Newtons' farm in silence.

Peyton and Brandon paced at the driveway. Nate whispered to Peyton, and she grinned as she pointed to Rosalie. "Girl power, Red," she said.

When they went inside the house, Henry rushed to Aimee Louise and hugged her. "Mama Sandra said you and Deputy Stuart are staying a while. I'm happy you'll be here a little longer."

Stuart knelt and wrapped the two of them in a hug.

"That's true, "Aimee Louise said. "We are staying for a while, but it doesn't really matter to you because when we leave, you're going with us."

As Henry gazed at her, a tiny tear slid down his cheek, and his lower lip quivered. "Really? Then you'll be my Mama Angel for always."

ACKNOWLEDGMENTS

Huge thanks to my husband for his patience, support, talented technical expertise, and guidance, and to my editor for her encouragement and eagle eye for a stray comma.

Thank you for reading. *You keep reading; I'll keep writing!*

What to read next?

DANGER IN THE FIELD

GRID DOWN SURVIVAL SERIES, Book 4

Stuart and Aimee Louise and their team defend against attacks on the Georgia farm. As the elusive enemy closes in, Stuart and Aimee Louise set a trap for the hate-filled killer who seeks revenge.

Subscribe to the newsletter!

Look for the Subscribe button on www.judithabarrett.com

ABOUT THE AUTHOR

Judith A. Barrett is an award-winning author of post-apocalyptic science fiction, thriller, and cozy mystery novels with action, adventure, and a touch of supernatural to spark the reader's imagination. Her unusual main characters are brilliant, talented, and down-to-earth folks who solve difficult problems and stop killers. Her novels are based in small towns and rural areas in south Georgia and north Florida with sojourns to other southern US states.

Judith lives in rural Georgia on a small farm with her husband, dogs, and chickens. When she's not busy writing, Judith is still busy working on the farm, hiking with her husband and dogs, or watching the beautiful sunsets from her porch.

Website   www.judithabarrett.com

Newsletter   *Subscribe* to her eNewsletter via her Website

Let's keep in touch!